THE MARRYING TYPE

EVERNIGHT PUBLISHING ®

www.evernightpublishing.com

Copyright© 2019

Megan Morgan

Editor: Lisa Petrocelli

Cover Art: Jay Aheer

ISBN: 978-0-3695-0045-8

THE MARRYING TYPE

DEDICATION

For the Club crew, who are always encouraging and
supporting me.

THE MARRYING TYPE

THE MARRYING TYPE

The Man Catalog, 1

Megan Morgan

Copyright © 2018

Chapter One

Libby Dawson clutched her best friend Kellie's hand so hard, the poor girl squeaked in pain. Libby realized she'd dug her nails in and eased her grip.

"Oops," she said in apology.

"Damn, girl, would you relax?" Kellie placed her other hand over their joined ones. "I don't think you should've had that latte before we came. At least we should have gotten you the half-caf."

Kellie was obviously trying to ease her nerves, but Libby couldn't relax. Heck, she could barely breathe.

"I'm about to do the craziest thing I've ever done in my entire life. Cut me some slack, huh? I'm a little wound up."

"You don't say?"

"Do I look all right?"

Kellie rolled her eyes. "You look fine, Libs."

"Maybe I should have worn more makeup."

"I don't think they're going to parade a bunch of

guys out for you to pick one right here in the office, so chill out. You look great."

Kellie's brown hair was tied in a perfect ponytail at the back of her head, and her face was flawless. She'd done Libby's hair and makeup and let her borrow one of her outfits, because Libby was clueless when it came to things like that. After all, college was the first time she'd been able to claim her own style, only to discover she didn't actually have one. High school was spent in uniforms and her parents rarely let her leave the house in anything they didn't approve of first. She needed a makeover to do this properly, because she couldn't look like some clueless little girl. She had to appear mature and sophisticated.

"Are you sure this is legit?" Libby couldn't stop herself asking the same questions over and over. "I mean, for real? I don't think this is legal."

"Oh my God, yes. My aunt did it, okay?" Kellie's phone chimed and she picked it up from her lap. Guys were always texting her. "It's legit, Libs, just calm down. You don't even have to agree to anything. This is just to see if it's something you want to try."

Libby drew a shaky breath. "I have to go through with it. I already stole the money."

"It's just a loan, you'll give it back."

"Don't you usually *ask* people for loans?"

"Depends."

"On what?" Libby's voice went up a notch.

"You know, on stuff." Kellie peered at her phone. "I don't think it counts as stealing if it's a family member."

"Oh God, I'm going to jail."

Kellie looked up from her phone and sighed. "Okay, you're going to jail. And some big linebacker broad named Bertha is going to make you her prison bitch. The next time I see you, you'll have a face tattoo and belong to a gang. Is that what you want to hear?"

Libby finally laughed.

But what if it happened?

Kellie shook her head and looked back at her phone. "Chill. Out." She paused. "Oh hey, Sean texted me."

"Is that the guy who's obsessed with soccer?"

"No, he's the one with the weird accent we can't figure out. Still say he's faking it." She started typing.

Libby crossed her legs and bobbed her foot, looking around the office. Sunshine poured through the windows. A huge vase of flowers sat on the table next to her. A bunch of framed pictures of happy couples decorated the desk in front of them.

"I mean, *how* is it legal?" Libby switched legs. "Isn't it prostitution?"

"Libby!" Kellie yanked her hand out of hers. "I don't know, okay? You'll have to ask her."

As if on cue, the door behind the desk opened and a woman stepped through. She was middle-aged and blond, wearing a smart red dress. Despite the fact she was the sort of pretty, intelligent-looking woman who usually made Libby feel like a sack of dirty diapers, her face was pleasant and her eyes kind. Her smile almost made Libby relax.

"Liberty Dawson?" the woman inquired in a lilting voice.

Libby jumped to her feet and rubbed her sweaty palm on her skirt. "That's me. It's just Libby, though. That's fine. You can just—call me Libby." She held out her hand and only realized as the woman shook it that it was the other, still-sweaty one. Why couldn't she stop being awkward for ten seconds?

The woman didn't seem to notice Libby's swamp

hand, or at least, she was polite enough not to mention it. "Hello, Libby, I'm Monica Hunt. I'm the director of SASS." She chuckled. "I love saying that."

SASS stood for Singles Arrangement Service Specialists, a clunky phrase that Libby suspected they'd shoehorned together to get the acronym. On the surface, it was a matchmaking service, but the kind of match Libby was looking for went beyond the usual internet dating and single's ad stuff.

"This is Kellie Smith, my best friend." Libby wrung her hands. "She's here for moral support. I'm a little nervous."

Kellie had tucked her phone away. "My aunt used your service a couple years ago. I convinced Libby to call you and set up an appointment. Thought she might benefit from it too."

"Really?" Monica spoke brightly as she sat down. Libby sat too. "Well, that covers my first question, how you discovered our services. And how are things with your aunt, Kellie?"

"Great. They're still together."

"I'm happy to hear that. Another success story." She focused on Libby. "So, Libby, tell me exactly what you're here for. Don't be shy."

Libby clutched the arms of her chair. The words sounded crazy before they even left her mouth.

"I need a husband. Before my twenty-third birthday, which is in six months."

Monica didn't burst into laughter. She and Kellie didn't crack up and reveal this was all a huge prank, as Libby feared.

"I see." Monica folded her hands on the desk. "Can you fill me in as to why?"

Libby didn't like this part at all, but she supposed she couldn't just walk in and demand a husband without an explanation. "It's … sort of a trust fund thing."

"Her dad is a complete dick," Kellie more succinctly corrected.

Libby glared at her, then looked back at Monica. "It's a complicated situation."

"It's not complicated." Kellie was relentless. "Her dad has a giant trust fund put away for her, but she can only have it if she's married before she turns twenty-three, 'cause like I said, he's a dick. And a misogynist. And a creep."

Libby squeezed the bridge of her nose. "Yeah, it's something like that. Complicated."

"Don't worry, I've heard things like this before." Monica appeared unruffled. "Before we get down to business though, Libby, I must let you know that this is an expensive service. We charge a hefty fee. That's why it works, because the men involved are handsomely compensated. We also insist the fee be paid in full before anything moves forward."

Libby nodded. "It's ten thousand dollars, I read the literature I requested." She fidgeted with the hem of her skirt. "I have that much."

"Ten thousand is the cheap package, the married-in-a-hurry package." Monica opened a drawer in her desk. "Many women use it when they have a deadline, as you do. However, while it's the cheapest package, it has some drawbacks." She pulled out a fat red ledger and plunked it on the desk.

Libby twisted her skirt. "What are the drawbacks?" *Besides ending up in prison, of course.*

"After paying in full, you need to move forward quickly. You must get married within a week of obtaining the license. That might make it difficult if you have people in your life you need to tell you're suddenly getting married to a man they've never met before."

Libby had a sort-of plan to address such a thing. She'd cross that bridge when she got there.

"The arrangement is only for six weeks before the annulment takes place. That is, of course, unless you decide to extend the contract, and that does get pricey."

Six weeks wasn't long, but hopefully Libby wouldn't even need it. "My dad gave my sister the money the week she got married as a wedding present, so hopefully, he'll do the same for me."

All the bridges she had to cross before she got to *that* one were rickety and traversed dangerous, shark-infested waters. But it would all be worth it, eventually.

Kellie reached over and squeezed her arm.

"I do have some questions." Libby tried to stay calm. "Mostly, like, is this even legal?"

Monica gave her a blank-faced, fake smile. "Of course. We're a matchmaking service that aims to provide companionship for lonely singles. We don't offer the promise of anything long-term. If two adults want to get married, that's their choice. Our commission is merely for the services we provide in helping them meet each other."

Libby narrowed her eyes. Legal, but not legal. "It's kind of like an escort service, then?"

"We provide discerning women with male companionship. There is no promise of sexual services and we do not promote prostitution." Her speech sounded well-practiced. "The fact that some of our clients end up getting married just shows we do our job very well."

Libby almost started laughing, but that would be impolite. She was here, seriously considering marrying a man she'd never met, so she didn't exactly have a platform to ridicule from.

"We don't handle anything with the marriage agreement." Monica picked up the red ledger. "That's between you and your companion. We take our fee and the rest of the sum is gifted to him." She plopped the ledger in front of Libby.

"Gifted?"

"Yes, it's not illegal, after all, for one consenting adult to give another consenting adult a monetary gift. We just handle the money for you, since it's so much."

So much gray area. Even Libby, who felt like she was in over her head in most things, could read between the lines. Of course, again, here she was, considering it. She could get up and walk out right now. She could find another, harder way to do this.

"Okay." She took a deep breath. "Well, I have ten thousand dollars. So, what do I do next?"

Monica patted the ledger. "Would you like to look at the catalog?"

Libby eyed it. "The ... catalog?"

"Yes. You came here to pick a husband, didn't you?"

Libby still stared at it. Finally, she sat forward and took it, slowly, and stared at the blank front cover. "I thought you would just sort of assign me someone..."

Monica chuckled. "I'm not that good of a matchmaker, dear. There are some stipulations. If you can't make a decision today and start the process with us before you leave, there's a five hundred-dollar deposit to keep the catalog for forty-eight hours. If you decide not to use our services, half of that is nonrefundable. If you do go ahead, the full five hundred is applied toward your payment."

Libby barely heard her. Was this really a book full of men for her to pick from, like a Sears catalog? Kellie leaned over and looked at it too.

"All that is merely to assure discretion," Monica said, "and to assure it's returned." She gave Libby a saucy wink. "It's a very exciting book."

Libby was too scared to open it.

"Would you like to fill out some initial paperwork?"

Twenty minutes later, Libby left the office with the book in her arms, clutched to her chest. Kellie placed a hand on her back. They stopped in the hallway and Libby turned to her, very much on the verge of freaking out.

"I can't do this. This is crazy. I should take this back in there and have her rip up the check. Do you think she'd refund me since I haven't actually left the building yet?"

"Libs." Kellie clutched her shoulders. "You can do this. You already stole the money from your mom, and I gave you the other half from my grant. You're too far in to back out now. Be brave."

"I'll give it back to you and I'll put the money back in Mom's safe." Hysterics bubbled inside her, making her queasy. "If Daddy ever finds out about this he'll murder me. Like, probably hire a hitman to kill me. I couldn't see him doing it himself, he wouldn't want to risk his reputation and—"

Kellie gripped her face, stopping her babble. "Libby, you're going to change the world. When you get that half-million, you're going to save lives with it. Imagine what you'll do. That's worth a little bit of craziness, right?"

Libby gazed at her.

Kellie went on, speaking calmly but firmly. "You'll pay me back, and your mom, and you'll make all your dreams come true. Okay?"

Libby tried to calm down and breathe.

"Your dad is a class-A douchebag and he deserves to get tricked. You're going to do so much good, Libby. You're smart and you're talented and you've got a brilliant soul. I believe in you. You've got this."

Libby was trembling. "I've never done something so insane. College must have corrupted me, just like Daddy said it would." She tried to force a smile.

"Yeah, corrupted you, in the best way possible." Kellie pulled her into a tight hug. "Just a couple weeks of crazy for a lifetime of awesome." She drew back and looked down at the catalog. "I'm dying to see what's in there."

Libby looked down at it too and let out a shaky laugh. "Ditto."

****

Libby sat on the couch in Kellie's tiny apartment—the spot where Libby was currently crashing while she lived out of a suitcase and duffel bag—knees drawn up, eyes big as she flipped through the pages of the book.

Kellie hustled out of the kitchen, carrying two glasses of red wine. "Shove over, I wanna see."

Libby lowered her knees and scooted over. Kellie sat down next to her and handed her one of the glasses.

"I can't believe my aunt picked her boyfriend out of a book." Kellie peered over. "Do you think she got a book like this? I never asked her."

Libby took a sip of the wine. She'd never even tasted alcohol until she went to college. Her mother always condemned the drinking of any kind of booze, and brought up her alcoholic father—Libby's grandfather—any time the subject arose. This was compounded by the fact that Libby's father was also a heavy drinker, and most of the time, Libby thought she was just using her own father as an example so she didn't have to condemn her husband out loud. Libby felt like she was doing something bad, drinking it up like some wanton lush, and she'd had so few alcoholic drinks so far she could still count them on one hand.

But she'd been doing lots of other bad things lately.

"This is mind boggling." Libby turned a page. "I mean, they're all so handsome. I didn't expect that."

"No kidding, look at him." Kellie gaped. "And him! Dang, I wonder if I can take more money out of my account?"

Each page of the catalog presented a different man. Two pictures were provided: a head shot and a full body shot. Beneath was a list of basic information—a first name only, their age, ethnicity, occupation, and interests and hobbies. So far, she hadn't come across any guys who were into geeky things like microbiology and humanitarian efforts.

Monica had told her this catalog exclusively contained men who were willing to enter into short and long-term marriages. The company strictly catered to heterosexual women, though they had a sister company that served the gay community. Were there really so many men out there willing to accommodate desperate people for money?

A dumb question.

"Of course they're hot, Libs." Kellie hung over her shoulder. "You can't charge that much for a scrub."

Libby clutched the stem of her glass and stared across the room, her other hand flat on the catalog. Panic rose in her once again. "I can't do this."

"Stop it." Kellie poked her in the ribs. "Yes, you can."

"My parents aren't stupid. They'll figure out what's going on."

"They haven't figured out you dropped out of

school yet, have they? Or that you moved out of the dorm and you're staying here with me?"

"Maybe I should go back."

Kellie gripped her arm. "Do you really want to be a schoolteacher? Come on. Tell me right now what you want. Say it."

Kellie made her do this when she started to doubt herself. She made Libby say it out loud, so she would believe it.

"I want to study microbiology and bacteriology so I can create a filtration system that helps provide clean drinking water in compromised areas." She spoke the words by memory. "As soon as I get my dad's money, I'm going back to school. I'm also going to start up a nonprofit that helps people in perilous situations where clean water is unavailable." She balled her hand into a fist on the catalog. "*That's* what I want to do. I don't want to be a teacher."

Libby's father believed women shouldn't be involved in fields like science and technology, and since he paid her tuition, she had to get her degree in a "feminine" field, such as education. But she'd had this desire since she was a teenager, even before, after she'd watched a documentary in fifth grade about the lack of potable water in impoverished areas. She'd done a science project on it her freshman year, something she'd never let her father see. She borrowed textbooks from the library and read them under the covers in bed at night, like they were some kind of shameful porn.

Kellie squeezed her arm. "Your parents are controlling assholes. This is your life, and you have a right to live it. Once you have that money, they can't touch you and they can't tell you what to do."

Libby looked at her. "How did I ever manage to find a friend like you?" She was still baffled by it, especially since she didn't make friends easily. She was much too shy.

"Luck." Kellie kissed her cheek. "Or maybe you have a guardian angel."

Libby lifted her hand from the catalog and looked down at the page she was on. Her stomach did a flip.

The man there was gorgeous, like the rest of them, but in a different way. Something intangibly unique stood out about him, something that captured her attention and made her blush, though it was just a picture. She couldn't articulate it, but she felt it.

He had heavy-lidded blue eyes, the type they called "bedroom eyes," she supposed. They seemed to gaze right into her. His smile was self-assured and almost mischievous, like he knew a secret. He had sharp cheekbones and a light growth of hair adorned his square jaw and upper lip. His hair was loose and wavy, dark blond, and curled thickly at his collar. Her dad would say he needed to sit his ass down in a barber's chair. She thought it was sexy.

Like the rest of the men in the catalog he wore a suit, tailored to his long, trim frame in the full-length picture. He was handsome, confident, and the type of guy she would turn into a quivering little bunny rabbit in front of.

She didn't realize she'd been staring at the page until Kellie giggled.

"He's pretty nice, huh?"

Libby's blush intensified. She skimmed his information. "Blaine." She rolled her eyes to hide her embarrassment. "That sounds like something out of a romance novel. I wonder if it's his real name?"

Kellie shrugged. "My aunt's boyfriend used his real name. It's John, by the way."

"John." Libby grinned. "How sensible."

Blaine was twenty-nine. A little too old for her, maybe. He was Caucasian with Irish and French heritage. She continued down his list of stats.

She scrunched up her nose. "He's a stockbroker." She didn't know anything about finance, another thing her father said was a man's domain. "He likes cooking, running, travel, and foreign films." She shook her head. "We'd have nothing to talk about during our short, weird marriage." She started to turn the page.

Kellie grabbed her hand and stopped her. She eased the page back down. "He caught your eye, though. That means something."

"Yeah, but there's a lot of nice guys in here. I need to find one I at least have something in common with."

"This is just a short list." Kellie indicated his stats. "Do you think this is the only stuff he likes? Besides, Libs, you're interesting. You could teach him a few things."

"Me?" She laughed. "I'm not interesting. Where did you get that idea?"

"He knows money, and you need to know about money to start your nonprofit, right? It's not all about helping people, you gotta know the ins and outs and technicalities of running something like that. And who knows, maybe he could help you invest some of your money and do even more with it."

Libby chewed on her lower lip and gazed at Blaine's pictures. God, his eyes were beautiful. She also imagined staring into them in person and how horribly weird she'd be.

"You should give him a shot." Kellie sat up and grabbed her wine glass from the stand next to the couch. "I mean, it's only six weeks, right? Not even that, if your father gives you the money sooner."

"I don't know. I need to think about it for a while. I mean, I should look through the rest of the catalog, right? It's not fair if I don't consider them all." She ruffled the remaining pages.

"Drink your wine and stop thinking so hard." Kellie urged Libby's glass to her mouth. "Obey your vagina."

Libby laughed, flushing again, and took a drink. She winced. She wasn't used to that burn. By half a glass she was usually tipsy.

"He's too old though," Libby protested. "I think I should pick someone younger."

Kellie craned her neck. "Oh God, twenty-nine. Yeah, he's *way* over the hill." She took a drink.

Libby sighed. "I need to think about it. This isn't like buying a pair of shoes."

Kellie got up. "I'm gonna go check the food." She headed toward the kitchen, but stopped and looked back. "You're doing the right thing, Libs. Get crazy, girl."

"You're a lot crazier than me. You are my inspiration." Libby flung her hand dramatically in the air. "You inspire me!"

Kellie headed into the kitchen, yelling back, "And you get to do it with a hot guy. Bonus!"

Libby looked down at Blaine. A mature, sophisticated stockbroker with socially acceptable hobbies. The kind of guy who would never be interested in a dumpy, sheltered college girl with delusional aspirations to save the world. Unless, of course, she paid him.

She turned the page. The next guy was generically handsome and an accountant. She studied him a moment, took a deeper drink of her wine, and turned the page again, back to Blaine.

This was going to be more difficult than she imagined.

Chapter Two

Blaine Parker stepped into the coffee shop on Stanton Street. The place was busy, packed with the morning rush. People filled the little tables and clustered together on couches, laptops open, cell phones out. He'd resisted the urge to bring work with him, though he could have. Skipping out on this morning would put him behind all day, but he wanted to make a good impression.

And, at this price, the least he could do was give her his full attention.

He tugged his collar to make sure it was straight. He'd dressed casually, but still professional, in a dress shirt and blazer without a tie. He held a bouquet of daisies and carnations.

Blaine scanned the room for someone fitting the description Monica had given him. His gaze finally settled on a table in the corner, where a woman sat alone. Judging by her hands balled in her lap and the way she was staring at him with a gaping, deer-in-the headlights expression, it was her.

He put on a smile and strode toward her. Her face paled as he approached and he slowed his walk, uncertain. Was this not her? Was he about to swoop down on some hapless woman?

She jumped to her feet when he was a few feet from the table.

"Libby?" he asked.

She clutched her hands in front of her. "Hi, Blaine?"

This was a change of pace, but not an unpleasant one.

Liberty Dawson—she preferred to go by Libby— was not the sort of obviously wealthy, confident, boisterous woman he usually worked with. Her shiny chestnut hair hung straight over her shoulders, cut in thick bangs across her forehead. She had big green eyes and a round, almost cherubic face, with plump lips. She wore a loose brown shift that hung off one shoulder and was cinched with a belt across her tiny waist. Her legs were long and shapely and she had curves, despite her slender frame. Overall, pretty as hell, in a sort of clean, fresh way.

It wouldn't hurt that the woman he'd be married to for the next six weeks was nice to look at.

He held the flowers out to her. "It's nice to meet you, Libby. I'm Blaine Parker."

She stared at the flowers, then took them. Her fingers trembled.

"Thank you." Pink blossomed across her pale cheeks. "I'm sorry, I'm super nervous."

"Understandable." He tried to keep his tone light and companionable. "I'm not as calm and collected as I look, trust me. Usually, when you meet your spouse for the first time, it's a bit less of a business transaction, huh?"

"Yeah." She sat down demurely and glanced up at him from beneath her bangs. Sweet and coy. This was not what he expected. The type of woman who typically used this service was a lot more forward and he rarely had to take the lead.

"I'm going to get a coffee." He gestured toward the counter. "Would you like anything else?" She already had a cup in front of her.

She shook her head. "No, thank you."

While he stood in line, he slipped his phone out of his pocket and checked the stock exchange. Things were fluctuating wildly this morning. He should have known, take a morning off and things got crazy. He resisted the urge to text his assistant, Emily. After all, he'd hired her for a reason. He'd let her take care of things.

Blaine glanced over at Libby while he waited. She'd set the flowers on the table and her hands were wrapped around her cup as she stared out the window. Her legs were crossed and she bobbed one foot, quick and frantic, like she might vibrate out of her chair.

Very unusual.

He returned to the table with a latte and sat down across from her. "So, you like to go by Libby? That's what Monica told me."

She sat up straight. The color had receded from her cheeks. A shame, as he found it charming.

"Yes, Libby. Just call me Libby."

"Liberty is a pretty name, though. I do have to say that."

She scrunched up her nose. "My parents are so pretentious. My older sister's name is Justice. I hate it, they're the only ones who still call me Liberty."

"Liberty and Justice." He propped his elbows on the table and laced his fingers above his cup. "Do you have a younger sister named Freedom, as well?"

She stared at him a moment, and he feared his joke fell flat. Then she chuckled. "I'm sure if they had another kid, that would have been her name. Or something equally dumb, like Truth or Patriot."

She seemed to relax a little, at least.

"What do you do, Libby? Tell me about yourself."

She gripped her cup and toyed with it, turning it on the saucer beneath. "I ... was going to school, at NYU."

"Was?"

"I dropped out three months ago." She bit her plump lower lip. Her eyes were bright in the light through the window. "I didn't like what I was studying." She added hastily, "I'm planning on going back, though. I want to study microbiology, instead of education."

"Ah, so you picked the wrong major?" He picked up his cup. "It happens." He took a sip.

"Yeah, I guess, something like that." She kept fidgeting. "I have some pretty big plans for the future, and I need to change my field of study to make them happen."

"Tell me about your big plans." He set his cup down. "What are they?" He was genuinely curious.

She looked down, and the blush crept back across her cheeks. "Well, it's kind of grandiose. I don't know."

"All dreams are grandiose. That doesn't mean they can't come true."

She looked up, and something in her face changed. Determination blazed through the shyness, a resolve that instantly told him she wasn't some shrinking flower, despite her current discomfort. Maybe here was the boldness he was used to.

She took a deep breath. "I want to start a nonprofit that helps people in disaster-stricken areas and places of extreme poverty to obtain clean drinking water. I have this idea for a filtration system that makes polluted water potable. I need some more education, though. I've learned a bunch of stuff on my own, but I don't think I can invent it without knowing more about the biological factors and the technical aspects that could make such a thing not only viable, but capable."

Blaine raised his eyebrows. Passionate, altruistic, and intelligent. This was *definitely* a change of pace, and not for the first, obvious reasons. "Wow. That sounds kind of amazing. Not kind of—really amazing." He was blown away.

"I've always wanted to help people." The passion lingered in her voice. "I want to travel the world and bring hope to people who need it the most. The concern of victims in crisis areas not having safe water is much bigger than most people realize. A human body can survive for much longer without food than it can without water." Her voice rose and grew stronger. "I think I can help stop that. I've got all these ideas. It's more a matter of creating something that's easy to transport and distribute *and* is easy to train volunteers on how to implement."

He was transfixed. He'd only known her ten minutes and he already liked her.

"That sounds like a noble and necessary endeavor." He wasn't sure how to respond in a more satisfactory way, one that conveyed the scope of just how impressed he was "I hope you get to do everything you're trying for. It sounds like you've got your ducks in a row. You have a goal and you know how to get there."

Her shoulders slumped.

"The problem is, it costs a lot of money to get something like that off the ground. You have to build and test prototypes. You have to pay someone to create the components for it. You have to apply for a patent. It's a good idea, sure, but it's not easy to realize."

"Of course." Now she was speaking his language. "I work in a field where I see people and companies with the need to build capital for projects every day. Trust me, I know it's not easy. But it is possible."

She bit her lip again. "That's why I need to get married."

He tilted his head. Surely, she wasn't marrying him for money? She didn't seem the shrewd and gold-digging type, unless he severely misjudged her. Besides, her money was flowing to him in this transaction.

She clutched her hands around her cup. "Have you ever heard of Dawson True Life Products?"

He blinked. "Of course." They were a large company that made innovative products for the home—kitchen gadgets, time-saving devices, leisure accessories, and things that were supposed to make home life "Easy, Convenient, and True to Your Lifestyle," as their slogan promised—and they had grown significantly in the past ten years as they had also branched into the technology market. He'd traded their stock many times.

She gazed at him. "Coleman Dawson is my father."

Oh, wow.

Blaine sat back. "The CEO of Dawson True Life Products is your father?"

She was *not* a gold-digger. She didn't need to be.

"Yes. He set up a trust fund for both me and my sister, half a million dollars each. He gave her hers three years ago."

Blaine was stunned. Perhaps this marriage would be more profitable for him than he thought.

"The thing is…" She chewed her lower lip, yet again. He wanted to kiss her and make her stop, before she hurt herself. "My father is kind of … old-fashioned. He has these ideas about how women should present themselves, how they should behave, what their place in life should be. His stipulation is, he'll only give me and my sister the money if we're married by twenty-three." She gazed at him again. "My twenty-third birthday is in six months."

The pieces fell into place. Blaine tilted his head back.

"Ah, I see now." He sat forward. "You need a husband to get your trust fund."

She ducked her head. "I'm sorry. I know it

sounds like I just want to use you."

He chuckled. "Libby." He slid his hand across the table and touched the back of hers. "This is a practical arrangement. I know you're going to use me. You're using me for what I put myself to use for. And it's not like I won't get something out of it too. You're paying me."

Her skin was soft beneath his fingertips. He stroked the back of her hand, to soothe her, but also to indulge in that silky smoothness for a moment.

She glanced up. "I didn't know what else to do. I've been desperate, trying to come up with something. Then my friend told me about the agency. Her aunt used it to find her boyfriend."

He withdrew his hand. "It's all right. I understand."

"When I get that money, I'm going back to school to learn the stuff I need to know. I'll be able to start my nonprofit and work on my project. It'll make things much easier. My dad is probably going to disown me, but I don't care. He can't take the money back." She frowned. "He doesn't think women should be involved in science and medicine. He doesn't even like that I went to school to begin with, and I had to choose some 'girly' field, as he called it. He wants me to get married and have kids like my sister."

Blaine folded his arms on the table. "I don't mean to be rude, but your father sounds like an unpleasant man." What sort of man treated his daughters that way? Not to mention put insane boundaries on their inheritance like that?

"He's not just unpleasant, he's horrible." She lowered her voice. "He and my mother got divorced when Justice and I were teenagers, but he never left our lives. That's when he went off and started making all his money and really got his company off the ground. My mother isn't much better, though. In fact, she can be just as bad." She paused. "I'm sorry. I shouldn't be dumping this on you. It's a bunch of awkward personal stuff."

Blaine reached over and took her hand fully this time, and squeezed it. "Libby, you sound like you have a good head on your shoulders. You want to do something important and you're willing to take huge risks for it. You seem very smart and very brave."

She smiled. "You sound like my friend Kellie. She always tells me things like that."

He rubbed his thumb over the back of her hand. Her nails were short and bare, as simple as the rest of her appearance. "A lot of people come from less-than-ideal families and still accomplish a lot of good. You don't sound like you let your father get in your head. I admire that."

The corners of her mouth perked up. "This is the most insane thing I've ever done."

He grinned. "Good. I'll be your partner in crime, you just tell me what role you need me to play."

She tightened her fingers around his.

"I guess we better get our story straight." Her smile got bigger, and it made her face even more beautiful. "I have to warn you though, it's probably not going to be easy. My parents are going to scrutinize you like crazy and ask a million questions. But I won't get the money if we don't make it seem real."

"I'm at your service." He bowed his head. "Trust me, I'm a good actor."

"I think we should work it all out in writing. Probably easier that way."

"I agree."

They fell into silence. She didn't stop smiling though, and she didn't let go of his hand. She was the first to speak. "You don't look like a stockbroker."

He chuckled. "Don't I?"

"No." She touched her own hair, but was obviously indicating his. "With the longer hair—which I like, by the way. It looks really nice on you." She touched her chin, her smile turning bashful. "And the scruff. It's dignified, but, well, you don't look like the guys who work for my father."

She certainly knew how to stroke a man's ego. He was smiling just as widely as her now.

"I don't like looking like a stuffy suit. Clean-cut has kind of given way to a hipper look these days. It's more the attitude you put forth than how you look." He squeezed her hand. "You're lovely too, by the way. Your hair is gorgeous. So is your smile."

Red burst across her cheeks. "Thank you." She paused, then quickly asked, "Is it fun being a stockbroker?"

"Most of the time. Depends on what you think of as 'fun,' though. I've always been good with money. Well, other people's money." He winked. "I don't plan to do it forever, though."

"We have to figure out how we met. I mean, it's not like I hang around the stock exchanges or anything."

"Maybe it was by chance, out somewhere?"

She narrowed her eyes, then perked. "I think I have an idea. We need paper." She let go of his hand and pulled her bag up from next to her chair, and drew out a notebook and pen.

By the time they left the coffee shop forty-five minutes later, Blaine was no longer thinking about work or anxious to get back to the office. He hadn't even checked his phone. He and Libby stepped onto the street, the sidewalk teeming with people and the traffic congested. They stood in an alcove near the coffee shop door, out of the way.

"I have my car." He rested a hand on the small of her back. "Can I take you somewhere?"

She wrapped her coat around her delicate frame. Fall had descended and the morning was chilly.

"No, I'll catch a cab. I'm just going back to the place where I'm staying. I don't want to keep you from work."

He looked down at her. He was about six inches taller than her, though she did have heels on, so maybe eight. The more time he spent with her, the cuter and endearing she became. Now, in stark contrast to when he first walked in, she was lively and relaxed, fired up with determination and the secret conspiracy they shared.

"Thank you." Her eyes gleamed. "I really hope this works out. I'm nervous as heck, but really hopeful too."

He took her by the arms. "I guess it's a go, then? We'll sign the paperwork and make the transaction?"

She smiled. "Oh, yeah. I guess this meeting was to find out if we really want to spend time together, huh?" She looked sheepish. "We need to get the technical stuff out of the way first."

"Though it may be business, I'm really looking forward to spending time with you, Libby."

Her hair fluttered around her face. Her cheeks were pink. He still wanted to kiss that swollen red mouth.

"I guess I'll call Monica," she said. "We can set up an appointment."

He nodded. "You sure you don't want a ride?"

She shook her head. "I'll be fine. I need to hash out everything in my head. I'll send you an email when I get it sorted out. I'll make you that script." She patted her coat pocket, which held his business card. He'd written his personal email and cell number on it too. "Thank you so much, for all of this, for playing along. For being willing to deal with whatever happens." She took a breath. "Sorry, babbling."

He hugged her. She was soft, incredibly so, and smelled like wildflowers. He snuck a sniff of her hair before he drew back. He would get something more than money from this, for a change. Mostly, the chance to be in her company. He had truly never met a woman like her before.

The color in her cheeks was deeper now, though it might have been just the sting of the wind. She pushed her hair out of her face. "I'll see you soon?"

"Of course you will, my darling wife." He grinned. "At least let me hail you a cab."

He walked her to the curb, his hand on the small of her back again. She didn't pull away. The jostling crowd forced them to keep close together.

Regrettably, there was a free cab coming their way. He lifted his arm and waved it down. The car slowed and eased up to the curb.

She turned her face up to him. "I'll see you soon, when we make it official?"

"Of course."

He opened the back door for her. As she got in, he slipped his arm loosely around her waist and guided her. She climbed in and looked out at him, and waved.

He waved back. "See you soon, Libby."

He closed the door and stepped back. Her cab slid off into the stream of other cabs and cars flowing down the street. He watched it go, hands jammed in the pockets of the long coat he wore over his suit. He realized belatedly he should have been a gentleman and given her fare. He was too off kilter to think.

Calm down, he told himself. *Take it slow. Don't start treating her like your wife just yet.*

He headed down the street in the direction of his car. He'd been imagining, in the back of his mind, walking her to his car and giving her a kiss in the shadows of the garage. But that was foolish, because he knew better than to kiss her, or to get involved beyond what they were there to do. This was about money. *His* money that he would get for playing the part, and *her* money that she would use to change the world, apparently.

Still, he had a spring in his step and he hummed a tune under his breath as he walked down the crowded street in the bright, crisp morning.

Chapter Three

"What kind of dress do you wear to buy a husband?" Libby stood in front of Kellie's closet, staring at the row of clothes that hung from the rod inside. She had so many, way more than Libby had, and much more colorful and fashionable than she could ever obtain for herself. She didn't want to look dumpy today.

"One that screams, 'I'm a wild and crazy rebel.'" Kellie sat on the bed, sorting through her makeup bag. She held up a tube. "I think you should wear bright red lipstick today."

Libby frowned and pulled out a dress. It was gray flannel, with a cute clasped collar. She held it up to herself and turned to the full-length mirror on the inside of the closet door.

"No way." Kellie jumped up and rushed over. "That's a winter dress, for going out on coffee dates." She snatched the dress and stuffed it back in the closet. "Let's see here…"

Libby sighed and slumped. "It doesn't matter. I just want to get this over with, so I can face my parents." She winced. "The sooner I get through that obstacle, the better."

She was a few hours away from signing the papers—and slapping down the money—that would start this whole crazy process. Once that was done, there was no turning back.

"Tell me more about Blaine." Kellie shoved hangers aside, as she sorted through the jam-packed offerings. "Was he as cute as his pictures?"

Libby's cheeks turned pink. She looked away from her reflection. "He was very handsome." His face danced in her imagination, his eyes vivid in her memory. They were so clear, so blue.

"And nice, I hope?"

"He said a lot of nice things to me." She recalled the sincerity in his tone, the earnestness of his interest. Maybe that was all for show, though, to make sure she picked him.

Not that it mattered. As he'd told her, this was a business transaction. A professional deal. What he was and wasn't held no weight, as long as he played his part.

"And was he sexy?"

Libby rolled her eyes, though her cheeks remained hot. "That's not really important, is it?"

Kellie yanked a dress out and turned, brandishing it at Libby with a flourish. "I think this is perfect."

Libby looked the dress over, skeptical. It looked more formfitting than what she usually wore, a sort of sweater dress with a cinched waist and long sleeves, and a scooped neck. The fabric was maroon, and she worried with her pale skin it would make her look like an open wound.

"I have a belt for it." Kellie turned and rummaged around on the shelf above the clothes. "This dress is kind of businesslike and slinky at the same time. It'll make you look hot, but sassy too. Like the kind of woman who buys a husband."

She pulled down a wide leather belt with a big gold buckle. So bold.

Libby held the dress up to herself and turned to the mirror again. She pondered. This would make her look confident and mature, at least.

"It's super important." Kellie propped her chin on Libby's shoulder. Her eyes glittered in the mirror.

"Huh?"

"If he's sexy." She poked her in the side and stepped away. "You need something to look at while you do this, right?"

Libby played with the material of the dress, surreptitiously tugging at it to see if it would be tight across her hips. "It wouldn't matter if he was ugly, as long as this works."

"Yeah, but he's not ugly." Kellie plunked back down on the bed. "I know if I was gonna fake-marry a man, I would want him to be eye candy." She rooted through her makeup again.

Libby turned, clutching the dress to herself. Her heart thudded in her ears. She couldn't seem to ease her anxiety below "raging out of control" level.

Kellie looked up at her, eyebrows raised, and frowned. "What's wrong?"

"I'm just so scared," Libby said softly.

"Oh, honey." Kellie set her bag aside and sighed. She held out her arms. "I know this is frightening, but you're doing the right thing."

Libby walked over and sat down next to her. Kellie wrapped an arm around her and Libby dropped her head on her shoulder. Kellie smoothed her hair with her other hand.

"I've just had so many disappointments." Libby clutched the dress harder. "So many things that blew up in my face, when I thought something was going right for a change."

"Don't worry, this time you have help."

Libby sat up, Kellie's arm still around her. An old memory came flooding back, one that made her stomach clench and her chest ache.

"My parents got divorced when I was fourteen and Justice was sixteen." She stared across the room. "I don't know how my mother found the courage to do it. She must have finally reached the end of her rope. She filed without my father knowing about it and had the papers served to him at work."

Kellie rubbed her back. "I'm sure he deserved it."

Libby looked down at her lap. "I think she was planning on taking us and leaving before he got home, but she couldn't bring herself to do it. And when he showed up he was … so angry." She swallowed, her insides going cold at the memory. "I'd never seen him that angry. And he said so many nasty things. He's always said nasty things, but those were the worst I'd ever heard."

Kellie tucked Libby's hair behind her ear. "He's a monster. I've never even met the man, but from everything you've told me, he's an absolute bastard."

"He hated losing control like that, having someone defy him." Libby picked at the fabric of the dress, then stopped herself so she didn't ruin it. "No way was he going to grant my mother a divorce. He swore he'd fight it, with his powerful lawyer, and she'd end up with nothing. He said he'd take custody of us and she'd never see us again."

Kellie lowered her hand and was silent.

"Mom took me and Justice and we stayed in hotels for a while. But he'd always figure out where we were and show up, usually drunk, and fight with my mom. Once the cops were called because he was making so much noise, but they didn't do anything. Finally, she ran out of money and we just … went home."

"God." Kellie shook her head. "That poor woman. Poor all of you."

"Then, like a week later,"—Libby lifted her head—"he just said okay. He gave in."

"Huh?"

"He granted my mom the divorce." Libby looked at her. "He stopped fighting, just like that. They ended up having a simple, no contest divorce. He gave her the house and custody of us, and she agreed to give up any right to his future earnings and waived the right to request alimony. I think she just wanted to be able to wash her hands of him. She didn't care."

Kellie furrowed her brow. "Why did he suddenly give in?"

"I have no idea." Libby smoothed her hands over the dress draped across her knees. "I never figured it out, and Mom never said. I've always been afraid to ask her, but maybe *she* doesn't even know."

"That's very strange." Kellie picked up her makeup bag. "Maybe she had some dirt on him?"

Libby shrugged. "It's not like he ever left our lives, though. Even though they got divorced and he moved out, he still insinuated himself as much as he possibly could. He insisted he had the right to help raise us. And now that we're adults, he still insinuates himself in all our lives, even my mother's."

"Of course, he's a total control freak." Kellie held up another tube of lipstick and squinted at it, looked at the dress, then looked back at it.

"But, anyway, I remember this one time, about a year after they got divorced." Libby's stomach clenched up again. "His business was booming then. He'd started it when I was a kid, but it didn't really get huge until after the divorce. It caught on and just took off overnight, and he started expanding his operations. He was making a lot of money, and he liked to lord it over us."

"Asshole," Kellie muttered, and tossed the lipstick back in the bag.

"He picked me up from school one day and told me he was going to take me to see his product testing facility." She smiled faintly. "I was so excited, even though I didn't dare show it. I loved learning how gadgets worked, and making my own. And it was easier, with him not living with us anymore, for me to work on my inventions. I was always creating things but I was terrified he'd find out and punish me."

"That's so sick." Kellie grimaced. "What kind of parent punishes their kid for being creative?"

Libby snorted. "Mine." She paused a moment, then pushed on, the memory as painful as if it happened yesterday. "So, he drove me to the plant where they made prototypes, and we walked through these big rooms. There were all these tables with half-made things on them, and diagrams drawn on whiteboards, and people tinkering with stuff and testing stuff. It was so interesting."

"Like a bunch of engineers?"

Libby nodded. "I'd already been playing with how to build different kinds of water filters and I was fascinated. I thought how these people must have such great educations and must be so smart. I wanted so badly to do what they were doing. I think my father knew that, he knew how I would react to it."

"I feel like this is going to a bad place…"

Libby fidgeted with the dress again, but tried not to pick at it. "I was so caught up in looking at all the gadgets and tools and drawings that I didn't notice it at first, but then I looked around and I noticed something." She swallowed. "All the people working on this stuff were men. All of them. Like, there were a few women around, but they seemed to just be doing secretarial and administrative stuff. And I remember one woman brought this group of guys coffee."

"Ugh." Kellie slapped the lid of her bag shut. "How the hell does your dad not get slammed for discriminatory labor practices?"

"He's shrewd and crafty. But that's when he came over to me, and he put his arm around my shoulders…" She could still feel the tight, cold grip of his hand. "And he said, 'Liberty, this is what I've created. This is what a smart man can build for himself.'" His words echoed in her head, every one memorized for eternity. "And then he said, 'I know it's hard to grasp, as a girl, but if you're unlucky enough not to get to stay home with your children and take care of your home, someday you can get a job in a place like this, supporting people like this.'"

"*Supporting* them?" Kellie said sharply.

She nodded. "He meant like as a secretary, or a coffee fetcher—like one of those women who were scurrying around like anxious mice."

Kellie made a sound of disgust. "God, I really kind of hope this man's head catches on fire. I know he's your father, Libs, but damn."

"I know what that day was about." Libby's vision blurred as her eyes welled up with tears. "He knew about my secret ambitions. He knew about my carefully hidden projects in my bedroom. He took me there that day to crush those dreams out of me. He took me there to show me only men could do that sort of job. He wanted to rub my face in it." A tear slipped down her cheek.

"Libs." Kellie grasped her face and wiped the tear away with her thumb. "It's *not* just men who can do those things. It's just that your dad only hires men."

"I know that." Libby sniffed, and more tears fell. "I was young though, and vulnerable, and it was such a huge disappointment, such an embarrassment. I went home and crammed all my projects in the back of my closet and didn't touch anything like that again for almost a year. He nearly broke me for good."

"You are not broken." Kellie pressed her forehead to hers. "You are stronger than that man, or any man, will ever be."

Libby wiped her eyes. "I'm just afraid. I'm afraid

this whole thing will end up like that day in the lab. I'll be crushed. I won't be able to try again. Just when I think something good is happening, it all falls apart."

Kellie gathered her into her arms, and held her while she cried for a few minutes. But a few minutes was all she gave it—she'd cried way too many times over that incident, and her father didn't deserve any more of her tears. Yet, they always came.

"You're not a fifteen-year-old girl anymore." Kellie drew back and stroked Libby's hair away from her face. "You're a hell of a lot wiser." She turned and plucked some tissues from the box next to the bed, and gave them to her. "Once you get your dad's money, you can put him out of your life for good. You never have to speak to that man again."

Libby wiped her eyes and blew her nose. She took a few deep, ragged breaths.

"He's a horrible man, Libby." Kellie spoke firmly. "And he's brainwashed and abused you for your entire life. That's why you feel this way now. Don't let fear stop you."

Libby looked down at the dress in her lap. The rush of tears seemed to have cleared out the tension in her chest and the block in her head. She felt slightly more optimistic. No, she wasn't fifteen anymore. And her father absolutely deserved to have control ripped away from him once and for all.

Kellie gathered up the dress and held it out to her. "Now, go buy a husband and get this wheel turning. And then use it to run your dad right the hell over."

Libby took the dress and managed a smile. "I don't know what I did to deserve you."

"You deserve a lot of good things."

Libby collected herself and went to the bathroom to try on the dress. She avoided her own eyes in the mirror over the sink, as they were now puffy and red and she hated how she looked after she cried. The memory settled again in the back of her mind, a dormant lump, but ready to spring out at a moment's notice. She would never be free of it.

The dress was indeed formfitting, but not in a racy sort of way. It clung to her curves and gave her a shape she didn't even realize she had. The skirt came to the knee, and the collar, while low, didn't show off anything inappropriate. After putting the belt on she had to agree it did indeed look professional and sophisticated, but maybe just a little naughty too. The color went well with her fair skin tone.

She stepped out of the bathroom with warm cheeks, which got even hotter when Kellie whistled.

"That looks even better on you than it does me, I'm totally jealous." Kellie walked over and inspected her, circling her. "I think that bright red lipstick will go perfect with it." She peered at Libby's lips.

"I've never worn bright red lipstick." She laughed. "I don't wear lipstick at all."

"Come on." Kellie grabbed her hand and dragged her back to the bedroom. "I'll do your hair and face. Man, maybe I should drop my business classes and just become a hair and makeup artist. I love doing it, and it would be less expensive and wouldn't take as long."

Libby chuckled, but of course it prickled in her brain that her father would approve of a woman doing that over business, because it was a "female" profession. She really had to get his programming out of her head if she wanted to get anywhere in life.

Kellie sat her down in front of her vanity mirror. Libby gazed at herself in it. She wished she had a knack for making herself look pretty the way Kellie did. She was so mousy and plain.

"I have a date tonight with Sean," Kellie said. "So I won't be here when you get back, but you have to tell me all about what it's like to buy a husband."

"Sean." Libby looked up at her. "The guy with the fake accent, right?"

"Turns out it's real." Kellie shrugged. "He's from Denmark, who knew?"

Libby grinned and looked back in the mirror. "Maybe when this is all over you can set me up with someone too, huh? I'm not very good at talking to guys. I need a blind date or something."

"Girl, you don't want to date guys blindly, trust me. I wish we could all pick them out of a catalog."

Something told Libby this whole adventure was going to underline how lonely she was, and she'd feel worse at the end of it, even if all went well.

"Now, tell me about Blaine." Kellie started getting her products and instruments lined up on the vanity. "*Really* tell me about him."

Libby smoothed her hands over the leather belt around her waist. She felt like one of those high-powered female CEO's in this outfit.

She took a deep breath. "He's really, really sexy."

Chapter Four

Blaine stared out the window and chewed on the end of his pen. The gridwork of Manhattan sprawled in all directions and glistened beneath the late morning sun. The view was so familiar to him, sometimes he dreamt about it.

When he tried to imagine never seeing it again, that was almost a dream in itself. Could he really walk away forever?

And if he didn't, how would the rest of his life play out? What would he become?

"You wanna grab lunch with me today?"

Blaine shook himself out of his thoughts and swiveled in his chair, away from the window. Rick, one of his sub-brokers, sat on the other side of the desk. He was a young, slick guy with blond hair and chiseled features, the kind of guy who went to the gym three times a week and never missed a cocktail party after work. He was still bright-eyed and enthusiastic, and believed this was a great job.

He kind of reminded Blaine of himself at that age—what, a whole five years ago?

"I'd like to, but I can't." Blaine twirled the pen between his fingers. "I have to meet someone."

"Oh yeah? A client?"

"Something like that. Honestly, I should have a working lunch." With an inward groan, he looked at the stack of folders on his desk. Portfolios to review, not to mention the actual trading he needed to do and the three meetings he had with perspective clients this afternoon. No rest for the wicked.

He couldn't exactly miss this appointment, though.

"Anything I can take over for you?" Rick rocked

his chair. "Looks like you got quite a workload." He eyed the stack. "Things have been lively lately, day and night. Money never sleeps."

Blaine rubbed his chin with the pen. He needed to shave. But Libby had mentioned she liked his scruff.

"Thanks for the offer, but I got it. Just have to play some catch-up this afternoon. I'll probably be here late." He snorted. "I *know* I'll be here late." Had he ever left the office on time? He didn't even remember what "on time" was supposed to be.

Rick leaned back in his chair. "So, you're really gunning to be out of here before the end of next year? That's still the plan?"

Blaine tossed the pen on his desk. "Yes. My personal investments are solid, I've been building my savings, I just need to sink the right money into this one last investment and it should pay out what I need." He grinned. "Then it's fun in the sun for the rest of my days. Maybe I'll buy a beach house in the Bahamas and drink piña coladas every day. Or hey, maybe I should buy a race car—do you think I could get into stock car racing? You know, go from stocks to stocks?" He thought that was damn clever.

Rick snorted, apparently unimpressed by his pun. "Retiring at thirty. You're living the dream, my friend."

"I'm only living the dream because I made it work."

"You know money, man, and you know investing. I'm envious. I wanna grow up to be just like you."

Blaine chuckled. His colleagues assumed he was some kind of financial genius, making himself enough money to retire with a cool million at thirty. The truth was, he had the money to put into the right investments at the right time, and that was the key—and he was disinclined to tell them exactly how he'd *gotten* that investment money. They believed he'd netted it from prior, smaller investments over time, ones he'd cleverly scoped out and jumped on using his savvy skills, and that assumption was fine by him.

They also didn't know he'd taken a hefty loss early this year, one he was still trying to recover from. Barring that, he might have been starting to pack up his office. This was his chance to make it up. Libby was his prayers answered.

"Something tells me I won't hang out on that beach for too long, though." Blaine raked his fingers through his hair. At work, he usually pulled it back, but having it this long made him look young and hip and dynamically appealing to young investors. Young money didn't want a stuffy suit handling their finances. Old money knew him by his reputation and didn't care, but he still tried to look a bit more professional around them.

Libby liked it too, and he wanted to look good for her. Even if they were just conducting a business transaction.

"Think you'll get bored on the beach?" Rick asked.

"I know I'll get bored." Blaine lowered his hand. "I'll need something to keep my brain occupied. Maybe I can open a tiki hut or something."

"I can't believe you want to get out so bad." Rick tilted his head back. "You're so damn good at playing the stock market." He looked back at Blaine. "You're a master investor. Young guys in the game are learning so much from you."

"Are you saying I'm fucking old?"

Rick laughed. "No, man. You set the precedent, though. You ought to write a book." He pointed at him, eyebrow cocked. "There you go. That'll keep your brain occupied."

"I don't know about that. Yeah, I'm good at it, but this line of work burns you out quick. You'll find that out soon enough." He paused. "It's a rough business, and it drains you. Don't let it drain everything from you, Rick. Don't let it drain your soul."

Rick flung up his hands. "I've been here what, three years? That whole time, I've watched you work. You thrive on this. How can you just walk away? I know it can be a pain in the ass sometimes, but it's exciting too, isn't it? It keeps your heart beating!"

Blaine had struggled with that dichotomy for the past few years. He needed to get out, before this constant hurricane sucked the life out of him and turned him into a monster, but it was like ripping off a particularly snug Band-Aid. Jumping from the familiar into the unknown was terrifying, no matter how much he'd carefully planned his exit.

He thought about Libby and her aspirations. She'd shown up just when he needed the inspiration and courage the most. Maybe she was the answer to his prayers in more ways than one.

"Listen." Blaine heaved a sigh. "I've been in this world since I was a teenager, I did it before I even made any money from it. I started out as a courier, worked in mail rooms, and I got my first internship while I was still in school. My father was a trader, I learned more from him than I did in college. He started teaching me the stock market when I was thirteen."

Rick chuckled. "Kinda sounds like my old man. He started preaching personal finance at me in the cradle, I think."

"My dad hooked me up with a lot of good clients, right out of the gate. I've always done well, by the grace of others and hard work. I've only been officially brokering for seven years but I feel like I've been at it for fifty. I've never known anything else in my life."

"Seasoned at the ripe old age of twenty-nine." Rick chuckled wryly. "You got decades left in you. You could probably become a multimillionaire if you put your mind to it."

Blaine shook his head. "Trust me, I'd probably jump off a ledge before then. There's so many assholes in this business. So many cutthroat people who would kick you down a stairwell to turn a profit. I've met every bastard in Manhattan, and it's left a bitter taste in my mouth."

"Yeah, but that's part of the game." Rick splayed his hands. "These are high-maintenance rich people. Successful people. They didn't get that way by being nice. You just kind of learn to live with it or overlook it, don't you? I can brush a lot off my shoulders, trust me."

"So can I, and I have for a long time." Blaine gazed at the desk, at the stack of folders. Some of those people, with their money and their success, were certainly not nice people, and he would have to talk to them today and put on his usual false charm. "But I don't want to lose my soul. I feel it slipping away, little by little every day."

Maybe he needed to create a nonprofit as well, really help people, like Libby wanted to. Maybe he would be happier dealing with the world's lowest instead of society's highest.

"You sound so dramatic." Rick scoffed. "Maybe you're just depressed, man. Go to the doctor, get some Zoloft. Stick around here and teach this young blood how to really swim the shark-infested waters."

Rick would feel differently, maybe in five years, maybe ten. He had the constitution that Blaine didn't, but it would eventually crumble.

"I can't." Blaine sat forward. "That's why I've been investing on my own behalf the past few years." He stood. "Making my nest egg, so I can bail. I probably won't rest for long, but I won't be dealing with the bastards anymore, whatever I do. It's time to learn something else. There's more to the ocean than sharks."

Skepticism was evident in Rick's eyes. "You're really going to be able to cash out and retire? You've really accumulated that much money? What are we talking, tens of thousands?"

"Hundreds, after I turn this next investment." Blaine smirked and buttoned his blazer. "The *very* high hundreds."

"Damn, man!" Rick's yelp followed him out of the office.

Blaine got ready in his private bathroom. He wasn't going to change clothes, as he felt his work attire was good enough for this meeting. He did straighten his hair out a bit and freshen his cologne, though—no need to be a caveman.

He gazed in the mirror. "It's almost over," he murmured to himself. "Let's put this money where it counts."

The loss he'd taken still weighed heavy on his shoulders. He'd been aiming to be out by the first of the year, had gotten overzealous, and made the wrong investment. When that loss report came back it stung like no other loss ever had, even when one of his big accounts had taken a dive. That negative mocked him, like God laughing at his plans. What right did he have to stop working at such a young age? He could hear his father grumbling about it in his head every day.

But it was just a minor setback. It would work this time. He would take the cash from the marriage and put it in the right spot this time.

"Let's do this." He ran his fingers through his hair again. *Be the man they all think you are.*

He walked out of the bathroom with his head held high, ready to go sell himself to his new wife.

****

"Blaine, darling. How are you?"

Monica's smile could light up a room. Her soothing, agreeable nature sometimes reminded him of his mother, and it gave him a warm and fuzzy feeling inside.

"I'm great, how are you?" He squeezed her hand and kissed her cheek. "Everything going well at the old brothel?"

Ever since he'd signed on with the agency, he liked to tease her about the nature of her business. No matter how much they sugarcoated it or twisted things around to fit through legal loopholes, at the end of the day he was selling himself and his services. Like an escort.

She chuckled. "Things are great here. And how's work? The stock markets all in order today?"

He tucked his hands in his pants pockets. "As in order as they ever are. Work is work, as usual." He tried to keep his negative feelings out of conversations with others. "I'm never bored, that's for sure."

"That's good. Idle hands, after all."

They strolled down the hallway together. Monica was carrying a stack of paperwork. Blaine calculated if he could get it all signed and get back to the office before his next conference call. He could always conduct it in the car on the drive back of course, but he didn't want to.

"I'm happy to see you and Libby hit it off." Monica smiled at him. "She seems like a lovely girl. She was so nervous when she first came to see me."

"She is indeed a lovely girl." He found himself

smiling too. "She's got some big dreams, very intelligent. And an interesting case."

"Aren't they all?" Monica stopped outside a door and opened it. They stepped into a dark conference room. "I've been doing this for a lot of years, you know." She flipped on the lights. "I see all kinds of things, so many complicated situations. I swear if it wasn't a huge breach of privacy I would put them all in a book. But as it is, I'm just happy to help and bring people together."

They moved to the long, polished table in the center of the room and took seats on either side of it.

"I just love … *love*." Monica sighed, setting the paperwork down in front of her. She gazed dreamily toward the ceiling. "There's something about seeing lonely, struggling souls coming together and finding strength in each other. It makes you believe there's something out there, doesn't it?"

Blaine furrowed his brow, bemused. "You set people up in fake relationships, though. That's not exactly true love."

She focused on him, an easy smile playing on her lips. "It happens more often than not around here, believe me. What starts out as fake becomes very, very real."

Blaine reached over and pulled a folder toward him. "Not for me though, huh?"

Monica just continued smiling. She checked the time on her phone. "Libby will be here shortly. We can get a head start on your paperwork."

Fifteen minutes later, a knock sounded at the door. It popped open and a woman peeked her head in. "Miss Hunt, Liberty Dawson is here."

"Libby," Blaine muttered to himself, writing.

"Come right in." Monica got to her feet.

Blaine got up too, to be a gentleman, but also because he was stunned. Libby had been pretty and charming when he first met her, but what walked in the door now was something else entirely.

She wore a slinky red dress that did amazing things for her figure. Her hair was pulled up on top her head but spilled down to her neck in thick curls. She wore bright red lipstick and it made her features look sharp and striking. Despite her knockout appearance, hesitation shone in her eyes, and she was gnawing on her lower lip.

Monica beamed at her. "Hello, Libby. It's so good to see you again. Please have a seat."

"Uh, hello." She clutched her purse in front of her. "Thanks."

Blaine quickly pulled out the chair next to his. She sat down, her posture stiff and shoulders hunched. He sat down as well.

"Hi." She gazed at him.

"Hi." He gazed back at her. "You look beautiful."

She burst into a smile. She had lipstick on her teeth, from chewing on her lip. Blaine inwardly winced, but also found it cute. He debated telling her, but she was already so wound up he didn't want to embarrass her.

"Thank you." She ducked her head. "It's my friend Kellie's dress."

"I've never met Kellie, but I'm going to declare unequivocally that it looks better on you."

She kept her head down, her cheeks as red as her lipstick, but she was still smiling.

The process only took about fifteen minutes, but Blaine was distracted by the scent of Libby's perfume, as well as her presence burning bright next to him. Half of his brain admonished him not to get swept up in this, not to get all starry-eyed, because it was the least romantic thing in the world. The other half argued back that it was okay to like her, to enjoy her company, and to look forward to spending time with her. After all, they were going to be attached to each other for six weeks.

His brain was so busy shouting back and forth he could barely pay attention to the task at hand.

Libby paid with a cashier's check, and Blaine respectfully pretended to be absorbed in the terms and conditions he was reading. Partly to make it less awkward for her, and partly because no matter how proper and businesslike this was all pretending to be, there was something seedy and base about someone forking over money for the company of another human being.

Papers were signed, agreements made. Monica reiterated sternly that this was not a transaction that carried the promise of sexual services, as she was required to say to cover her ass.

"If you change your mind before the marriage, the money is nonrefundable," she informed Libby, and pushed a paper over for her to sign and acknowledge that she understood this. "This is our policy."

Libby nodded. "I understand." She quickly grabbed the paper and signed it.

Blaine would feel terrible if she changed her mind, though. He would give her the money back on his own.

He surprised himself with this line of thinking. Since when had gotten so selfless?

Maybe the world of money hadn't corrupted his soul after all. Maybe he could still get out unscathed.

When the papers were all signed, they rose and both shook hands with Monica. He was on the hook now, and would see the numbers rise in his bank account in the next few days. He'd wait to get the investment rolling though, until Libby actually said "I do."

After exiting the conference room, Libby went to

the ladies' room and he and Monica stood in the hallway.

"I hope it all turns out well for both of you." She squeezed his arm. "The money will be transferred as soon as the check clears."

"Thanks, Monica." He heaved a sigh. "You know, I wish I'd figured out in my early twenties how profitable it was to sell myself. I might not have gone into stocks." He winked.

Monica laughed. "We're always recruiting bright, beautiful young men for our catalog. If you have any handsome friends, be sure to refer them to me."

He thought of Rick. He would probably love to date women for money, but at the same time, Blaine would have to admit what he was doing and it might tarnish Blaine's image of him as a shining investing star.

Monica left, but Blaine waited outside the ladies' room for Libby.

When she emerged, her cheeks were flushed and her lipstick gone, her lips back to their soft pink color, which was also lovely.

"Oh my God, I never wear lipstick." She was flustered. "I had no idea it was all over my teeth. I feel like such an idiot."

Blaine kept a poker face. "Was it? I didn't even notice."

She looked at him, doubt in her eyes, but he maintained his blank demeanor. She seemed to relax.

"Well, it's done." She let out a breath, her shoulders sagging.

"Not quite, we still have to get married." He smiled and offered her his arm. "Can I walk you out?"

She demurely took his arm. They started slowly down the hallway together. He had to get back to work soon, but suddenly he was more open to doing that conference call in the car.

"I read the email over a couple times," he said. "I think I can pull it off with your father." She had sent him a detailed email covering the things he needed to say and do, and the story they were going to run with.

Consternation strained her features. "My father is incredibly strict, and ruthless, and shrewd. You're really going to have to play this up. I'm so sorry."

"It's all right." He hesitated. "I hope you don't think I'm out of line when I say that your father sounds like a gigantic jerk."

She huffed, tightening her arm through his. "I could think of a few other stronger words for him."

"I researched him a bit, just to see what I'd be up against."

She looked up at him. "Did you?"

He nodded. "While he's a dynamo of a businessman and I found lots of compliments and praises in that area, it seems personally he's not so well-lauded."

"Imagine that."

"There's rumors about unfair labor and hiring practices, and compliance issues. Nothing that's actually blown up or been heavily documented, but it's out there."

"I'm super *not* surprised." She spoke bitterly. "My dad is really good at hiding things and getting around things. I'm not shocked that it hasn't become a big deal yet."

"It might though, someday."

She sagged against him a little, and he had the urge to slip his arm around her, but didn't.

"I don't think he'll ever get caught." Her tone turned weary now. "He'll never have to pay for the things he does. I don't think people like him ever really get what's coming to them."

Blaine's concern was growing, not so much for himself but for her—he couldn't imagine how such a bright, gentle creature had come from a man who sounded like such a demon. She was a rose growing in gravel, that was for sure.

"You're going to make him pay." Blaine patted her hand on his forearm. "You're going to get that money. People like him, that's the only place you can really hurt them."

She looked up at him again and smiled faintly. "We'll see."

He walked her to her car in the parking lot. She had a compact, but newer model and decent car. Blaine had the sneaking suspicion her father had probably bought it for her, and he was sure in return she was expected to be ever-grateful and groveling.

"So, I guess we go get the marriage license next?" She stood on the other side of her open door, poised to get in. "I have to tell my parents first." Worry shone in her eyes, which was barely an overlay for the pure terror behind it. "That's not going to be pleasant."

He touched her hand, where she was gripping the top of the door. "If you need any support, just call me."

She glanced at his hand and smiled. "Thank you, Blaine."

He smiled back at her in return, gazing into the frightened, beautiful depths of her eyes. He wanted to throw his arms around her, tell her everything would be all right, and protect her. His brain was still arguing wildly about impracticality and hastiness versus the simple matter of being nice to another human being. Denial was a deep river.

"I'll see you soon, Libby. Be well." He stepped around the door and kissed her cheek.

The taste of her skin lingered on his lips—as did the smell of her perfume in his nostrils—as he watched her drive away. *Focus on the money, not the girl.* Easier said than done.

He checked the time on his phone and sighed heavily, then turned and walked toward his car. Back to reality.

At least he would have the image of her in that red dress to dwell on the rest of the day.

Chapter Five

"You're getting married?" Libby's mother slammed down her cup of tea, so it made a loud crack on the countertop. Libby flinched.

Libby sat in a chair at the kitchen table, her fists balled and stuffed between her knees. The familiar kitchen of her childhood loomed around her like the walls of a prison cell, one with flowered wallpaper and teakwood cupboards. Every time she stepped back in this house she immediately felt like she couldn't breathe. The scent of the air, the way the light fell through the windows, the old furniture, and the never-changing décor—nothing but bad memories.

"Liberty Dawson, you'd better not be screwing with us." Her father's voice came scathing and harsh through the phone on the table. Getting the two of them together in one place was nearly impossible now. "This isn't funny, young lady."

"I'm not joking, Daddy." She fought to keep her voice calm and even. "I'm telling the truth."

"We didn't even know you had a boyfriend." Her mother clutched the edge of the counter, like she might collapse. She was dressed immaculate as always, in a plain, high-collared dress, her hair pulled into a tight bun. She looked like an old schoolmarm. "We've never even met him."

"I know." Libby dug her nails into her palms. "It's been kind of a whirlwind thing. I haven't had a chance."

"Clearly." Her father's voice remained droll and severe. "So whirlwind you couldn't even tell us about him until you decided to get married. This is absolutely unacceptable."

She could do this. She *had* to do this. She tried to

recall Kellie's words, and Blaine's, about being brave and making a difference, and about her father deserving this deception.

"We're in love." She managed to squeak the words out.

Her father blustered. "Does this boy not know he's supposed to ask me for your hand first? That's how you do things. I know you kids these days like to be all wild and free and disrespect your parents, but that's not how we raised you, Liberty Ann. There's a lack of tradition in this country, but I won't put up with it, not in my household. Things have to be done a certain way, especially when it comes to my damn daughter."

Libby looked down at her clenched hands. They trembled. She squeezed her knees around them.

"What is this boy's name?" her mother demanded. "Did you meet him at school?"

"His name is Blaine." She lifted her head. "And he's not a boy. He doesn't go to my school, but I met him at school."

"He's not a professor, is he?" Her father sounded incredulous.

"No. He's a stockbroker. He came to our school to give a seminar on the importance of financial planning for our future. After it, we—we talked, and we just sort of … we connected. And we started dating."

Her mother stared at her, her face blank. Her father was silent.

Libby pushed on. "I know I should have told you. It happened so fast, and I've been so distracted. I'm sorry. I was afraid that—"

Her father cut her off. "How old is this man?"

"Twenty-nine."

Her mother clutched her chest. "Thank God, I thought you were going to tell us he was your father's age or something. I've read about older men preying on young girls. It happens all the time, especially in college settings."

Libby shook her head. "He's kind and intelligent, and he treats me very well. He brings me flowers." She wasn't good at lying, so using half-truths came much easier.

Her mother huffed. "It takes more than flowers to make a marriage, Liberty." She glanced at the phone on the table. "Marriage is difficult. It's a commitment, and there's a lot of trying parts. It doesn't always work the way you want it to." The last bit sounded accusing.

"We sort of decided on it together, spur-of-the-moment." Libby kept talking, because if she didn't, she would lose her nerve. "We think marriage is a good idea, even though we haven't been together that long. We're in love and we make a great team. He didn't propose all fancy or anything. We just made a practical decision."

"Even though he hasn't met your parents." The anger in her father's voice made her blood run cold, even as an adult. "Very disrespectful, don't you think? What kind of man is that?"

"I think you should meet him, then." She twisted her hands between her knees. "Daddy, I know you usually have a short day on Wednesdays, so we thought we'd have a little get-together this Wednesday night so you can meet him, both of you."

Her mother frowned. "I have book club on Wednesday nights, Liberty."

"Oh."

"We'll be there." Her father spoke sharply. "There's no way I'm letting you plan a wedding without meeting this guy. You can miss your damn book club, Marge. Those trashy romance books aren't as important as your daughter's future."

Her mother glared at the phone, but didn't protest. Even divorced, he still commanded her, as he did all of them.

"Can't you have a party next week?" she suggested to Libby, lowering her voice. "Book club is only once a month and it's so nice to get together with the girls."

Libby was so stiff she was about to topple over. She had come this far, she couldn't turn back now.

"No." She gripped her knees. "Because we're getting married this Saturday."

For a moment, there was heavy, ominous silence. Then her mother and father both started shouting at the same time. Libby winced and dug her fingernails into her knees.

"Saturday!" her mother shrieked over her father, who was swearing through the phone. "Are you playing a joke on us right now? This is ridiculous!"

"No." Libby tried to speak over them. "We think the sooner, the better. We want to get it done right away."

Her mother stared wide-eyed at her, and suddenly blanched. She clutched her bosom again. "Liberty Ann Dawson, are you *pregnant*?"

"You better not be!" her father roared.

"No, no!" Libby leapt to her feet. "I'm not pregnant, calm down." Adrenaline surged through her, making her tremble harder, but also giving her courage and conviction. "It's just—you're right, Daddy, and I finally understand that." She steeled herself, though the words cut her apart inside, where she had no defense. "I've finally taken your advice to heart."

Her parents fell silent, and then her father spoke. "About what, exactly?"

Libby smoothed her shaking hands over her hair

and tugged on a strand of it. "The older a woman gets, the less appealing and marriageable she is. I don't want to end up an old maid. I don't want to get all dried up and useless so no man will want to take care of me. I'm almost twenty-three, and I see what you mean now, Daddy. A woman doesn't make a very good companion for a man when she gets past a certain age. She doesn't bring anything to the table. The older she gets, the more likely she is to be soiled, right? Even if it's not true, it's the impression it gives."

These were all exact phrases he had said to her as a teenager.

Her mother pinched her lips together and turned to the counter. She snatched her cup up.

Libby dropped her hands in front of her and fidgeted. "I've been thinking about Justice and her husband and kids, you know? I want that. I want it so much. I know that's the life I should have, Daddy. I want to get married while I still have my shine. I want to make a man happy."

Her father heaved a sigh. That, at least, was a resigned rather than angry sound. Maybe this was working.

"Liberty, I appreciate you've finally come to your senses. I'm relieved, truly." His voice was softer, but still stern. "And I understand your panic. But this is very fast. Sudden, even. I don't want you to make a poor choice."

She told the worst lie then, her ace in the hole.

"He's a good man, Daddy. He reminds me of you." She had only met Blaine once, but he didn't seem anything like her father. Still, that line would work on him.

Her mother turned from the counter. She sipped her tea and stared across the kitchen, her eyes glistening.

"Liberty, dear heart, I want you to be careful."

Her father sounded kind now, but it was fake. He had never been truly kind a day in his life. "Have you considered this man may be rushing you into marriage for the money? You're a naïve little thing."

She pulled at her thumbnail. She had to tread carefully here. "He … doesn't know about the money, Daddy. I wanted it to be a surprise when we got married. I wanted it to make him even happier that he'd chosen me."

Her mother glanced at her. Libby avoided her gaze and stared at the phone.

Her father sighed again. "I wish you had told us about him before this. I mean, I'm glad you finally found someone. I was starting to worry about you. I know how college can corrupt a young woman."

She didn't know specifically what he meant by that, but she was sure it was a hodgepodge of concerns he had voiced when she first enrolled—that she would take drugs, drink alcohol, have promiscuous sex, and perhaps become a lesbian, or worse, a feminist. So far, the only thing she'd done was drink wine.

And of course, buy a husband and concoct a scheme that would get her disowned eventually.

"When we get married," she spoke carefully, "I think I may quit school. I'll become a housewife and have kids like Justice. I think that's for the best."

This, more than anything, would sweeten the deal for her father. Technically, she had already fulfilled part of it. Her mother fixed her with a hard, glittering glare, and there was perhaps a touch of panic there as well. But if her mother wanted to hang her abandoned hopes and dreams on her, it wouldn't work. Libby wasn't a coat hook for her issues.

As predicted, her father's voice brightened. "Well, it does sound like you're getting your head on straight at last, Liberty. Maybe letting you go out in the world and see how harsh and cruel it is did you some good after all."

"I'm ready to settle down, Daddy, and I've found the right man to do it with. I was scared to tell you before because I was afraid it might not work out and you'd be disappointed in me."

"You know I love you, Liberty. You were more difficult than your sister growing up, but I blame that on your mother leaving me. I know you had a hard time with our divorce. I should have been there for you more."

Her mother plunked her cup down again. "You swear you're not pregnant, Liberty?"

"No. I'm saving that for my wedding night."

That was true as well—at least, her real wedding night, with a real husband, someday.

"We'll meet this man on Wednesday, then, Marge." Her father's tone was decisive. Libby knew from experience you couldn't argue with him after his mind was set. "And if I like him, I'll give you my blessing. That's the condition. If I don't approve of him, you're not marrying him."

Panic rose in her chest. She was really going to have to coach Blaine on how to hit all her father's buttons. He *had* to like Blaine. If she married him and her father didn't like him, she wouldn't get the money.

"I think this is foolish and brash," her mother informed her. "You shouldn't rush into things like this, Liberty." She glanced at the phone. "I don't want you to regret it down the line."

Libby swallowed. The next words out of her mouth hurt as much as the rest had, but by now she was numb to it. "I think fate sent him to me, to show me Daddy was right."

Of course, *she* knew, better than anyone, how to

hit her father's buttons.

Her mother turned and stalked out of the kitchen. She always walked away, instead of standing her ground. Even now.

"All right, darling." Her father's voice was all sugar and honey now, and it made her stomach turn. "I'll make sure my calendar is clear for Wednesday night."

Libby waited until she was in her car and a few miles from her parents' house before she pulled over on the side of the road and burst into tears. She ground her teeth and dug her nails into her arms.

He deserves this. He's an awful man and he deserves to be lied to. He deserves it if I take his money and never see or speak to him again for the rest of my life.

"I hate you," she spat through her sobs. "I hate you so much. Asshole!" She slammed her hands on the steering wheel.

She grabbed her phone from the seat next to her and held it in her shaking hands, and stared at the screen through blurry eyes. She wanted to call Kellie and tell her everything, let her reassure her and support her, like she always did. Kellie was good at boosting her resolve. It could wait, though. Wait until tonight. She had somewhere to be. And her resolve was strong, because she couldn't turn back now. The hardest part was over, thankfully, somehow.

She looked at the paperwork on the passenger seat. The filled-out form, her birth certificate, all the necessary stuff. She took a few deep, shaky breaths to calm herself, hot tears still slipping down her cheeks. A look in the rearview mirror revealed that her eyes were red, her nose running. She couldn't show up looking like this.

She dug some tissues out of her purse to mop her

face, and rolled the window down so the air would dry her cheeks and clear her eyes. For once, not wearing makeup was to her advantage. At least she didn't have any mascara to smear.

"You deserve this, Daddy," she muttered as she pulled back onto the road. "For all the years you told me I could never be anything but a possession."

She sped back toward the city, her throat thick, eyes burning, heart pounding.

When she arrived at the clerk's office, she checked herself in the mirror again. Her eyes were almost back to normal, though they were still a little bloodshot. She fixed her hair and put some lip gloss on. After a few bracing breaths, she gathered up everything from the passenger seat and climbed out of the car.

Despite the euphoric rush of having done something so absolutely bold, she was incredibly nervous, so much so she was light-headed and her knees shook. Part of her still wanted to turn around and run. She didn't even care about getting her money back. This was too wild. She was going to destroy her parents' lives. She was going to destroy her own life.

However, she pictured her mother's pinched face as she stalked out of the kitchen. The way she still obeyed him even though he wasn't her husband anymore. Libby was not going to live her life like that. She was going to wiggle out from under her father's iron fist, no matter how difficult the fight.

Blaine was waiting for her outside the building, near the front steps. As she approached, she slowed her pace and her breath caught. She thought after meeting him twice already, she would have a less visceral reaction to how handsome he was, but that wasn't the case.

He leaned against the side of the building,

looking down at his phone. At least he wasn't watching her, so she could take a moment to compose herself. She forced a smile and strolled up to him—casually, she hoped, and without looking like a maniac who was about to start screaming.

He looked up. All her composure went out the window. His eyes were vivid and so clear blue. His hair fell in soft, honey-gold waves around his face and curled against the collar of his white dress shirt. He also wore trim black slacks that hugged his marvelous hips, and she tried not to stare.

"Hey." He pushed away from the wall and slipped his phone into his pants pocket. "It's good to see you again."

He gave her a light hug. His musky cologne filled her nose and she found it even harder to unlock her tongue, or control her nervousness.

He drew back, holding her arms, and looked her in the face. That didn't help. He was painfully handsome, and she was mesmerized by the sharp lines of his cheekbones and jaw. He furrowed his tawny eyebrows, the same color as the hair that graced his chin and upper lip.

"Are you okay?" His voice was deep and soothing like a backrub. "You look a little stressed out."

She let out a short, sharp laugh. "Yeah, this is kind of stressful. But I'm ready."

"You told your parents?"

She nodded. "They're a little … surprised. But that's to be expected, right?" She forced out another laugh. This one wasn't as genuine.

"I'm sure." He continued to study her face, and she wished he'd look away before she blushed herself to death. Could you literally die from embarrassment?

"You're absolutely, positively sure you want to

do this?" he asked.

She kept smiling. "I don't think I can get my money back at this point, can I? No refunds."

He chuckled and finally looked away. He placed a hand on the small of her back, as smooth and comforting as his voice. "I wouldn't trap you like that. I don't abide by the 'no refunds' policy."

She arched an eyebrow. Had he done this before?

"So." He turned them toward the stairs. "Shall we? Did you bring everything you need?"

She clutched the papers. "Uh huh." She gazed up at the stoic brick building. This was all so formal, so clinical. They'd sign a few papers, pay a fee, and she could legally change her last name in a couple of days.

She hadn't thought much about that part. Liberty Parker. That didn't sound so bad. But should she take his last name or keep her own? After all, it was only six weeks.

She started to internally freak out. She hadn't considered these practicalities. Given the short duration of the marriage, she should probably keep her own last name. Didn't they charge to change your name back after a divorce? Her mother had kept her father's, but she wasn't sure if that was about money.

Blaine started up the stairs, but stopped and looked back at her when she didn't follow. "Libby? You okay?"

"Yeah, I was just thinking, I thought the day I got a marriage license would be more romantic." She felt lame. "I mean, if I ever got married for real."

Blaine smiled. "I can take you to lunch after, if you like? It may not be romantic, but we can be friendly, can't we?"

She squared her shoulders. Romance wasn't important here, the future was. The future of all the people she would someday help.

"Absolutely." She strode up after him. "Let's do this."

He offered her his arm. Her cheeks warmed again.

He was smiling still. She loved his smile. It was easy and kind and … sexy. His whole laid-back demeanor was sexy, in fact. She took his arm. It was sturdy.

"Come on." He led her up the stairs. "There's nothing to be afraid of. This will be easy."

None of it would be easy, especially not the aftermath, but she had to fight for what she wanted.

Time to grow up and be a big girl.

Chapter Six

Blaine reserved a table at Gramercy Tavern, his favorite restaurant in the Flatiron District of Manhattan. The place was upscale, but not too fancy, still formal enough for casual dress but nice enough to prove he had decent taste. He wanted Libby's father to be impressed but not *too* impressed. If he was obviously showing off, things would look phony. On the other hand, he had to appeal to the man's sensibilities.

This exercise took delicate balance, like walking a high wire. He'd told Libby he was a good actor, but this was the first time he'd ever had to play such a precarious part. To his surprise, he found he almost relished the challenge.

"You look very nice." He swept Libby with an apprising look. "That color suits you."

She wore a dark blue chiffon dress with a flowing skirt and high waist, with a boxy top that had shoulder straps instead of sleeves. He tried not to check out her figure, though the fabric clung to every curve and it was hard not to. Her hair spilled over her pale shoulders, and she wore a thin silver chain with a sparkling diamond heart on it.

Almost as nice as the red dress. She looked good in everything.

"Thanks. It's Kellie's, again." She twisted her silver clutch between her hands. As always, her nails were bare and shiny, he face fresh and mostly free of makeup. Despite the obvious terror in her eyes, she looked stunning in a subtle, natural way.

He drew her chair out next to his at the table. "Don't panic, okay? We got this. Take a few deep breaths."

She sat down and arranged her skirt in her lap,

and pulled in a couple breaths. He sat down as well and touched her arm. She looked at him with those beautiful green eyes.

"This is a really nice place." She bobbed her knees under the table. "I should have dressed up more."

"You look gorgeous." He leaned in closer. She wore that same delicate, flowery perfume. "The dress is perfect." He wore a blazer and a black dress shirt, business-casual style. That's what this was, after all. A casual business meeting.

"I should have worn more makeup." She opened her clutch and pulled out a mirror. "But Daddy says women who wear too much makeup are trying to hide something. Is my lip gloss too dark?" She puckered her lips in the mirror. They were shiny, but barely had any color other than their own deep pink.

Blaine rubbed his thumb across his eyebrow. "Stop worrying, all right? My parents will be here soon. I think you'll like them."

Libby lowered the mirror and looked at him. Her gaze softened a little, but fear still tensed her features. "What are you going to tell your parents when this is over? I mean, my parents will never speak to me again, but I'm ready for that. I don't want to screw things up with your family."

"Don't worry about it." He squeezed her arm. "I'll figure something out. I have six weeks to come up with something, right? If I didn't want to put myself in this situation, I wouldn't have signed up with the agency to being with."

She pushed the mirror back into her clutch. "Should we go over the details again? I hope I don't forget anything."

He rubbed her shoulder, and then her back. She was so nice to touch. He withdrew his hand, because he didn't want to cross the line from being soothing to inappropriate. "Don't worry, we'll do just fine. I remember everything. If you forget something, just stay quiet, and I'll take over and help you out."

"That'll be for the best anyway." She plopped her clutch on the table. "Daddy will like it that you're speaking for me."

The more she told him about this man, the less he liked him. He already kind of hated him, as a matter of fact. But he wasn't being paid to get involved in her personal life. Besides, it seemed like she was about to take care of herself just fine.

"Would you like me to order some wine?" He grabbed up the wine list. "It might relax your nerves."

She held up a hand. "No, my parents don't know I drink. I mean, I *don't* drink, I've just had a few glasses of wine with Kellie, but I can't drink in front of them."

This was going to be a long night.

Libby's parents arrived first. Even if Blaine had never seen a picture of Coleman Dawson, he would have known it was him by the way Libby stiffened. Blaine squeezed her knee under the table and got to his feet.

"Mr. Dawson." Blaine put on a bright and open face—his working face—and stepped around the table, hand extended. "I'm Blaine Parker. It's a pleasure to meet you."

Coleman was a tall, long-limbed man with mahogany brown hair streaked with a hint of silver at the temples. He wore a perfectly tailored charcoal gray suit and a red power tie. His eyes were the same color as Libby's, but not nearly as wide and innocent. His face was tanned and clean-shaven, and both his expression and gaze were no-nonsense and commanding. He stared Blaine down as he took his hand in a strong, firm handshake.

"Yes, I would hope so," Coleman said, and his voice was as lofty and intimidating as the rest of him. "It should definitely be a priority to meet the father of the girl you're planning on marrying. This Saturday, no less."

Blaine wasn't cowed. He met guys like this all the time in his line of work, suits who threw around their position and power to make themselves look inflated. What this blowhard didn't know was that Blaine was already trying to calculate future stock losses in the back of his head, when all his unfair practices finally came to light—and they would, because things like that always did in Blaine's experience.

"Ah, yes." Blaine tucked his hands in the pockets of his pants, elbows out, keeping his body language open and casual, and making it clear he wasn't intimidated. "I'm sorry about that, I realize I should have spoken to you first, but I was afraid someone else might snag Liberty up if I waited too long."

Libby insisted he call her by her full name in front of her parents.

Coleman swept him with a cold, regarding gaze, then turned to the narrow, tight-lipped woman at his side. "This is Marge Dawson, the mother of my children."

Blaine kept his expression passive, not reacting to the strange wording. Libby had told him her parents were divorced, but he supposed Coleman didn't want to acknowledge that. Blaine had only known this man ten seconds and he already understood the self-important way he operated.

"A pleasure to meet you, Mrs. Dawson." Blaine held his hand out to her. He had a feeling he'd better use "Mrs." over anything else.

She was a stern-looking woman, with glasses and a pointed chin, her hair wrapped tight on top of her head.

She wore a long-sleeved prim black dress. She reminded him of a stereotypical librarian. However, beneath her dour and reticent expression he saw Libby's beauty, that soft open-faced look which had long been covered with heavy lines of unhappiness.

She shook his hand briefly, her fingers bony and cold. "Liberty hasn't told us much about you."

"She hasn't told us anything about you." Coleman focused on his daughter, who still sat at the table, shoulders hunched and eyes downcast. "Until just a few days ago."

"I know this must be a huge shock." Blaine hurried to pull out Marge's chair. "And I know it's incredibly irregular, but I hope tonight you'll let us explain."

Marge gave him a sharp, though curious look, and sat. Blaine went to his chair. Coleman was the last to sit, and he kept his piercing gaze on Blaine as he did.

"Your sister couldn't come, Liberty," her mother said. "She doesn't have a babysitter."

"That's okay." Libby continued to stare at her lap.

"I must say, it's a pleasure to meet you, for other reasons." Blaine made his voice a little more anxious and high, in a mimicry of gushing. "Dawson True Life Products is such a powerful company on the exchange. I work with your stocks every week and they always seem to be climbing. You've built a strong and thriving business. I followed your rise to success in the periodicals. Amazing how it took you less than a decade to climb to the top."

Coleman tilted his chin up, a glint in his eyes. Of course, his ego would be the easiest thing to grab.

"So, you're a stockbroker?" Coleman remained frosty in his demeanor, however. "How long have you been at it? Who do you work for?"

"I own my own firm, and I've been on the floor of the stock exchange for seven years. I jumped into it right out of school." He smiled. "Though, I got into trading as a teenager, thanks to my father. He's a broker as well. I've always enjoyed working with money and futures. There's something thrilling about knowing you help keep the business world turning."

Coleman grunted. "So, you thought you'd marry the daughter of a powerful CEO, is that it? Do you think if you do this I'll get you some upper-level management position in my company? Is that your angle?"

Libby lifted her gaze, her eyes wide beneath her thick fringe of bangs. She was pale. "It's not like that, Daddy." Her voice came out squeaky and small.

"No, it's not like that at all." Blaine reached over and took Libby's hand from her lap. She was trembling and she closed her fingers tight around his. "In fact, Liberty didn't even tell me who you were until I was already in love with her. And I quite like what I do, I'm not looking to make any sort of career change. I'd rather stay in stocks."

Coleman was not easily swayed. "It would certainly help your career for investors to know who your father-in-law is though, now wouldn't it?"

Blaine had prepared himself for this, but maintaining a cool and collected demeanor suddenly didn't come easy. He reminded himself he'd run into many self-important guys like this in his time and he knew how to handle them. The problem was that usually, he didn't have to take care of their scared, timid daughters at the same time.

"I don't need your name to help me attract investors." Blaine squeezed Libby's hand. "I can ride on my own reputation, thank you."

Coleman tilted his head, narrowing his eyes. If there was one thing guys like him respected, it was an ego as big as their own.

"We're in love, Daddy." Libby's voice was a little stronger. "He's not trying to get your money or your name. Please stop being rude to him."

Coleman focused his burning gaze on his daughter, and she looked down at once. Blaine got the sick feeling that if she were younger—or he wasn't there—he might have reached out and slapped her.

"He's not being rude, darling." Blaine squeezed her hand again. "It's perfectly normal for him to be worried about you. He's never met me before. I could be any sort of predator. He has a right to be suspicious. Just calm down." As the condescending tone fell out of his mouth, he immediately regretted it. But it was fake, and it was on purpose.

And it worked.

Coleman refocused on him, and the ice in his expression melted a bit, as if he'd just recognized one of his own. Blaine felt even sicker.

Marge spoke up. "Liberty said it's been a whirlwind romance. Are you sure you're in love? It's so hasty, you haven't known each other long."

Blaine smiled at her. "Yes, I agree it's hasty, Mrs. Dawson, but sometimes love is like that. I'm sure when you fell in love with your husband, you knew it was fate."

Marge pressed her lips together and stared down at the tablecloth. Coleman gave a humorless chuckle.

"You fell head over heels for my daughter?" He gestured to Libby. "Why? She's hardly a prize. She's extremely willful. I've done my best with her, but…" He sighed heavily. "It's not easy to raise a daughter, let alone two of them. There's so much you have to keep them from, so many paths they can wander down that you don't want them on, especially in this day and age. If I'd only had a son, it might have eased my burden a bit. But God saw fit to saddle me with girls, so I make do."

Blaine stared at him. He couldn't believe in the first five minutes of conversation he was speaking this way, to a stranger, about his children.

Libby was looking down at her lap again, her long lashes fluttering. Blaine flexed his fingers around hers.

"Well, sir." The words tasted like bile on his tongue. "We'll just have to work on that, won't we?"

Coleman raised his thick eyebrows.

"I see potential in her. I think I can shape her into the young woman she's truly meant to be. I think I'll be very good for her in that respect."

The tiniest of smiles touched Coleman's thin lips. Libby's hand eased around his, but he didn't know if it was relaxation or despair.

At that moment, Blaine saw two familiar faces across the restaurant, and a wave of relief swept through him, mostly because this conversation could now be derailed.

"Ah, my parents are here." He let go of Libby's hand, got to his feet, and waved to them.

Libby lifted her head.

They were a stark contrast to Marge and Coleman, and in much better disposition, but then, probably everyone was. His mother had a head of artfully arranged silver curls and wore a colorful but distinctly fashionable dress. His father was tottering and short, nearly bald and sporting a bushy gray mustache. He wore a suit, though it wasn't nearly as tailored as Coleman's.

"My parents," Blaine introduced them. "Sherri and Robert Parker."

Hands were shaken all around. His mother cooed over Libby and made her stand up, and looked her over.

"Oh, aren't you just a gorgeous thing. Blaine showed me a picture, but it didn't do you justice."

Libby's cheeks were pink.

"This is for you." His mother held a small package wrapped in white wrapping paper, with a green bow. "Welcome to the family, Liberty." She pulled her into a hug and kissed her cheeks.

Libby's eyes were wide as she clutched the present. Blaine smiled at her.

"It's nice to meet you, Liberty." His father had a jolly, good-natured voice. "Good to see my boy finally settling down." He clapped Blaine on the arm. "And with such a striking young woman too. She's lovely, Blaine."

Blaine chuckled. "Thanks, Dad."

Coleman was scrutinizing Blaine's parents. Marge seemed taken aback.

"So, you only just learned about this as well?" Coleman strong-armed his way into the conversation. "You haven't met Liberty before tonight?"

"Oh no, no." Blaine's father sat down, between him and Coleman. "But we were very keen on meeting her when he told us."

Marge eyed Blaine's mother as she sat down between her and Libby. "This doesn't bother you at all? It's so sudden. It's crazy."

"I think it's very romantic." Blaine's mother beamed at Libby. "Oh, to be so young and spontaneous again."

Libby plucked at the ribbon on her present and for the first time, a smile broke her lips.

"Go on and open it, dear." His mother patted Libby's arm. "And then I want you to tell us all about yourself. Blaine has only told us a little and I'm dying to know more about you."

"This is madness," Marge muttered.

Blaine's father poured himself a glass of water from the pitcher in the middle of the table. "Mad indeed, and risky for both of them, but then, without risks one never succeeds, or gets very far in life. That's how it works in the business world, doesn't it, Mr. Dawson?" He grinned wryly at Coleman. "I know who you are, everyone in my line of work does. You're a bit of a legend, if you don't mind me saying. And I think you're a man who knows about taking chances when they're right in front of you. The good things slip away fast."

He had Coleman's attention. Blaine breathed an inward sigh of relief.

"It's about hard work and dedication, mostly." Coleman looked haughtily to his daughter. "Are you willing to put that into a marriage, Liberty?"

Libby was tugging the ribbon open. "Yes, Daddy."

"We should order some wine!" Blaine's mother clapped her hands together. "Dinner is on us. Let's order something nice to get us started and we'll all get to know each other."

Libby glanced at Blaine. He held his breath.

Coleman smirked and shifted in his seat. "Yes, why don't we? I think there's a lot to get to know."

****

Despite the tension that never seemed to fully abandon the table, and the stress of navigating polite conversation with an egomaniac, the dinner was going better than Blaine expected.

Blaine and his father kept Coleman wrapped up in conversation about finance and business through the salad course and the first half of the meal. No one else got many words in edgewise, despite this being about "getting to know each other." Coleman grew more boisterous and talkative as he polished off glass after glass of wine, and he was on his fourth by the time the server cleared their dinner plates. Libby and her mother were the only two at the table not drinking. Blaine limited himself to one and sipped slowly.

"I still think you should extend your engagement," Coleman said, when dessert arrived. He was much more amicable now, though the wine had not dulled his jagged edge. "There's no need to rush into things so fast."

Libby had finally gotten the floor to talk about herself to his parents during the second half of the meal. She stuck to the story that she was still in school and studying to be a teacher, and mentioned nothing of her future plans or real interests. Her father, of course, interjected often and provided details—specifically, how she went against his wishes by going to school and how she was too headstrong, and how this occasion was a fine example of it.

"I'm a man of action," Blaine said. "If we're in love with each other, and we fit perfectly together, why should we waste time?"

He had his arm draped around Libby's shoulders. She toyed with the diamond tennis bracelet around her wrist that his mother had given her.

"I don't want to wait," Libby spoke up. "I'm getting older, Daddy. You always said it was my duty as a woman to find a good man and make a life with him. I think Blaine is pretty good."

Blaine knew Coleman most likely suspected he wanted her inheritance, so he had to keep feeding the idea that he knew nothing about it and wouldn't care if he did.

"I can provide for her." Blaine rubbed her

shoulder. "I know I'm not as wealthy as you, sir. I mean, who at this table is?" He chuckled. "But I make decent money. I have a nice house, and several cars. I don't want for anything. Money is immaterial when it comes to love, but do know that I can provide for her just fine. I grew up in money, and I understand it." Growing up in it was a lie, but he did understand it now. Also, he did have two cars, if his good one and the backup beater counted—and his apartment was pretty nice.

"He's telling the truth." Blaine's father dug into his cheesecake. "He's doing quite well for himself. Better than his father these days, if I might say."

Coleman gazed at Blaine over the rim of his wineglass as he took a drink.

"I'm sure she'll be taken care of financially," Marge said. She'd spoken little compared to her ex-husband, and her rigid exterior had not eased even a bit. "It's her emotional well-being I'm more concerned about. I want her to be happy."

Coleman scoffed and plunked his glass down. "She's got a lot of growing up to do, that's what *I'm* worried about. I want to make sure she's ready to be a wife and that she'll perform her wifely duties like she should." He fixed Marge with a disdainful glare. "That's still important to most men."

At least Blaine would have a reason to give when they got divorced, though the thought of using that reason made him feel slimy. Almost as slimy as the man sitting across from him, if that was possible.

"I'm ready to be a wife." Libby picked up her fork and poked at her cheesecake. "I'm ready to settle down, Daddy. I've thought really hard about it."

Marge sighed. She didn't touch her dessert. "It's just so fast."

"Like I said, I'm a man of action." Blaine took

Libby's fork from her, broke off a bite of the cake, and held it up to her mouth. She gazed at him with wary eyes as she took it.

"I think they're perfect for each other." Blaine's mother gazed at them with sparkling eyes. "They're so cute. I can tell Blaine is in love. I've never seen him look like this. It's almost magical."

Blaine smiled and placed Libby's fork down on her plate. "I am in love. And it's wonderful."

Coleman made a derisive sound and sat back from the table. He studied his daughter across it.

"You're going to have to set her right." Coleman tugged at the knot in his tie. "You should encourage her to drop out of school. If you're planning on having children in the future, she needs to get these willful ideas out of her head and take care of her home. You can't bring children into a world where their mother is never there for them."

Libby played with her fork, staring at her plate. Marge shifted and took a drink of water. Blaine's father continued eating, looking between Blaine and Coleman.

Blaine slipped his arm from around Libby and stroked the back of her hair.

"I understand." Blaine could barely force the words out, and the disgusting feeling in his gut was even worse now with food and wine in there. He looked Coleman directly in the eye. "I'll make sure she understands her place. That's what a man does, doesn't he?"

The tension at the table was palpable. Everyone subtly stiffened. Everyone, that was, except for Coleman. A smug, easy smile spread across his lips, and his face, for the first time, sagged into a relaxed expression.

"I believe you will, Blaine. I believe you will."

Blaine excused himself to the restroom. When he

stepped in, the room was quiet, shadowy, and cool, and he could finally breathe. He bent over the sink counter and propped his elbows on the black granite. He held his head in his hands and closed his eyes. Tears burned behind his eyelids. He felt sick, physically and mentally. He thought he might actually throw up.

Someone cleared their throat. "Rough night?"

Blaine opened his eyes. The bathroom attendant held out a facecloth. He was an old man with a soft, wrinkled face and deep-set eyes.

Blaine stood up and took the cloth. It was damp and warm. "You could say that, yeah."

He rubbed his face with the cloth. When he lowered it and considered his own eyes in the mirror, guilt overwhelmed him. He'd kept up a good act, but in here, faced with himself, it crumbled.

"Anything I can do to help?" the attendant asked. "I do have some bottles stashed in here, if you need a nip of something."

Blaine dabbed his face again. "No, I think I need to be clearheaded right now. I'm meeting my fiancée's parents for the first time."

"Ah, nerve-wracking, isn't it?" The old man brought him a fresh, dry towel. "Not going well?"

"They're … very difficult people." He exchanged the cloth for the towel. "Especially her father."

The attendant chuckled. "They often are. Just remember, you're not marrying her father. Take her for who she is and don't judge her based on where she came from."

Blaine rubbed his face dry, then looked in the mirror again. He raked his fingers through his hair to fluff it up a bit.

He handed the towel to the attendant. "Can I ask you a question?"

The old man smiled. "Well, if it's about grooming, I might have an answer." He turned to his table of products. "You need a good cologne?"

"It's a bit deeper than that." Blaine tugged at his lapel. "Do you think it's okay to do something really shitty, to say really nasty things and pretend to be something explicitly against your nature, if it'll help someone?"

The old man raised his bushy white eyebrows. "Depends on how much it's helping them."

"A lot. Like, it'll change their life." He paused. "By doing this thing that feels all wrong to you, you'll help them escape something terrible. You'll help them make their hopes and wishes come true."

"I think that's the best reason to do something shitty and nasty and against your nature. The only reason."

Blaine relaxed his shoulders, letting some of the tension drain out. He was doing the right thing, saying all those awful lines, acting like he wanted to own her. She would be so much better off after this. She would be her own person. He only had to keep it up for a few weeks and help her get out. Once again, he reminded himself he wasn't being paid to get emotionally involved or solve the many-layered psychological issues her family had.

This was far more complicated than he expected, though.

He used the facilities, washed his hands, and stuffed a twenty in the old man's tip jar. "Thank you for the wisdom. And the towel."

The attendant smiled a bright smile, one full of obviously false teeth. "Remember what I said, you're not marrying her father."

Blaine left the bathroom. At least they were at dessert. It wouldn't be much longer he'd have to remain in Coleman Dawson's self-important, smarmy presence.

As he turned the corner, Libby came around it. She stopped short. So did he.

"Oh, hi." She fidgeted with her bracelet. "I was just…" She glanced at the ladies' room door. "I need to take a quick break."

Blaine gazed at her. She stared back at him, eyes questioning and cautious. Even in the dimly lit hallway, she was radiant. Despite her father's best efforts to dull her shine, it couldn't be hidden. Blaine was suddenly overcome. Regret, guilt, but also a strange possessiveness filled his chest.

He walked over to her and gripped the sides of her face—gently, but firmly. Her eyes popped wide and she sucked in a breath. He didn't want to scare her, and he tried not to look as demented as he felt.

"Libby." His voice was thick. "I don't mean any of those things I'm saying out there. Not a single one."

Her gaze turned from alarmed to shy. Her face softened. "I know," she whispered.

"I'm just trying to appeal to your father and impress him." He swallowed around the lump in his throat. "This is harder than I thought it would be. Because frankly, he's … he's not a very pleasant man." He wasn't sure she was ready to hear the words he wanted to use to describe him.

"To say the least." She clutched his wrists. "I know you're just acting. Thank you, for what you're doing. I know it has to be difficult." Doubt tinged her voice, though. She had heard this crap for so long she believed it anyway.

He lowered his hands, though he wanted to pull her to him and hold her tight, tell her she was worthwhile and that her father was completely out of line and a hateful bastard.

"I grew up with him." She held onto his wrists still. "I've put up with that my entire life. I know how to manipulate him, but it only goes so far."

"I can't imagine. I'm sorry, Libby. I'm so sorry."

"Thank you." She looked down. "If you want, when he gives me the money, I'll pay you extra. You deserve it for putting up with this."

"No." He pulled gently out of her grasp and took her hands instead. "I don't want any of your money. For God sakes, you've earned it. Keep it."

She looked up.

"I want you to take that money and get as far the hell away from him as you can. Make your life magnificent and put him behind you where he belongs."

A faint smile touched her lips. They were shiny under the overhead light. He wanted to lean in and kiss them.

He dragged a hand through his hair. "Hopefully this meal doesn't last much longer, though, or I might just tell him what I think of him." Fear flashed across her face. "I won't do that though, I promise. I won't mess this up for you." He squeezed her hands. "I should, uh…" He looked at the ladies' room door. "I should let you go."

Her smile widened. "Yeah, sorry." She glanced down at their joined hands.

He let go of her. "I'll see you back at the table." On impulse, he reached out and stroked her hair. "Just breathe, it's almost over."

Her cheeks pinkened and her smile remained. He liked seeing that.

Thankfully, he was right about it almost being over. When dessert was through and Coleman had polished off another glass of wine, they made ready to go. Out on the sidewalk in front of the restaurant, they waited for their respective Ubers and said their good-byes.

"I still wish you would wait a while." Coleman gripped Blaine's shoulder. "But you seem like you have the right intentions for my daughter. You seem like a man with a good head on his shoulders, and that's what she needs to get her life on track."

Blaine stood with his arm linked with Libby's. He forced a smile. "Are you giving me your blessing, sir?"

Coleman wobbled, leaned in, and gave him a self-satisfied smile. "I'll be there on Saturday," he stage-whispered.

Marge stood several feet away, still relentless and stiff as she had been the entire night. Blaine's parents' Uber arrived first and Blaine left Libby to walk them to the car at the curb.

"Thank you." Blaine opened the back door for them. "You did great tonight. It was very convincing."

Robert let out a huge breath, as though he'd been holding it all night. He looked over at Coleman and shook his head. "That is one prickly bastard. You got your hands full there, Blaine. I don't envy you. I thought guys like him only existed on TV."

Blaine slipped a hand into the breast pocket of his jacket. "Yeah, well, I've seen plenty of guys like him in my line of work, unfortunately. They're real, and they're everywhere. Ruthless as hell and don't care about anyone but themselves, not even their families. Why do you think I'm trying to retire early? I'm gonna get old before my time watching this parade of assholes go by."

Blaine pulled an envelope out, thick with a wad of cash, and pressed it into the older man's hand.

Robert glanced at the envelope, nodded, and tucked it into his own jacket. "I hope she gets what she's after."

"I do too. That's why I'm playing this shitty part." He glanced at Libby. "It's the best reason to do something shitty, after all. To help someone else."

"You take care, Blaine. Give me a call soon." He patted him on the back.

Blaine saw them into the car and closed the door. He waved as they pulled off.

As he walked back to the others, Libby gazed at him, a quizzical expression on her face. Blaine put a smile on and rejoined them.

"I can get Liberty home, if you like." He stopped next to Coleman.

"Oh no, we'll get her back to her dorm." Coleman flashed him a syrupy, and drunk, smile. "We'll see you on Saturday for the big event."

Blaine's phone went off, indicating his car was pulling up. He looked at Libby.

"Saturday," he said softly.

She managed a smile as well. "Saturday," she said.

Chapter Seven

"I always thought my wedding day would be a little more magical." Libby fluffed her dress sadly. "I thought I'd look like a princess and be in a church with all kinds of flowers and candles and they'd play the wedding march as I walked down the aisle and—"

"Stop." Kellie fussed with the pins in Libby's hair. "This is more important than a princess wedding. Soon you're gonna be a half-millionaire and you're going to change the world and never have to see your dad's stupid face ever again. How is that not magical?"

Libby looked at herself in the full-length mirror. They stood in a drab, bare room in a dingy corner of the courthouse. A couch sat behind her, a coffee table in front of it, with a tray of cookies and candy. That was the extent of Libby's bridal shower, which incidentally, was taking place immediately before her wedding. All very quick and convenient, and the only guest was Kellie.

Libby sighed. "I just thought it would be more impressive than this, you know?"

She wore her new white dress, and it was acceptably pretty, even if it wasn't an actual wedding dress. More like a prom dress, or a bridesmaid's dress. The top was formfitting silk, cinched at the waist, with a calf-length lace skirt embroidered with silver thread. The top had sleeves, which were made from sheer fabric so they were see-through. She also wore a pair of chunky white heels with straps. She wasn't good on heels, but she was trying to stand up straight and proper.

"This isn't a real wedding." Kellie continued to work on her hair, which was pulled up in an elegant knot, with curls that spilled down to her neck. "I mean, you'll get married for real someday, to someone you love." She looked at Libby in the mirror. "In a church and stuff, with flowers and a princess dress."

Libby took a deep breath, which made the bodice of her dress tighten. She'd made sure it wasn't too sexy, since her father would be there. You weren't supposed to be sexy on your wedding day anyway, right?

Kellie wore a green silk dress, like the ribbon on Libby's present from Blaine's mother, which incidentally, was also her favorite color. Kellie was her only bridesmaid and maid of honor all in one.

"Blaine seems really nice." Kellie brushed her fingertips across Libby's cheek as she scrutinized her makeup. "I mean, I only met him for a few minutes earlier, but he seemed really cool." She grinned. "And even better-looking than in his picture."

"Yeah, he's nice." Libby played with the tennis bracelet on her wrist. She loved it. "He played my father so well, said everything he wanted to hear, stroked his ego, acted like he wanted to own me and tell me what to do—it almost seemed real." She frowned.

"That's a good thing, right? I mean, you gotta make it look legit."

Libby thought of Blaine holding her face, the worry in his eyes, the guilt in his expression. "It wasn't real though, he was just acting." She chose to believe that. She *had* to believe that. If he turned out to be as much of a monster as her father, this whole thing would be a disaster. She wouldn't be able to bear it.

"You're doing the right thing, Libs." Kellie walked to the couch and grabbed her makeup bag. "Once you're married, your father can't control you anymore. And once you got that money, it's bye-bye Daddy." She wiggled her fingers.

Libby still didn't believe it would be so easy. But it had to work—after all she'd gone through, after all she'd done. If it didn't work out, she wasn't sure what she'd do, or where she'd land. She could only imagine how bleak the rest of her life would be if she failed and had to answer to her father.

She looked at her nails. Kellie had taken her to get them done and they were shiny with French tips. She'd never had her nails done professionally before.

"Just focus." Kellie dug through her makeup bag. "Focus on the future. One step at a time, you'll get to your goal. Be strong."

Something ate at Libby though, something that kept poking at the back of her brain. She couldn't shake it.

"I saw something weird that night, after dinner, when we were all leaving."

Kellie walked over, compact and brush in hand. "This whole thing is weird, Libs. Here, let me put some more blush on. You look pallid."

Libby let her apply it, though she was sure her father would say she was made up like a whore. She recalled again the envelope Blaine had passed to his father. Maybe it was nothing. Maybe it didn't matter. Still, it stuck in her head for some reason. Kellie would probably tell her she was being paranoid, and really, it *didn't* matter. *It just didn't matter.* In six weeks, this would all be behind her. She simply had to hold on until then.

"Yeah, this is definitely weird." She stood passively as Kellie worked on her. "But I can't stop now."

Kellie finished getting her ready and handed her the bouquet they'd made together: white roses and lilies, and a few pansies for color. The arrangement looked nice. Maybe like a bouquet a princess would carry at her wedding.

Kellie turned her toward the mirror and smiled

over her shoulder. "Today is the first day of the rest of your new life."

Libby clutched the bouquet and gazed at herself. She did look good. She looked like a person about to do something bold, but necessary.

"Let's get this show on the road." Libby braced herself. "I paid huge money for this, after all."

Kellie chuckled. "Just like a real wedding. See?"

They were having a simple ceremony in front of a judge. Libby's father didn't complain, given the buttering-up Blaine had applied. After all, the sooner his daughter was under a husband's control, the better. On top of that, he didn't have to pay for an actual wedding.

Libby held her breath as she stepped through the doors of the courtroom. Her hands were sweating around the handle of her bouquet. Kellie stood at her side.

This certainly wasn't a glamorous and well-attended affair. Her parents and Blaine's parents were attending, and beyond that, just Libby's sister. Justice had her kids with her, sitting to the side on a bench, baby on her lap, toddler fussing at her side. Her husband had to work.

No wedding march. No flower girl. Kellie led her to the front of the room, up to the judge and Blaine, on her arm.

Blaine looked good, and momentarily distracted Libby from both her nerves and disappointment. He wore a suit—she was yet to see him in anything else—with an emerald green tie to match her "wedding colors." His hair was pulled back in a conservative yet somehow sexy little knot at the back of his neck, which showed off his strong, handsome face even more. His smile was tender. As he took her hand, her heart fluttered despite how romantic none of this was.

Her parents stood beside her, Blaine's parents

next to him. His parents were both much like him, amicable and easygoing, though she didn't think they looked much alike. His mother dabbed her eyes with a fabric handkerchief. His father smiled widely. In stark contrast, her own parents were grim and stoic. She expected nothing less.

"You look beautiful," Blaine whispered.

She smiled at him. "You look good too." The room was so quiet, apart from her nephew whining.

The judge was a broad black woman with a bright smile. She looked at them over her glasses. "Ready?"

Libby nodded. She was, and she wasn't.

The ceremony was short and to the point, like everything else. When the judge asked who gave her away, her father stepped forward.

"I do." He spoke loudly. He looked at Blaine. "Take care of her."

Blaine nodded. "I absolutely will."

She felt like a chain that had been wrapped around her for years started to give, just a little.

Libby's head spun. She barely heard the judge's words, or herself saying "I do." Before she could center herself and catch up, the woman was pronouncing them man and wife.

Blaine turned to her with that kind smile on his lips. His eyes shone.

She smiled back, and then, her breath caught as he leaned in.

The kiss was unexpected, though that was the silliest thing ever. It was her wedding, of course her husband was going to kiss her. Blaine's lips were soft and warm, and he pressed them firmly against hers. His facial hair tickled her nose and chin. She was so stunned she didn't know what to do for a moment, then she kissed him back. She thought in a brief flash she would love to make out with him, right there, in front of everybody. He smelled so good.

She'd had a boyfriend in high school and had kissed him, as well as another guy one time. This wasn't her first time, but it felt like it was. Her heart and stomach both jumped like it was.

When Blaine drew back, her lips tingled and her face burned. He took her hand.

"Yay!" Kellie threw a handful of confetti in the air. The judge gave her a stern look and she turned meek. "Sorry, I'll clean it up."

And that was that.

Everyone hugged. Her father hugged her the hardest, tight enough to make her squeak, and then placed his hands on her shoulders and looked into her eyes.

"You need to be a good wife to him. Be like your mother was, when you were a little girl, before she got all headstrong. If you need any advice, call me." He hugged her again and murmured in her ear, "Don't mess this up, Liberty."

Her mother gave her a much briefer, light hug. "Congratulations, Liberty." She didn't look her in the eye.

Blaine's parents swept her up in blustery, happy hugs. They both smelled good, like him. She smiled.

Her sister was the last to hug her, baby still on her hip and toddler clinging to her leg.

"Congratulations, Liberty." She sounded tired. She looked like their father, with dark hair and the same wide, boxy face, but her demeanor was much more sagging and beaten, like their mother. "Sorry Dave couldn't be here, he had an account to close today."

"It's okay." Libby played with her niece's tiny hand. "How's things going?" She didn't get to talk to her sister nearly as much as she'd like.

Justice sighed. "Don't ask." She gave her a weak smile. "Blaine seems nice. I hope you guys are happy."

Libby smiled back at her. "I think we will be."

They were having a party after, at least. Blaine had booked a small banquet room in the hotel where they were staying tonight, at his own expense. Libby planned to get her things from Kellie's place tomorrow and would stay with Blaine until the marriage was over. They had agreed it was the best course of action, so her father didn't become suspicious. Also, she was very much floating on the wind right now and needed a place to stay, until she could rent an apartment of her own.

They walked downstairs together, Libby on Blaine's arm. When they reached the lower floor she looked at him, her heart pounding so loud in her ears she could barely hear. "I just need to go to the ladies' room before we get in the car."

He kissed her cheek. Again, she received a heady dose of his cologne. "I'll be outside."

Libby headed to the ladies' room, thankfully found it empty, and stood in front of the mirrors, trying to compose herself and catch her breath. Then, she burst into tears.

A moment later, the door opened. She quickly stifled her sobs and wiped her eyes, pretending to check her makeup.

Kellie hurried up beside her and flung her arms around her. "What's wrong? You did it, girl!"

Libby dissolved into tears again. She clamped her hands over her face.

Kellie squeezed her. "I know this is an emotional moment for you, but you did it. You really did it."

"It was all so fast." Libby drew a shuddering breath. "It just … happened. Just like that, I'm married. It was all so businesslike."

"Honey, it's all for show." Kellie rubbed her back. "It's not about romance, it's about doing what you have to do."

Libby tried to calm down and stop her tears. She wiped her cheeks. "I know, I just thought … I just—"

"I know." Kellie kissed her shoulder. "But you know this doesn't mean you can't get married for real someday, right?"

Libby looked at the two of them in the mirror through bleary eyes. Her sobs tapered off. "And my father won't be there for that one."

Kellie smiled. "No, he won't. And he won't be giving you away like you're an object he's trying to get rid of cheap."

Libby's cheeks were red, her eyes bright, mascara running. Yes, someday she'd be over this, long past it, and doing what she was supposed to do with her life. She'd find the right man and she'd get married in a romantic, elaborate ceremony, for love.

"I messed up my makeup." She dabbed at her eyes. "Oh, man. This is why I don't wear this stuff."

"Hold on, I'll fix it." Kellie let go of her and pulled her purse off her shoulder. "I'm the master here."

A short time later they emerged from the restroom, Libby's makeup fresh, her blotchy cheeks hidden. She put on a smile. Everyone was waiting for them outside.

Her father looked at his watch. "It's about time. I have a conference call at six, so I'll have to leave early."

Blaine took her arm. Concern filled his eyes. "You okay?" he asked softly.

She nodded. "Yeah, just had to fix my face."

Much to Libby's surprise, Blaine had rented a limousine for the ride to the hotel. She'd assumed they would just take his car. She stood at the curb, staring in shock. She had never ridden in one before.

"Everyone is welcome to come with us," Blaine said. He grinned at her father. "There's a mini-bar inside. We can come back later and pick up the cars."

Her father held up a hand. "I'll take my own, in case I have to leave even earlier than I'm expecting. Never know when I'll get a call. I'm never off the clock." He turned to her mother and sister. "I'll meet you two there."

Libby's heart soared. Suddenly, she was excited.

She and Blaine got in, as well as his parents and Kellie. The interior was roomy, and indeed, there was a bar along one wall. She sat close to Blaine, almost snuggled up to him.

"Want a drink?" He grinned at her.

She looked at the bar, then at him. "I shouldn't."

"You're a married woman now, you can do as you like."

She bit her lip, then smiled. "Well, if there's some wine, I wouldn't mind that."

Kellie slid over and started rummaging through one of the cabinets. "Found some!"

A few minutes later Libby was drinking a glass of wine in the back of a moving car, which felt incredibly decadent and naughty. She eased a bit closer to Blaine. He took her hand.

"We're married." His eyes were clear and pale in the muted sunlight through the windows and they held her spellbound. "I'm happy to be doing this with you. When do you think he'll give you the money?"

Her heart jumped into her throat and she glanced in alarm at his parents.

"They know what's going on." He squeezed her hand. "They know this is an arrangement we made. It's okay."

She looked at them again, and thought of the envelope.

"It's all right, darling." His mother smiled. She held a glass of wine as well. "Blaine told us all about what you're trying to accomplish. We won't breathe a word of it."

"Coleman Dawson is a ruthless man." Blaine's father held a beer. "I commend you for what you're trying to do. It sounds like a good cause. Sometimes to get what you want, you must get creative. There's nothing wrong with that."

"It's a shame though." His mother sipped her wine. "You're such a cute couple." She winked.

Libby blushed.

Kellie giggled. "You are. Super cute."

Libby drank her wine.

Blaine slipped his hand from hers and put his arm around her shoulders. "We're going to have fun today, so try not to worry. Just relax and enjoy it. You deserve a break. Everything will work out." He rubbed her arm.

She gazed down into her wineglass. "He gave my sister the money the week she got married, so I'm hoping he does the same for me." She hesitated. "We don't have to go the full six weeks if he does."

"You paid for six weeks, I'll give you six weeks." He continued rubbing her arm. "You're going to need some time to get your thoughts together and figure out what to do next. I don't want you having to deal with a divorce on top of that."

Kellie smiled over at her, and it was a knowing kind of smile, and equally sly. Libby couldn't stop her face burning, which was embarrassing in itself, so she continued drinking her wine.

When they arrived at the hotel, Libby's spirits

lifted even higher. The place was swanky and modern, the type of place she'd seen on TV but never stayed in before. She stood on the sidewalk in front of it, gazing up at the glass façade that pierced the bright blue sky. They were in an upscale part of Manhattan.

Blaine held his arm out to her. "Shall we, honey?"

She took his arm. Maybe the wine had loosened her up a bit, but she was indeed ready to have some fun.

"I got us a suite for tonight," he said as they walked up to the front doors.

She tensed. Tonight was her wedding night, technically. Well, more like actually. She hadn't dreamed much beyond her princess wedding, but of course, there would be a wedding night attached to that as well.

"There's an extra bed," Blaine said. "I'll let you sleep in the big one."

She relaxed. Also, a twang of disappointment sounded deep in her chest. What was *that* about? Their business arrangement didn't include personal services, after all. That was prostitution.

The banquet room was decorated with flowers and there was a small buffet, champagne, and a small but cute three-tier wedding cake, decorated with green icing.

Libby stood in front of the cake, hands clasped over her open mouth. She looked at Blaine.

He laughed. "What? It's a wedding. We have to have a cake."

She lowered her hands. "You didn't have to go to all this trouble. I mean, it wasn't necessary." She kept her voice down, though her parents weren't there yet.

"It has to look real, right? And besides, you deserve it."

She threw her arms around him, before she realized what she was doing. Then, she drew back shyly.

He kept an arm around her waist. "You're going to be okay." He gazed into her eyes. "Trust me on this."

She recalled their kiss in the courtroom and found herself staring at his lips. He was her husband, after all, why shouldn't she want to kiss him?

"Wow, look at this cake!" Kellie zoomed over. "It's so pretty."

Libby pulled out of Blaine's grasp and caught her breath. "Yeah, let's have a party, huh?"

"I brought my laptop." Kellie grabbed a bottle of champagne. "Can't have a party without music, right? And you guys have to have your first dance."

"Yeah, I guess we do." Libby pulled out her phone and took a picture of the cake. Even if this wasn't real, she wanted the memories. "Thank you, Blaine." She smiled demurely at him.

He stepped up beside her and gripped her hand holding the phone. He lifted it up in front of them, over their heads. "We need a man and wife selfie."

Libby laughed, turned the camera around, and took a picture.

They did look cute together.

As Libby expected, the party was less like a party and more like a wake, as half the guests were grumpy, unpleasant, angry, or all of the above. Libby's mother didn't unwind the entire time, and she sat far away from her father. Her sister was grouchy with the kids, who seemed to get more and more temperamental as the day went on. Her father drank champagne and complained that if they hadn't gotten married so fast, more of her relatives could have attended.

"Your Aunt Mary is going to be so disappointed," he informed Libby as she brought him a gin and tonic from the bar outside the room. He'd decided to switch up to the hard stuff. "Her daughters were bridesmaids in your sister's wedding, they could have been in yours as well." He grabbed the glass from her.

Libby smiled tightly. "Maybe we'll have a bigger ceremony later on, Daddy. They can be in it then."

She tried to have fun. Kellie played music and she and Libby and Blaine's mother danced, giggling, with glasses of champagne in hand. Libby couldn't look at her father as she drank it, terrified of his disapproval despite the fact he was getting drunk himself.

But she was a married woman now, her own woman, and she could do as she liked.

The food was good. She and Blaine cut the cake together and his mother took pictures. They laughed as they forced chunks into each other's mouths and smeared it over each other's faces. Blaine licked the frosting from her chin and she tittered and grew bashful.

Kellie put on a sappy love song and insisted they have their first dance. Libby was reluctant, but Blaine took her hand and led her onto the small dance floor in front of the buffet table.

"Adorable," Kellie proclaimed, and took a picture as they swayed together.

Libby bit her lip. "I'm not a very good dancer," she murmured. She felt clumsy and stupid, and everyone was staring at them.

Blaine pulled her closer. "It's okay, just follow my lead."

She did, and it wasn't that hard after all. Her father watched them shrewdly, sipping his gin, and she tried to ignore him because it made her even more nervous.

"Are you having a good time?" Blaine settled his arm around her lower back. "I tried to make the most of this for you." They were far enough away from everyone they couldn't be heard over the music.

"It's very nice." She smiled at the cake, which was now carved up. "I hope we can take the rest of that home."

"We'll take it up to our room and eat the rest of it tonight. It'll make for a nice sugar rush."

Libby laughed. "We'll be sick if we eat all that. We should give some to Kellie." She was a little floaty, though she wasn't sure if it was from the champagne or how good Blaine smelled. "You look very nice."

"So do you." He shifted his arm behind her back. "That's a pretty dress."

"I always imagined I'd be wearing a wedding gown. A real wedding gown."

He was staring into her eyes, and for once she held his gaze without getting bashful and turning away.

"You will wear one someday," he said. "You'll meet the right man and have a proper wedding. With a much bigger cake."

She glanced toward her parents. "And they won't be there." She wasn't sure if that made her happy or sad. It was a difficult tangle of emotions to navigate. "But this isn't so bad, really. As far as fake weddings go, it's pretty awesome."

Blaine turned her around on the dance floor, so her back was to them. "You'll be world-renowned for your contributions. Everyone will come your real wedding."

She shook her head. "I don't know about that."

He drew her even closer, so she was pressed up against him. His body was firm, and warm, and his arms felt so strong and comfortable around her. She gazed into his gleaming blue eyes, into his handsome, striking face.

"You're unlike anyone I've ever met," he said, his voice low and intimate between them. "Unlike any woman. I know this is a weird situation, but I'm glad to be in it right now."

She looked at his lips. She wanted to kiss them so badly, wanted him to kiss her, for real, a full, deep kiss that wasn't for show.

She looked down. "I'm not super special. I have a lot of thoughts and ideas, but they're going to take a lot of work to make happen." She tightened her arms around him.

"All ideas take work." He put a finger under her chin and lifted her face to his. "You'll get there."

Her heart was pounding so hard, he had to feel it against his chest. He was looking at her lips as well. Maybe it wouldn't hurt, just one kiss, to make it look more real. She licked her lips.

He gave her a squeeze. "Stay strong," he whispered. "I'll help you get through this."

The song ended. She realized Kellie was filming them with her phone.

"Whoo!" Kellie hollered. "Aww, what a happy couple."

Everyone clapped, a small, polite sound. Libby quickly pulled away from Blaine and tried to act natural.

Why did she have such an ache inside her? She never meant to make this personal. She needed a boyfriend, obviously. Maybe she'd work on that when this was over.

"I need to go to the restroom." She touched Blaine's arm. "I'll be back."

As she passed her father, he lifted his glass to her. "We should have the father-daughter dance when you come back. It's tradition. And I have to leave soon."

She hurried off.

In the restroom, she tried to compose herself. She felt warm inside, low in her stomach, and she could have squirmed right out of her dress. She knew what that feeling was and she had to control it, because she might do things she'd regret if she let hormones take over. She was embarrassed she was letting herself feel this way.

After freshening herself up, she was about to leave the restroom when her mother came in. Libby quickly returned to the mirror and pretended to check her hair.

Her mother plunked her purse on the counter between them and pulled her lipstick out. Silence hung heavy between them as she reapplied it. Libby kept messing with her hair.

"You seem happy with him," her mother finally spoke, as she shoved the tube back in her purse. "He reminds me of your father."

Libby wanted to turn on her and shriek that Blaine was nothing like her father, but she stayed in place and bit her tongue.

"This is impulsive." Her mother fiddled with her own hair. "But I knew I couldn't talk you out of it. I hope you didn't make a mistake."

"I know what I'm doing, Mom." Libby turned to her. "He's very good to me." And he was, so far.

Her mother huffed. "Men seem very charming when you first meet them. They act so sweet and thoughtful toward you. You're caught up in a storm of emotion right now. But that wears off, and reality starts setting in. Next thing you know, you're married to a megalomaniac drunk, like your father, like my father. It's true what they say, women marry men just like their fathers."

Libby ached for her, deep down in her heart. She knew, even after being free of their father all these years, her mother was still bound to him, still unhappy, and still under his control. Sometimes Libby boggled that the two of them had made such a life when they were obviously unsuitable for each other. But then, sometimes her mother seemed more matched with her father than she liked to admit.

Or, maybe he had just made her that way over the years.

"Mom." She braced her hands on the counter. "Will you tell me something?"

Her mother didn't respond, but Libby pushed ahead.

"When you and Daddy got divorced, he fought it like crazy. But then all the sudden, he was okay with it and just moved out. What … what changed?"

Her mother looked at her in the mirror, eyes flashing. "It was a long time ago. Don't worry about it."

"But—"

"You need to focus on your own marriage now. Worry about the suffering you might have ahead."

Libby sighed and turned to her. "I'll be happy, Mom." She touched her shoulder. "Don't worry about it."

Her mother glowered at her, lips pursed. But behind the seething disapproval in her eyes something else peeked through—worry, fear.

"Everything is going to be okay." Libby squeezed. "I promise. Now, come back and have some cake and champagne."

Her mother looked away. "You know I can't drink in front of you father. He doesn't approve. He can pound them down but the second I take a sip, I'm a raging lush."

"Mom, you don't have to answer to him anymore."

Libby squared her shoulders.

"Neither of us do."

The words were soft, but they were powerful. She

walked past her mother to the door, and went back to her husband, carrying that confident feeling with her. She *never* had to answer to him again.

Never.

Chapter Eight

Blaine watched Libby spin around the small dance floor in the arms of her father and tried to stop clenching his teeth. His entire body prickled with anger and outrage. He wanted to go over and yank her out of his grip, but he stayed put, clutching the stem of his champagne glass. This would be the last time that bastard had a hold of her like that.

The scene was awkward for everyone in the room, to an absurd degree.

The guests sat plastered to their chairs, watching them. Libby's mother stared past them, toward the front of the room, as if in a trance. Kellie sat next to her laptop, hands balled in her lap, glancing between them and Blaine as the song Coleman chose played. The only other sound was one of Justice's kids fussing.

Coleman stumbled his way through the steps, as he had now consumed a full bottle of champagne and probably most of the gin at the hotel bar. Libby smiled up at him, but it was a clearly forced, fake smile, so much she looked like a doll. A few times Coleman almost knocked them down and Blaine nearly lurched out of his chair to rush over and catch her.

When the song was finally, blessedly over, everyone clapped politely. Kellie quickly turned to her laptop.

Coleman stood tall but wobbling in the middle of the room, holding his daughter's hand, chin tilted up.

"I want to say a few things," he announced, the edges of his words slurred.

Blaine groaned inwardly. *Play it cool, you guys are almost there.*

Libby remained at his side, her face still a plastic mimicry of happiness.

"I don't approve of the swiftness of this wedding." Coleman couldn't possibly start with something positive. "But I much more don't approve of my daughter becoming a spinster. I'm happy, if nothing else, that she's fulfilling her obligation as a woman. I'm sure she'll make a fine wife and mother." He looked imperiously toward his ex-wife. "Despite her lack of role models."

Blaine flexed his fingers around the stem of his glass.

"I hope you'll have a life like your sister." He turned to Libby, swaying. "I hope you'll be able to make the sort of joy that she's made for herself, that you'll follow in her footsteps."

Libby's frazzled sister smiled tiredly, shifting the whiny baby in her lap.

"And Blaine." Coleman swiveled toward him. He yanked Libby's arm in the process. "I trust you to take good care of her, and teach her everything she needs to know. I believe you'll make a fine woman out of her."

Blaine lifted his glass, forcing a smile. He wanted to throw it at his head.

Coleman flung his hand in the air. "To my daughter and her new husband!"

Everyone clapped again. Blaine downed his champagne. The room felt stuffy and the walls were closing in. He was more exhausted from keeping up this act than he realized.

Coleman released Libby and stumbled over to his table, announcing that they needed another bottle of champagne. So much for being "needed at work" today. Kellie rolled her eyes and started up the music again.

Blaine got up and went over to Libby. He took her hand, the one her father had been holding, gently and carefully. Her palm was sweaty.

"Want to get some air?" he murmured.

Her mask fell away and she looked relieved, if somewhat traumatized. "Please."

They slipped out of the room together.

Blaine had scoped out the hotel when he rented the room and their suite. He knew there was a courtyard off the lobby and he steered her toward it. When they stepped out, the light had slanted into late afternoon and a chill tinged the air. He immediately slipped off his jacket and put it over her shoulders.

She smiled, touching it. "Thank you. Aren't you cold, though?"

"Long sleeves." He rubbed one. "I'm fine."

The courtyard was circular, with a bubbling fountain in the middle surrounded by concrete benches. Trees and bushes lined the walls. A few people were out there, but it was quiet, the air was fresh, and most importantly, Coleman Dawson was not lurking in the foliage.

They sat down on one of the benches and Libby peered into the rippling pool beneath the fountain. She looked good with his jacket over her shoulders, and a sudden surge of protectiveness filled him.

"I'm sorry this is such a fiasco," she said flatly as she stared into the water. "I'm putting you through so much."

He reached over and took her hand. She looked at him.

"Libby, if anyone deserves to be apologized to, it's you. Your father is unbelievable." He smoothed his thumb over the ring now on her hand. They'd gotten simple, cheap bands for the ceremony. "I wanted to get up and throttle him during that dance."

She turned away from the fountain, her hand slipping from his, and groaned. "I thought he was going to kill us a couple of times." She slumped forward and folded her arms on her knees. "I can't think of a worse way to die, smothered beneath my drunk father on my fake wedding day."

Blaine tried not to wince at that. After all, she wasn't bemoaning the fake wedding, but her father's behavior.

"I have something that might cheer you up." He scooted closer to her. "I got you a present."

She looked up and perked slightly. "You did?"

"Yep." He reached over and tucked his hand inside his coat. She looked down at it, but he was careful not to accidentally touch anything as he slipped something out of his breast pocket.

He held it up, a small white box.

Her eyes shone as she gazed curiously at it. "What is it?"

"Well, you know, it's tradition that the bride and groom get each other gifts."

She sat up straight, her mouth falling open. "Oh gosh, I didn't get you anything." Worry filled her eyes. "I didn't know that!"

"It's okay." He patted her hand. "I didn't expect anything. I wanted to get you something though, because I knew this would be difficult and you'd need something to cheer you up."

"You didn't have to." She gnawed on her lower lip.

He was going to kiss her, and kiss her hard one of these days, to get her to stop doing that.

"I think after what you just went through, you need it." He held the box out to her.

Doubt filled him as she took it. What was inside certainly wasn't a traditional wedding gift, and she might think it was strange, or quite possibly insane. Though he'd been filled with a sense of his own cleverness when he bought it, now he worried he'd made a mistake.

She pulled the top off the box. Inside, wedged in Styrofoam, was a thin glass plate, about three inches long. She furrowed her brow and plucked it out. On the center was a smear of purple, trapped between two layers of glass, one end covered in opaque tape so it could be gripped without harming the specimen. She'd probably been expecting a piece of jewelry. He should have done that instead, as it was less bizarre.

She looked at him, eyebrows raised.

"It's a microscope slide," he explained.

"I know." She looked back at it. "What is it, exactly?"

He reached over and pulled a piece of paper from the bottom of the box. He read from it. "It's *vibrio cholerae*, the bacteria responsible for cholera."

Yes, this was the most insane gift he could have come up with, and now he was panicking. Any moment, she would run screaming out of the courtyard.

Instead, she lowered the slide and smiled at him again. "Okay?"

He took a breath. "It's the bacteria most often found in polluted water systems, and it kills thousands to hundreds of thousands of people each year in countries where sanitation is a concern." He'd done his research. "For such a small thing, it does a lot of damage."

She lifted the slide again and peered at it, her smile unwavering. "I've seen this in textbooks. Maybe Kellie can sneak me into the university to check it out under one of the microscopes in the lab."

"I know it seems like a really weird gift."

"I admit, I didn't expect to get cholera on my wedding day." She laughed. "But this is actually really cool and thoughtful, Blaine." She lowered it and looked at him. Her eyes were practically glowing. "You learned all that for me."

"So, you don't want to file a restraining order against me?"

She laughed again. "Nope." She sat forward, her elbows on her knees, and gazed at the slide between her fingers. "This is my enemy." She said this with reverence and awe. "Trapped in glass."

Blaine swallowed. He leaned toward her.

"I wanted to give you this to remind you of something too." He reached over and touched the edge of the slide. "Monsters can do a lot of damage, but sometimes they're also smaller than they seem and they can be overcome with determination."

She looked up at him, into his eyes. Their faces were so close. His heart seemed to still in his chest.

"You will overcome the monsters in your life," he said softly. "You have that power."

She continued to gaze at him, then glanced at his lips, like she'd been doing when they danced. The urge to lean in and kiss her was overpowering. The simple kiss they'd shared during the ceremony wasn't enough, and it made him want to do it again, properly.

She's not really your wife, you don't have the right to do this. It's an arrangement. Don't get this mixed up.

Though it almost physically hurt, he made himself sit back. Her cheeks were red, her eyes bright. She looked back down at the slide.

"Thank you," she spoke softly, but there was also a huskiness in her voice that gripped him right in the gut.

"If you want, I can get you a microscope too." He tried to shake his urges off. "They sell all kinds of slides like this at a store not far from where I work, and a bunch of scientific equipment. I didn't even know it was there until I came up with the idea to search for this."

"No, that's fine." She sat up. "You don't have to spend more money on me." She clutched the slide to her chest and smiled at him. It was a warm, real smile and he was so happy to see it on her face. "This is the best gift ever, thank you."

Blaine let out a laugh, the tension leaving him with it. "I really worried you'd think I was crazy."

"It's something important to me, and like you said, it's a reminder." She leaned toward him. "I'll look at it when I need to be reminded."

He held his breath, but she just gave him a quick kiss on the cheek. He had to lock up every muscle so he didn't grab her head and plant one on her.

"Maybe you can make a necklace out of it," he teased. "I'm sure no other woman on the planet would have such a unique piece."

She laughed and tucked it back in the box. *"What's the new fashion this season?"* She spoke high and mocking. "Oh *dah-ling*, it's wearing bacterial intestinal infections around your neck. It's all the rage in New York."

They both cracked up. She placed the box in her lap and touched it gingerly, as if he'd gotten her a string of diamonds. He was quite pleased with himself, after all.

"Do we have to go back?" She gave him sad doe eyes. "I don't think I'm ready. Maybe if we hide long enough, my dad will pass out and have to be carted away."

"No, let's stay a bit longer." He took her hand and gave it a squeeze. "We need a break."

They strolled around the courtyard together, checking out the plants, many of which had plaques in front of them to describe what they were. Libby told him certain plants could be used as water purifiers, such as bulrushes and waterlilies. He hadn't known this and was impressed. The more she talked about it, the more passionate she became, and the more of the real Libby he saw shining through.

"There's so many ways you can work toward clean water and eradication of disease." She held his arm as they strolled around the fountain. "The filter I'm trying to make takes into consideration that implementation has to be practical as well. It's not good if it can only be effectively used by an aide worker. The people in the dangerous areas have to have access to it and be able to use it easily as well."

Blaine smiled at her, spellbound. "You're so smart and sensible. It's kind of a turn on."

She giggled. "I had to sneak around to get that way. I'd never take books out at the library, I was afraid my father would find them. I would just go to the library and write all kinds of notes. Then I'd hide them in my schoolwork."

Blaine felt prickly again. Maybe if Coleman was drunk enough, Blaine could get off a punch and he wouldn't remember it.

"When you get that money, you should build a lab of your own. Get a microscope."

"First, I'm going back to school." She rested her head on his shoulder, and his stomach fluttered. "A sneaky education isn't as good as a real education."

Blaine paused and turned to her. She lifted her head and looked up at him. He cupped her cheek.

"My job sucks." He stared into her eyes. "Because it's full of jerks and cutthroat monsters, people who only care about money and getting ahead, and about themselves. But you remind me there's still something good in the world, that there's people who want to help, not slash the throats of everybody they see."

She smiled. Her cheek was warm in his palm. "I'm sorry you deal with so many people like my father."

"Thank you, Libby. I needed the reminder that you give me. And I hope you get everything you want in life, I truly do. Even when this is over, I want to stay in touch with you and know how you're doing."

She pressed into his hand, like a kitten. "That would make me happy."

He wanted to kiss her so badly his chest ached. The way she was looking at him, he knew she wanted him to do it, but still he hesitated. He was so afraid of taking advantage of her, of taking advantage of the situation. With every moment, with every touch, he was weakening, but he tried to remind himself to let her make the first move. Let her be in control for once. He wanted her to realize as well that not everyone in the world was like her father.

He withdrew his hand, but pulled her close again and took her arm. "Unfortunately, we should probably go back soon. We can't skip out of our own wedding reception."

She sighed. "Yeah, and I don't want my father to come stumbling in here looking for us." She dropped her head on his shoulder again. "I wish I could dance with my mom. I know you don't really do that at weddings. She's just so sad and uptight all the time, and I wish she knew how much I want to help her."

Blaine strolled with her toward the exit. "Would you like me to ask her to dance?"

She looked up at him. "I'm not sure she'd say yes." Doubt clouded her eyes. "She probably wouldn't in front of my father."

"Never hurts to try, right?"

They returned to the banquet room. Coleman was sprawled in a chair, a fresh bottle of champagne on the table in front of him. He was talking loudly to Justice as one of his grandchildren tugged at his jacket. He didn't even seem to realize the little boy was there.

Kellie sat next to her laptop, eating a piece of cake. She eyed them as they came in the room.

Blaine let go of Libby's arm and walked over to her mother, where she sat stiff and miserable, away from the others.

"Mrs. Dawson, would you like to dance?" He held his hand out to her.

She looked up sharply at him, then peered at his hand, as if he was going to slap her. "What?"

"I think it's fitting that I should dance with the mother of the bride. Would you like to? It's traditional."

She gazed at him warily. So much of Libby shone through her rigid exterior, and she had the same sort of cowed fear in her eyes that hurt his heart. She glanced over at Coleman, hesitated a moment, and stood.

"I suppose." She took his hand. Her fingers were cold and bony.

Blaine walked them out on the dance floor. "Kellie, will you play something appropriate for a mother dance?"

Kellie grinned and set her cake aside, and turned to her laptop.

Blaine smiled at Libby's mother. She seemed nervous, and kept looking over at Coleman, though he wasn't even paying attention to them. Blaine wanted to throw him out of the room so everyone could have fun without looking over their shoulders.

"I promise you." Blaine lifted her hand in his. "I won't hurt your daughter."

She looked back at him and stared for a long moment, and then, for the first time since he'd met her, some of the ice around her melted.

"You swear it?" she whispered.

"Yes." He pulled her in, though only close enough to dance while remaining appropriate. "I swear I'll let her reach her full potential."

As the music started, he looked over at Libby, standing next to the cake. She held the little box in her hands, clutching it in front of her. She smiled widely at him, her face aglow. If she was this beautiful now, he could only imagine how she'd look on the day she did reach her potential.

Chapter Nine

Somehow, Libby made it through the reception. Somehow, she did it without screaming or losing her mind. However, as she stepped into their suite, she let out a huge, relieved sigh and let the tension drain from her. She could have melted into the floor.

"We did it." She was giddy and anxious, and more than a little terrified despite the accomplishment, but she was also tired and wanted out of her dress that was starting to get too tight and itchy. "I can't believe we pulled it off."

Blaine stepped in around her. "Yes, we did. And no one punched anyone. Shocking, because I wanted to sock your father a couple of times."

Blaine had brought a bottle of champagne with them. He walked into the room and grabbed an ice bucket off a table.

Libby looked around, taking the place in. "This is nice."

"Check it out. I'm going to grab some ice."

The suite wasn't enormous, like something a president or celebrity would rent, but it was bigger than any hotel room she'd ever stayed in. It was made up of three separate rooms: the bedroom, a living room type area, and a huge bathroom, all connected by short hallways. The windows were huge and provided a stunning view of the star-splashed evening falling over the Manhattan skyline. The décor was rose and beige, with plush cream-colored carpet. An extra twin bed had been set up in the living room, and she supposed that was where Blaine intended to sleep.

Both the living area and the bedroom had TVs, and she discovered, hilariously, that there was one in the bathroom as well.

"This is bigger than my dorm room was," she said when Blaine returned with the ice. She sat down on the king-sized bed, which was draped with a pale rose-colored bedspread. She bounced on it.

"Nothing but the best for my new wife." He jammed the champagne bottle in the ice bucket and sat down next to her. "It's been one heck of a day, huh?"

She pushed her shoes off and wiggled her bare toes. Kellie had taken her for a pedicure as well and her toenails were seafoam green. "I can't believe it. It hasn't really sunk in yet."

"How do you feel?"

"Like I did something insane." She laughed. "And brave."

He squeezed her hand on the bed between them. "You did, on both counts."

"It's not over yet." She glanced down at his hand, then stared out the window next to the bed. She could see their reflection in it. "Not until he gives me the money. And then the really hard part begins—trying to escape him and live my own life."

"You will." He tightened his grip. "If you can do this, Libby, you can do anything. There's no stopping you."

She looked back at him. His eyes were bright in the soft yellow light from the lamp.

"You've been so nice to me. You didn't have to play this insane game with my father, but you have, and I can't thank you enough for that."

He leaned forward. Her heart skipped a beat. He just kissed her cheek, though.

"Believe me…" He drew back. "I know I barely even know you, but I want to see you happy."

Awkward silence fell. The room was so quiet. She couldn't hear anything from the rest of the hotel, nor from outside.

"So." Blaine let go of her hand. "What do you want to do?" He gestured to the TV on the wall. "You want to watch a movie or something?"

She wiggled her toes again and grinned. "Let's drink some more champagne and dance."

She felt more confident than she had in a long time, maybe ever. Blaine cracked open the bottle and turned on some music. They danced around the living area, barefoot and crazy. Blaine taught her a few dance moves. She made a video and sent it to Kellie.

She texted back, **What, no wedding night nookie?** along with a winky emoji. Libby shook her head.

Eventually, they did decide to watch a movie. Libby's head was spinning and she knew it was time to lay off the champagne. She was also dying to be out of the confines of her dress.

"I'm going to change," she told Blaine. "I think I've had enough of being dressed up."

"Same here." He grabbed up the remote control in the bedroom. "You can have the bathroom, I'll change in here."

She grabbed the bag she'd brought with her and took it to the bathroom. In the mirror, which spanned almost an entire wall, her cheeks were flushed and her eyes bright. She put her bag on the counter and giggled at herself. The taste of champagne danced on her tongue.

She took her slide out and placed it carefully on the sink counter, propped up against the tissue box. It might have been the weirdest wedding present anyone ever got, but it was also the best.

Blaine was the best.

She'd considered buying a cute nightie for tonight, but ultimately didn't have the guts to do so.

After all, it wasn't a real wedding night, and she would probably die of embarrassment, trying to act sexy in front of Blaine.

As she pulled on her regular pajamas—oversized and pink, consisting of pants and a button-up shirt with long sleeves—she found herself considering everything, though. The moment she was in, and about Kellie's text.

Her family wasn't particularly religious and she hadn't been saving herself because of some promise to God. She was just … too awkward and too timid. Also, the terror she'd held for years that if her father found out she had sex before marriage—it made her stomach go cold and heavy. He'd call her a whore, tainted, a disgrace. Her innocence was for her husband, that's what he'd told her all through her teenage years, every time he caught her so much as looking at a boy.

But *that* was her husband, out there in the room. She had saved herself for *tonight.*

She continued thinking about it as she brushed her hair and took off her makeup. Her plain, clean face was something she was more comfortable with, though the makeup did look nice. She reapplied some lip gloss, at least.

When she padded back out to the bedroom, Blaine was sitting on the bed in a pair of jogging pants and a loose, soft-looking gray t-shirt. It was the first time she'd seen him in anything less than a suit, and somehow it made him even more handsome, in a snuggly way. His hair rested in sandy waves against his neck.

"You look cute." He held up the remote. "What do you want to watch? A comedy? Something romantic?"

She crawled onto the bed. "A romantic comedy?"

"Perfect compromise."

"What about a foreign film? You said in your

profile you like foreign films."

He tossed the remote aside. "Too pretentious right now."

She was nervous, and the sensation intensified as he moved up to the top of the bed with her, so they both sat against the headboard and piled-up pillows. They sat close, but not touching. The scent of his cologne hung on the air.

"We can order room service later," he said. "If you get hungry."

She shifted around on the pillows. "I've never had room service before. It seems fancy."

"It's really for when you're too lazy to go out and get food for yourself. So, the opposite of fancy. Kind of bummy."

They started watching the movie. It was a standard, formulaic romantic comedy about a woman who was about to marry the wrong guy but met the man of her dreams shortly before her wedding. Hijinks and awkward romantic encounters ensued. At least it was cheesy, or she wouldn't have been able to handle sitting there watching it with him.

Eventually, she shifted around on the pillows again, a little closer to him. He glanced at her. She held her breath, debating.

Then, in her boldest move of the day, she scooted over next to him and cuddled against his side. He draped his arm around her shoulders.

"This okay?" he murmured.

She nodded and draped her own arm across his middle.

She couldn't concentrate on the movie after that. Blaine's body was firm yet supple, hard yet soft at the same time, something she could just sink into. His heart beat next to her ear, a heavy, reassuring thump. She felt every breath he took and every slight movement of his muscles.

He rubbed her shoulder and spoke, his voice vibrating in his chest. "You know I'm not trying to take advantage of the situation, or of you, right?"

She tilted her face up. "I know." She closed her eyes and wished.

Her wish came true as he rolled toward her and pressed his lips against hers.

The movie was entirely forgotten.

She wasn't very good at kissing despite her prior experiences with it, but Blaine was patient and slow, and she caught on quick, like she had with dancing. As the kisses turned deeper she even parted her lips and brushed her tongue against his. She was a virgin, but she wasn't clueless. So many things she'd imagined trying with a guy, and French kissing was one. Her old boyfriend was just as inexperienced as her and their kisses had always been rather chaste. She found it a little wetter and sloppier than she expected, but pleasant.

He caressed her side and hip as they made out. The warmth she'd felt earlier during the reception flared up again and spread all through her, making her ultra-sensitive to his touch. That warmth made her press tighter against him and pay keen attention to the long, lean line of his body against hers, how it made her feel both vulnerable and protected at the same time.

He broke the kiss and stroked her hair. His face was close to hers and he gazed into her eyes. She gazed back at him, her heart hammering, stomach fluttering, and that needy want building ever hotter between her legs.

"I know this is our wedding night." He switched to dragging his fingers through her hair, slow and smooth, which made the heat rise, and made a tingle spread down the back of her neck and across her shoulders. "But I'm not expecting you to do anything. It's definitely one of the rules of the agency that no physical intimacy should be expected or coerced."

"I'm not being coerced." She placed a hand on his broad chest. "I want to do this. But I'm not trying to pressure you either. I'm not expecting you to do anything for me."

He licked his lips. They were plump and wet and she just wanted him to go back to kissing her, harder this time, and with more tongue.

"I don't want to overstep any boundaries, Libby. I'm not sure what you want and I need things to be clear between us."

She wasn't used to a man giving her the lead, much less a voice to say what she wanted. Her father had told her real men didn't do such things. They didn't capitulate to women and they knew what to do at all times.

But he was wrong, and somehow she always knew that.

"It's my wedding night." She curled her fingers in his shirt, which felt just as soft as it looked. "And I don't really know how far I want to go, but if I want to stop, I'll tell you. I saved myself for this, and well, here it is." She was much more confident saying those words than she would have imagined.

He placed his hand back on the curve of her side. "I promise if you say stop, I will."

"I know." She tugged at his shirt, pulling him back down. "More kissing, please."

"As my wife commands."

She loved kissing, she'd quickly decided. It was the best. Blaine rolled her onto her back, so he was half on top of her, and kissed her deeper and harder. She sucked at his tongue. His mouth tasted like champagne and also mint, which meant he'd sneaked and brushed his teeth, or chewed some gum or something, which meant he wanted this too.

She stroked her hands all over his body—across the wide girth of his shoulders, down the curve of his back, tentatively across his hips. She brought them back up and caressed the hard bulges of his biceps. She wanted to touch more, but despite the feeling inside her that was now inarguably horniness, despite her building desire, she was still too shy.

He touched her as well, and his hands never strayed to illicit places either, but part of her wished he would do it first so she had a reason to reciprocate.

You're a grown woman and this is your wedding night, she reminded herself. *He's eager and willing. You're not afraid, you've proven that. Let's do this.*

She put her hands on his bottom, and squeezed. It was as firm as the rest of him. He gasped into her mouth.

"Sorry," she murmured. She was about to take her hands away, but he moved one of his own onto her thigh.

"No need," he whispered.

After that, their hands were everywhere.

Blaine's touch was gentle and distracting. She shivered as he stroked his fingertips across her stomach, as he traced the curve of her hip and then clutched her bottom as well. She shuddered when he cupped one of her breasts. Her nipples were hard and even more sensitive than the rest of her. When he squeezed one she let out a soft squeak, not of protest, but of surprise and delight.

She'd been aroused before, of course. She'd touched herself. She'd had orgasms. But she'd never had another person's hands on her to make her feel this way.

The situation was both thrilling and anxiety-inducing at the same time, mostly because she needed to get past the block in her head that told her this was wrong, it was disgraceful, it was bad.

No. It was oh so right, and this was the exact right time to enjoy it and allow it.

Blaine's pupils were darker now, his eyelids drooped heavy over his eyes. He looked even more breathtaking with each passing moment, so much so he barely seemed real now. She tried to catch her stuttering breath.

"Are you sure?" he asked.

She nodded. Part of her was grateful he was asking for permission, and part of her wanted to shake him and yell *"please!"*

He smoothed his hand down her quivering stomach and then tucked it between her legs, over top her pajama bottoms.

She fought the bashful urge to clamp her legs shut. His hand made that ache inside her even worse. She pressed up against his palm instead.

"You've never done this before?" he asked.

She shook her head, biting her lip.

"Just relax and enjoy it. I'll treat you right."

He removed his hand and she almost whimpered. But then, he tucked it into the top of her pajama bottoms, and she gasped instead. He stroked his fingers over the crotch of her panties and she was overcome with embarrassment, because she could feel they were damp.

He kissed her neck, below her ear. "You're so beautiful."

That made her blush hotter. Beautiful? She'd never thought of herself as *beautiful*. She was pretty enough, she supposed, but plain, and at the moment, wearing a pair of dumpy pajamas that did nothing for her figure. She really wished she'd bought that nightie now.

Blaine tucked his fingers inside her panties. She held her breath. Her thighs trembled.

He stroked her folds open, and his fingertips moved smoothly, as it became clear she wasn't just damp but soaked. She eased her legs apart, because it felt good and she didn't want him to stop. He pressed against that nice little spot at the top of her slit with two fingertips and started rubbing, slow and firm.

The desire inside her blazed bright, igniting her limbs, raging in her stomach, and flashing white-hot behind her eyelids. She was still flushed, but she wasn't sure if it was from embarrassment or arousal. The deep ache in her core throbbed and sharped, until it became all she could think about.

He kissed down her neck, his breathing hard. She could feel he was erect, pressed against her hip, and she wanted to touch him as well. She couldn't make herself do it yet though, she was still too unsure of herself. Too bashful, somehow, with a man's hand down her pants. She almost laughed.

Instead she moaned and tilted her chin back. Her stomach tightened. The insistent stroke of his fingertips was unlike any of the times she had done it herself, much more vital and intense, much more erotic. She stiffened, nearing the edge, helpless to stop herself from tumbling over. She was ashamed and elated at the same time.

"Blaine."

She clutched his shirt as she came. He pressed his mouth to her ear and let out a deep, rich moan of approval that only made her come harder. She shook and bucked and clamped her thighs around his arm. Strained whimpers passed her lips. She wanted to shriek, to scream, but she couldn't get the sounds out.

He lifted his head and kissed over her eyes and

cheeks, his breath hot across her skin. He pressed his hand tight over her mound as she continued to quake.

When she opened her eyes finally, her entire face was hot, and sweat slicked her neck. He gazed down at her, a tiny smile on his lips.

"Thanks," she whispered, and smiled too.

He laughed.

"Still feeling all right?" He pulled his hand out of her pajama bottoms.

Despite the fact she was still shivering from her orgasm, she wanted more. She wasn't sure what she wanted, but she wanted *him*—to touch her more, to make her feel more.

"Yes." She gathered the courage to slip her hand down and press it over the bulge in his sweats. He was long and thick, and very stiff. This was her first time touching a penis and it was strangely unlike anything she could have prepared herself for. While it was hard, it still felt pliable.

He groaned and rolled off her. "May I?" He indicated her bottoms, and mimed pulling them down.

"Yes," she said, though embarrassment gripped her again.

Blaine sat up and pulled her bottoms and panties down over her hips.

She couldn't look down at her bare legs and exposed—everything—as he worked them off. She'd trimmed down there, as she usually did, though she wasn't a hairy girl to begin with. Her inner thighs were warm and wet. Were they really going to do it? Was it really going to happen?

He tossed her bottoms and panties aside. His blue eyes were vivid.

"Want to come again?" he asked.

She blinked a few times, confused. Again? So

soon?

He spread her legs open, and the next thing she knew, he was at the bottom of the bed and his head was buried between them. She let out a surprised gasp when his tongue touched her. That felt even better than fingers, hers or his.

He lifted his head, his hair spilling around his face. "This okay?"

She nodded mutely, her thighs trembling anew.

He went to work. That *definitely* felt better than fingers. His tongue was shockingly hot and soft, and yet he could still use it firmly enough to make her squirm. Despite the fact she'd already come, she was immediately chasing it again, quivering and clenching inside, wanting it as much as she had the first time. Everything felt so wet down there.

She was self-conscious though too, and frantically wondered what he might be experiencing. Was she clean enough? Did she taste okay?

Soon the pleasure—and his obvious approval—overwhelmed her worries and all she could focus on was another orgasm.

He used his fingers as well, almost pushing them inside her but not quite. She tried to keep her legs apart even though she wanted to wrap them around his head. She touched his hair, tentative and unsure, then rested her hand on the back of his head. The strands were damp with sweat. He gripped her other hand, next to her hip.

When she came again it was so much deeper, so much harder, that it made her vision go gray and her whole body seemed to float right off the bed. She couldn't keep from writhing beneath his face. He held her hips and licked her through it.

This time she couldn't hold back the wails. They tore out of her, frantic and primal. She was both numb and hypersensitive at the same time.

He sat up, flushed, his hair a wild and sexy mess, his chin and lips glistening. He wiped her juices out of his facial hair and grinned down at her, his chest working hard.

Tears had sprung to her eyes from the intensity of her release. She tried to catch her breath.

He crawled up over her. "God, you look even more beautiful now." His voice was low and husky.

"I need a moment." Her voice shook with her shuddering breath. "Can we rest a moment?"

"Of course."

He lay next to her and held her while she calmed down. His breath was still labored, his skin hot. The air smelled musky. The sheet beneath her was wet.

She debated if they should stop, but that wouldn't be fair, not to him, after he pleasured her so much. He deserved something too.

And she didn't really want to stop.

She rubbed his erection again, through his pants. She traced the long, stiff line with her fingertips and bit her lip.

"Can I?" she murmured, tugging at the elastic of his pants.

"Yes."

He helped her push them and his underwear down over his hips. She shyly looked down.

She'd seen penises before, on the internet, but seeing one in person was quite different. It was thick and curved toward his belly. The head was plump and red, and it glistened. The scent of arousal came from him too, stronger and different than her own, and more enticing.

"Can I touch you?" she asked.

"Please."

He showed her how to wrap her hand around it.

The skin was hotter than the rest of his body and surprisingly silky. He guided her hand, teaching her how to stroke, to keep her fingers tight but not too tight. The fluid that leaked from the tip was slippery and thick and made the movements easier. Eventually, he removed his hand and let her take over.

He kissed her neck and nuzzled her hair, making soft sounds, faint grunts and breathy moans. He moved his hips as she stroked him. She became surer of herself and moved faster.

She could put him in her mouth too, she supposed, but she wouldn't be good at it and it would be terribly disappointing for him. Also, he seemed—just too big, and she didn't know how she could do it, not really. Not without choking to death or making an idiot of herself.

He finally gripped her wrist, gently, and slowed her hand. He whispered in her ear, "Do you want me to put it inside you?"

A hint of urgency filtered into his voice, the same sensation that was once again sparking in her. His voice was like a hook, pulling even more desire up from the depths of her body, from places she'd never explored or even known about before now.

She considered it, but not for long. Yes, she wanted him inside her. She wanted to know what it felt like.

Blaine undressed. She stared at his naked body and she thought she had never seen anything so gorgeous—and he called *her* beautiful. He was tight and toned, and something about the broadness of his chest and the span of his hips entranced her, made her want to climb him, to claim him. His thighs were thick and covered in light blond hair, the same as on his chest. He was prefect.

Though still self-conscious, she took off her pajama top too. She didn't have huge boobs, not even decent sized ones like Kellie, but Blaine seemed to like them just fine as he fondled and squeezed them and pinched her hard nipples.

"I'll get a condom." He kissed her temple. "I … always keep some on me just in case." It sounded like an apology.

She grinned. "I'm glad you do."

While he went to fetch a condom from his bag, she lay gazing at the ceiling, knees drawn up, acutely aware of both how naked she was and how wet she was between her legs. She subtly moved out of the wet spot beneath her, and then wondered if she should stay there instead, so they didn't make another one. She cringed, thinking of the housekeeper who would have to change the bedclothes.

Blaine returned with the packet and she watched him open it and roll the condom on. Frankly, it looked a bit silly, but she forced herself not to giggle. She rested her hands on her stomach and realized they were shaking. She was shaking all over, in fact.

"Will it hurt, do you think?" she asked. "I mean, I've read about it and stuff, I know it doesn't hurt for every woman. There's a lot of factors involved." She was starting to babble.

He crawled over her and stroked his fingertips up her slit, making her gasp.

"You're soaking wet and you've had two orgasms, it probably won't hurt much, if at all."

He settled on top of her, and she liked the reassuring weight of his body, the way everything about him seemed to engulf her. He kissed her and his mouth tasted like her. She had her legs spread around his hips, her arms over his shoulders.

He gazed down at her. "If it does hurt, and you want to stop, just tell me. You can tell me to stop any time."

Her heart was in her throat, making it impossible to speak.

He went slow. From the moment he breached her, she was startled by how he felt even bigger than he looked. She relaxed and tried to let him in.

She experienced some discomfort at first, but it wasn't real pain. Just pressure, as he pressed in, seeking for her to yield. She was tight. A few twinges, nothing to make her want to stop, and then he finally slid in, all the way up inside her. She gasped.

He groaned loudly. "Oh, God." He pressed his cheek to hers. "You feel so good."

She could barely think or breathe. She clutched his shoulders. He was inside her. He was filling her up, her husband. She was no longer a virgin.

He rocked inside her, thrusting shallowly. At first there was more pressure and discomfort, and then the pleasure surged in as she opened up to him.

"Oh my God." Her voice came out weak. She twisted the sheet in one hand, clutching his shoulder with the other. "Oh my God, that feels so good."

He let out a growl, a more feral sound than anything she'd heard from him yet, something transcendent and otherworldly. "God, yes it does."

So, this was sex. This was how it felt.

And it was *awesome.*

He braced his arm above her head and started thrusting. This pleasure was so much more intense and consuming than before. It was what she'd been craving all along without understanding it was what she needed. He reached that need deep inside her, filling it better than even an orgasm could.

She whimpered and yelped as he fucked her, unable to control her voice. He moaned, nuzzling her hair, kissing her face, biting gently at her neck. Their skin was slick and slapped together. She moved her hips to meet his, no longer reluctant or shrinking. Each thrust was sharp and good and plunged high and hard up inside her.

"Blaine." She clutched at his burning, sweaty skin, her nails slipping on his flesh. "Oh…"

He pushed all the way in and fucked her like that, barely pulling out, just pumping deep inside. He stared down at her face, his a beguiling mask of pure pleasure, his eyes on fire.

"You gonna come again?" he asked in that husky sex voice he'd developed.

She didn't know. She felt like she might, but it was different than during the rubbing or licking, different than being touched on the outside. The feeling was more elusive and yet, everything was so new and amazing it pushed her toward the brink again, somehow, deliriously, deliciously.

She was frantic. "Yes, I think so." She snapped her hips, urging him to go faster.

He did. That was exactly what she needed. Her pleasure built, so intense she could no longer think.

This orgasm seemed to drain every ounce of strength out of her, all at once. She came deep and powerful like last time, but he was inside her and she could feel her inner walls squeezing around him. She screamed, truly screamed, as she couldn't hold it back this time.

"Oh my God," she sobbed, nearly out of her mind. "Oh my God, Blaine."

He plowed into her, making the bed shake. The

pounding was almost too much, but he didn't keep at it for long. He slammed his hips against hers with a rough, loud groan and held still.

Feeling him come was almost as amazing as her own orgasm. His entire body trembled, his breath coming out stuttered and ragged against her throat, in little bursts. He throbbed inside her, a thick pulse in her still-clenching passage. She marveled at it, completely inundated by the wonder of the moment.

He slumped over her, panting, and she realized for the first time she was burning hot and desperately wanted some fresh cool air and a drink of water. Maybe a gallon of water.

"You okay?" he gasped out. He kissed her ear. "Everything okay?"

She gave a shaky laugh. "Everything is fucking great." She squeaked and clamped a hand over her mouth.

He laughed, then reached down and pulled out of her.

Feeling him go was strange, that long heavy length slipping out of her, and everything was soaked. She felt gaping and sore in his wake, and she couldn't control the aftershocks that continued to riot through her.

He slipped the condom off, tossed it in the wastebasket next to the bed, and collapsed beside her. She was rather glad he didn't drape himself across her body. The air felt wonderful on her sweaty skin. They both lay silent, panting.

Her entire body tingled. Her head spun. She was starving.

"Gosh." She touched tentatively between her legs. So much wetness. Surreptitiously, she checked her fingertips for blood. The fluid was clear.

He twisted his head toward her and smiled lazily.

"Thanks."

They both laughed. She rubbed her hands over herself, feeling super sexy. The movie was still on. She'd barely noticed it since they started making out.

Blaine rolled toward her and pressed his hand against her chest, between her breasts. She smiled at him and stroked his fingers. He looked so good, all tousled and depleted. She felt a twinge deep inside her that wasn't at all sexual, but affectionate.

"Even if this is difficult, I'm glad we're making the best of it." He patted her chest. "Might as well pass the time, huh?"

She grinned and took his hand in hers. "Can we get that room service now? I'm so hungry I could eat a horse."

"You bet."

Chapter Ten

Blaine sat at his desk, but he wasn't doing any work, despite the loads and loads of it piled on top. Instead he had his chair turned to the window and was staring out over the city, daydreaming. Time was ticking, but he couldn't concentrate.

All he could think about was Libby.

The ghost of her scent lingered in his nose and the memory of her taste stayed on his tongue. He could see her face in the throes of pleasure, her soft pink lips parted, her eyelids heavy over her green eyes, her silken hair scattered wild across the pillows. A beautiful, nubile creature beneath him, so hot and snug inside, so brilliant and eager, him being the one giving her those feelings for the very first time. Her moans and whimpers echoed in his ears and stirred heat in his loins. That heat, truly, hadn't faded a bit since last night.

"You skipping lunch today?"

Blaine turned his chair around. Rick leaned in the doorway, a cup of coffee in hand. He smirked at Blaine. "You have a wild weekend or something? You've been spaced out all morning."

Damn, is it that obvious? He could always play it off as a hangover, he supposed. But hangovers were for Sunday mornings, not Monday, in the orderly and proper business world.

"No, I can't, I have a lunch meeting." Blaine scooted himself back up to the desk. "I guess it's just hard to settle back in after a weekend. I didn't do anything productive for a change. Just chilled out. Now I have to play catch-up."

"Really? You didn't do any work over the weekend? You really *must* be ready to retire."

Blaine smirked. "I made my days off my *days off*,

I know. How sinful of me."

Rick strolled in and plopped down in the chair on the other side of the desk. Blaine wished he could tell him what he'd really been up to over the weekend. Even though he liked Rick, they weren't fast and trusted friends. He could tell Rick a few things outside of work, but they were by no means buddies.

Did Blaine even have any "buddies?" Had he ever made time for it?

"What can I do to make you stay?" Rick sipped his coffee. "I've been thinking about it. I don't want you to go, even though an early retirement like that is cool, and you'll be happier. I want to learn more from you."

Blaine snorted. "Yes, your advancement is much more important than my happiness. Thanks for that."

Rick rolled his eyes. "I didn't mean it that way."

"You literally just said 'I know you'll be happier.' And I will."

Rick held up a hand. "I'm sorry. I want you to be happy, man. I just really need help understanding why, I guess."

Blaine shifted some things around on his desk, one stack to another. He should work through lunch, but he wasn't going to cancel meeting up with Libby. He couldn't, wouldn't. The tug in his gut wouldn't let him. The ache in his groin forbade it.

"Explain it to me, fully," Rick demanded.

Blaine didn't have time for this today. He was aggravated.

"I met a man, not too long ago." Blaine dragged a hand through his hair. "A powerful man. A man with tons of money. He has it all—success, stability, a growing company, a lovely family." Blaine grimaced and propped his head on his hand, staring down at the desk. "And he was the worst human being I'd ever had the misfortune of spending time in the same room with. An evil, twisted snake in the grass. If I believed in souls, I'd say he doesn't have one. As it is, he's just a failed excuse for a human being."

Rick grunted. "Sounds like a lot of people we deal with, day in and day out."

"Right." Blaine looked up at him. "Every day, one of those snakes slithers in that door." He gestured to the office door. "And we help them make more money. We help them grow as monsters."

"Sounds a little dramatic." Rick drew back. "They're not all bad, either."

Enough of them were bad. Enough of them were like Libby's father that Blaine sometimes felt like he was standing at the edge of a deep, dark pit, staring down into the unfathomable blackness. One little push from behind, and he would tumble in. He would never be able to scramble back out either.

"I've done this for all of my twenties, and it made me really old." Blaine shuffled through the stacks of paper again, not really looking for anything, just distracted, agitated. He wanted to see Libby again. Looking into her beautiful eyes, hearing her gentle voice, would soothe his heart. He needed her to wrap a rope around him and pull him away from the pit. "I'm getting out before I get any older, literally and metaphorically."

Rick shook his head and sipped his coffee.

"You'll figure it out eventually," Blaine said. "I hope sooner rather than later."

Rick lowered his cup. "I think I have a much stronger backbone than that. I know these people are ruthless, Blaine, but I learned how to shut it out."

"When you shut it out, you become complacent to it." Blaine rested his hands on the desk and fixed him with a hard stare. "Some of these people who come in here are making their money off the backs of people they wouldn't even pay minimum wage if they could get away with it. People who live in trailers while they buy their second mansions."

"So now you don't like capitalism? You don't like progress and making your own way?"

Blaine pinched the bridge of his nose. "I'm not talking about that. I'm not saying people don't have the right to make money or buy things. I'm saying that they don't have to treat other people like dirt while they do it."

"Have you been watching too many sad movies or something?"

Blaine lowered his hand and glared at him.

"You've turned into such a mopey complainer over the past year." Rick plunked his mug on the desk. "You used to be the sharpest, shrewdest man here. Now you shiver because people are being mean." He mock-pouted at him. "So many big meanies out there, with all their money."

Blaine could easily tell him to go fuck himself. He could throw him out of his office. He could avoid him for the rest of his time here and give him the cold shoulder. But Blaine didn't want to go out like that, and he didn't want to give anyone any fodder to mock him with. Rick couldn't, or wouldn't see it right now, but eventually the looming grimness of it all would cast a shadow across him.

"Listen." Blaine held his hands out in supplication. "I appreciate that this is your livelihood and it doesn't bother you. You want to advance, you want to climb to the top. There's nothing wrong with that. But you don't have to get down in the filth with them, that's all I'm saying. Look those smarmy assholes in the eye every chance you get, and don't let them talk down to you."

He wished he could do these things with Libby's father right now. He wished he could stand up to him. Maybe when it was all over, he would get his chance.

Rick stood up. "I don't consider them smarmy assholes. They put their money in my hands and even give me a chunk of it for my time. That's called business." He jerked at his blazer.

"Just go, I have work to do." Blaine waved him off. "I don't want to argue with you about this anymore. I'm going, and nothing you say is going to stop me. I pray you never really understand why, but if you do ... you will."

"Yeah, good luck, man." Rick turned and stalked out of the office.

Blaine sighed and slumped in his chair. He checked the time on his phone. He really, really needed to see Libby right now. He tried to shift his thoughts back to last night, as those thoughts were much more pleasant.

Rick popped back in the office. Blaine scowled.

"I'm sorry." Rick held up his hands. "I don't want us to have bad blood like this. I still think you're amazing. I still wish you'd at least write a book to leave me with."

Blaine shook his head. "I'm not very good at writing." He held up a folder. "You wanna take on some of my workload today? I could really use the help."

Rick's whole demeanor changed. He hurried into the room like an excited puppy. He took the folder from Blaine with a wide smile. Apparently, his former admonishments were just posturing.

"Hell yeah." He flipped through the folder. "I need to start making connections with your clients anyway. Thanks for the opportunity."

Blaine hardly considered it passing on an opportunity. If he didn't get through some of this work today, he'd be here until midnight. And he definitely wanted to go home as early as he could to his darling new wife.

"I'll do the major stuff when I get back from lunch." Blaine got up from the desk. "I might pass you some more stuff this afternoon. You going to be around late tonight?"

"I can be if you want me to be."

"It's not so much that I want you to be as I need you to be."

Rick opened his mouth, but Blaine's assistant buzzed in.

"Mr. Parker, there's a Libby Dawson here to see you."

Blaine's heart jumped. Right on time. He was in deep, way too deep, already. Since when did he get so excited over a woman, especially one he didn't have a real relationship with?

"Thanks, I'll be right out," Blaine told his assistant. He looked at Rick. "I know this is all still bright and beautiful to you, and that you've got a lot of spine. But it's heavy, and it's dark, and it's going to bend your back eventually. You believe in everything else I say, and you respect my advice and counsel, so I hope you'll respect that too. I hope you'll take my words to heart."

Rick closed the folder and fixed him with an intense gaze. "I will. I know you've seen some shit, man. I'll try to listen to your advice. Sorry I went off like that."

Blaine walked around the desk and clapped him on the shoulder. "It's good for you. You should always question authority and wisdom. It makes a better man out of you."

"You should put that in your book. *Quotes from Blaine Parker, CFA.*"

Blaine adjusted his collar, smoothed his hair, and headed toward the door. "I could never be that pretentious."

Rick followed him. "Want me to join you for your lunch meeting? Double team?"

"No, I got this. Start working on that stuff, if you will, please?"

"Right on."

In his office foyer, Libby stood gazing at one of the overpriced paintings on the walls. Blaine stopped for a moment and took her in, a work of art in his eyes as well.

She wore a knee-length pink dress and a denim jacket. Her hair was soft and loose on her shoulders, a thick, silky curtain that he wanted to plunge his face into. She clutched her purse in front of her and chewed on her lower lip. He wished he could pull her into his arms and suck on it.

"Libby." He strode over.

She turned and smiled widely at him. Her cheeks were pink like her lips. She was wearing makeup.

"Hi." She sounded happy and upbeat. He swore she had a glow about her, a new easy confidence that she lacked before.

He reasoned it was probably because she *was* feeling more confident and more comfortable with him, not because he had divested her of her virginity. The thought gave him a quiet sense of pride though, and did nothing to turn off that heat inside him. If anything, it only stoked the flames.

He took her by the arms and kissed her cheek. Her light, flowery perfume filled his nose.

"You ready to go to lunch?" He drew back, still holding her arms. "I'm afraid it'll have to be somewhere close, I can only take forty-five minutes. It's a hectic day." He gave her a sheepish smile. "I wish I could spend more time with you, I really do."

"It's fine." She brushed her bangs out of her eyes. "Anywhere you want to go is fine by me."

Rick eyed them as he slipped past and left the office. His assistant was peering over her computer as well.

"Come on then." Blaine put his hand on the small of her back. "I know a nice little café nearby."

In the elevator on the way down, Blaine surreptitiously checked his appearance in the reflective doors.

"So, this is where you work." Libby stood close by his side, staring at the doors too. "It's a really big building. Lots of people, super busy." She seemed to be chattering to fill the silence.

"There's a lot of office space here." He smoothed his hair and looked at her. "When you get your nonprofit up and running, I could help you rent a space if you need it."

Her eyes were bright. "Really? Yeah, I guess I'm going to need offices and stuff, huh? I've got a lot of planning to do."

"Indeed."

They fell back into silence as the elevator sank.

"Did you get all your stuff packed up?" Blaine asked.

"Yeah. I didn't have much to begin with, and most of it is still in boxes from when I moved into Kellie's place a couple months ago." She chewed her lip. "I could stay with her, you know. You don't have to put me up at your place."

He slipped his arm around her shoulders. "I want you to stay with me. I like having you around."

"I guess since we're married it's only appropriate, huh?"

He finally gave in, swooped down to kiss those shiny pink lips, and suck at that bottom one she was worrying so much. She kissed him in return, hard and eager, confident in that as well now too. He caressed his hand down the curve of her back.

The elevator doors opened. They were on the bottom floor and being stared at by a group of waiting people.

Libby promptly broke away, her cheeks flashing a darker shade of pink. They hurried out of the elevator. A few sly looks were directed their way.

He really needed to remember this was *business*, not pleasure.

****

Blaine took Libby to the café down the street, the one where people in his office often grabbed lunch in a hurry when schedules were tight. The place had a reputation for being fast even during peak hours. The dining area was starting to fill up, but they managed to grab a two-seater table in a corner by the windows. Blaine went up to the counter to order them soup and sandwiches. He really wished he didn't have so much work to catch up on and could just sit with her for a while.

When he returned with the tray, her legs were crossed under the table, her dress up over her knee. He tried not to stare, or remember how they felt wrapped around his hips.

"Thanks." She beamed as he handed her a wrapped sandwich and a Styrofoam cup of vegetable soup. "I like Manhattan so much." She looked out the window, and the light brightened her face and shone in her eyes. "I'd only been here a few times before I started going to school. My parents never really took us anywhere. But we did come and see a Broadway show when I was ten."

"It's pretty hustle and bustle." He glanced out the window at the cars and people rushing by. "Easy to get swept up."

"I know, that's what I like about it. It feels like the real world."

Blaine smiled. "I never thought about it that way. Where did you grow up?" He suddenly realized he knew very little about her, and he wanted to fill in the blanks.

"Yonkers. Near the Hudson River. How about you?"

"The Bronx." He unwrapped his sandwich. "I spent most of my teenage years here in Manhattan though, tagging along after my dad and doing odd jobs for the people he worked for."

"Sounds exciting."

"It was, back then."

Blaine pulled a set of keys from his blazer pocket, took one off the ring, and dangled it in front of her. "The key to your new kingdom, Madame."

Her cheeks darkened again. He loved how much she blushed, another one of those sweet and charming things about her.

"You really don't have to do this." She took it demurely. "I absolutely could stay with Kellie, I don't mind sleeping on her couch. Intruding on your life like this is a big deal."

"It's not an intrusion at all. You're my wife, right?" He peeled the lid off his soup. "You need a place to stay and my apartment is huge. I'm also hardly ever there. It needs some life in it."

She toyed with the key. "I'll try to be as quiet as a mouse."

"The doorman knows you're coming, just tell him who you are when you go in the building. He'll be behind the desk. He'll have someone show you up and even help you bring your stuff in. Everything is arranged."

"This sounds like a really fancy place. A doorman?" She placed the key on the table beside her.

"It's not as fancy as I'd like, trust me. It's home though, at least for now. I have a spare room you can stay in, for as long as you'd like. It's no problem at all. I mean, you're paying me a lot of money for this experience, it's not like I'm giving you a handout. Right?"

She picked up her spoon and smiled. "I can't thank you enough. You're going above and beyond what I paid you for."

He was, in some unexpected ways, and he couldn't help but grin when he thought of those ways. "My pleasure."

Her cheeks remained pink. She ate her soup.

After a few minutes of eating in silence, Blaine spoke again. "You know, after this is all over, after the divorce, you can keep staying there if you want."

She blinked a few times. "I won't intrude on you for that long. I'm going back to school. I'll be able to stay in the dorms like I did before."

"Well, if you need a place to stay until then, you're welcome to. I'm not just going to kick you out on the street."

Libby stirred her soup and gazed out the window. "I'm so afraid this won't work out." Her voice fell a notch. "Even though we got through the hard part I'm worried it'll still fail."

"Your father will give you the money, don't worry. We were realistic, right? We fooled him."

"Yeah, but what if I can never do what I want with it?" She looked at him. "What if all these big dreams I have fall flat? I could get the money and still not accomplish anything."

Blaine thought of his work, and of the way his own hopes and goals had changed over time. "You're shrewd, Libby. I think, one way or another, something will work out for you. Maybe not what you envision right now, but maybe something even better. Something you can't imagine right now. You've learned to take risks and do what your heart says. That's the first step in making any dream come true. You'll get there."

She stared down into her soup. "I still don't know how I'm going to tell my father the truth after he gives me the money. I know he'll find some way to hurt me, or sue me, or get it back." Panic filled her voice. "He won't ever let me go. He'll make me pay."

Blaine reached over and clutched her hand on the table. She was trembling, and his heart ached for her. "I'll be there with you, if you want me to be."

She looked up at him. Her hand relaxed.

"And I know lawyers." He squeezed. "Good lawyers, ones who can strike down anything your father sends your way. I know places you can put your money that makes it damn hard for other people to touch it, even when they want it really bad. Trust me, I know ways to make sure your father can't take it back." He released her hand.

She sighed. "This won't be pretty." She scooped up a spoonful of soup. "But I expect that." She ate.

"At least we're having some fun, huh?" He winked.

Her smile returned.

Lunch flew by way too fast. Every minute he spent with her, he wanted to stretch it out longer. Time didn't care about his feelings, though. Before he knew it, he regretfully had to head back. They stepped out on the street, hand in hand. It was a natural gesture already and having her by his side made him feel quiet and calm inside. How long since he'd met a woman who made him feel that way? How long since he'd *felt* that way, period?

The sunlight fell on her face. She squinted. "Can I see your office where you work? I don't really know what stockbrokers do."

His heart sped up at the idea of spending a few more minutes with her. "Sure. But I warn you, it's really boring. You're not going to be impressed."

In the elevator back up to his office, he slipped an arm around her waist. She fit comfortably against his side. He rubbed her hip and glanced down at her.

She gazed back up at him and played idly with his lapel. He didn't kiss her this time, because there were other people in the elevator, coming back from lunch break like them.

His assistant was out for lunch as well when they returned.

"See, it's not that interesting." Blaine closed his office door behind them, after ushering her in. "I know it looks like I'm not organized at all, but I swear this cluttered mess makes sense to me. I know exactly where everything is."

Libby walked around, peering at his desk, looking at the bookshelves and filing cabinets piled with papers and folders. She batted at the leaves of the ugly potted plant next to the window. The drooping, sad, horticultural abomination wasn't his idea, just something that got stuck in here because no one else wanted it. She stopped in front of the window and gazed out.

"You have a nice view."

He raked his gaze down her body, over her curvy backside and her long, sleek legs. "Yeah, I do." He walked over next to her.

The sunlight picked out golden highlights in her hair and made her lips shimmer. He couldn't tear his gaze from her face.

"I guess I should let you get back to work." She played with one of the buttons on her jacket. "I'll take everything over to your place and I'll see you tonight?" She bit her lip.

He couldn't fight the temptation any longer, couldn't push back the desire that crashed over him like an all-consuming wave. He pulled her to him and sucked on that lip, and then claimed her mouth in a deep, hungry kiss. She locked her arms around his shoulders and pressed up against him, the entire length of her soft, lithe body. Wild thoughts rushed through his head, crazy, dangerous notions fueled by lust and the shiny newness of their situation.

When they broke the kiss, he found it hard to catch his breath. Her eyes seemed darker, full of need, full of the same demanding want that raged in him.

"I can't stop thinking about our wedding night," she said, her voice low and breathy. "About everything we did."

"I can't stop thinking about it either." He slipped his hands down her back and onto her bottom. Arousal flared bright in him, his will no longer able to hold it in check. His cock, which he'd been previously concentrating hard on keeping down, perked against her stomach.

She glanced toward the door. "I don't want to get you in trouble."

Those dangerous thoughts raced faster through

his head. The fact he'd apparently awakened the beast inside her as well made it harder to think rationally. He still had time, didn't he? At least ten minutes. His phone calls could wait, he could push his afternoon schedule back a little bit more…

He let go of her, walked to the door, and locked it. She widened her eyes as he walked back to her, with purpose and intent, stalking like an animal on the scent of prey. She let out an adorable squeak when he picked her up.

"Blaine." His name on her lips certainly wasn't adorable, though. It was the most mature, hottest, womanly thing he'd ever heard. She wrapped her arms around his neck as he carried her to the desk.

"I don't have much time." He plunked her down on the edge of it. He'd never fucked a woman in his office, but wasn't that a normal fantasy? "I've been thinking about you all morning. I can't get any damn work done."

"Sorry." She didn't sound it.

He pushed his hand up under her dress and caressed her smooth inner thigh. He worried she might flinch or shy away, but instead she opened her legs for him. The light filled her eyes, revealing the desperation behind them. She parted her lips and he kissed her hard, and plunged his tongue into her mouth. She sucked on it with a moan.

Not all her sweet naivety was gone with her virginity. She fumbled with his belt and pants button, but her movements were awkward and uncertain. He helped her by undoing the buckle, but let her unbutton and unzip him, just to feel her do it. He gripped the waistband of her panties over her hip and tugged them down. His heart beat so loud in his ears it was all he could hear.

She sat back on both hands and tilted her bottom,

so he could drag her panties down over her hips and thighs. Her body was eager and yielding as she lifted her hips to assist in his task.

"I haven't been able to concentrate either," she said. One of her sandals slipped off as he yanked her panties down over her ankle. She curled her bare toes, her toenails painted pastel green. "I admit, I thought about doing this when I came here. I kinda planned it." She bit her lip, which was now swollen and wet. "Is that okay?"

"I don't know, what do you think?" He dropped her panties on the carpet next to her sandal, then stepped between her legs and worked his stiff cock out of his pants and underwear. It popped out rather abrupt and embarrassingly.

She giggled. "Um." She glanced down. "I would say yes?"

He kept some condoms in his desk drawer—not that he ever expected this current scenario to unfold, but he went out with coworkers for drinks after work sometimes, and he never knew when he might get lucky. Well, he hoped anyway.

"Is it wrong?" She gazed at him, locking a leg around his waist. "To want to do this again?"

He shook his head. "I'm your husband." He grinned. "Hold on, one second."

He loathed pulling away from her, making her lower that long lovely leg wrapped around him, but he had to in order to retrieve a condom from the drawer. As he ripped open the package she watched him closely.

"Do you do this a lot in your office?" She sounded half joking, half worried.

He smoothed the condom down over his cock. "No. I promise, this is the first time. Do you believe me?"

She nodded and locked that leg around him again, and then the other one, and any remainder of good sense still left in his brain vanished. Hopefully, nobody called or needed him for the next few minutes. He thought he should have turned off his cell phone, but he didn't have the presence of mind to find it and turn it off now.

Her dress was gathered around her waist, her ass near the edge of the desk. He stroked his fingers up her slit, and she was slick, ready for him to slip inside. She whimpered, a sound that made his cock give an involuntary jerk.

"Are you sore?" he murmured. He dipped a finger into her. So hot.

"Just a little." She clutched his arm. "We better hurry." She glanced over her shoulder. "Can't you get fired for this?"

"Probably just yelled at, I'm the boss." He drew his finger out of her and sucked it clean. She tasted like heaven. "But it would be worth it."

Her wrapped an arm around her waist and hauled her forward. He slipped right up into her, into that snug, slick warmth that seemed to swallow him whole. He groaned as he sank in, much easier than last night. She really did want him, wanted him so much with all of her, like this, with reckless abandon and a shamelessness that was still somehow innocent and endearing.

She gasped and buried her face against his shoulder, clutching his arms with both hands now, her fingers curling in the fabric of his blazer. Her scent filled his nose, a mixture of her perfume and the heady smell of her arousal.

He tried to not make any noise as he started fucking her. The office was quiet and he could hear the slick sounds of his cock slipping in and out of her pussy, quick and rhythmic. God, she was so wet. The desk squeaked. Her breath was ragged against his chest, interspersed with soft whimpers and whines. She tightened her legs around his hips. Though he knew he had to make this quick, he wished he could fuck her for hours.

"Oh," she moaned, and dropped her head back. He caught her lips in a sloppy kiss.

He moved faster, desperate for the satisfying rush of release. He'd almost jerked off in the bathroom earlier and was now glad he hadn't. This was so good, so furtive, he wouldn't last long. He wanted her to get off too, though.

He braced one hand on the desk and pushed the other between them. He found the hard nub of her clit and flicked it fast and firmly with his thumb.

She pushed her face back into his shoulder. Her thighs trembled around his hips. He felt delirious and wasn't sure he could hold out long enough to make her come. He vowed if he didn't, no matter how much it increased the risk of getting caught, he would eat her out until she did.

As it turned out, thankfully—or perhaps regretfully—he didn't need to. She must have been on the edge as well because in less than a minute her inner walls pulsed around him. She squirmed like crazy. His hand was soaked as her juices gushed out around his cock.

"Blaine!" she shrieked, muffled against his shoulder. He hammered into her, too far gone to stop now.

He had to bite back hard on a groan as he came, and still, some of the sound slipped out between his teeth. He wrapped his arms around her and pulled her tight against him as he buried his throbbing cock deep inside her. He felt like his entire soul rushed out of him with his release, every ounce of his strength and need. Somehow, amazingly, he was already lost to her.

She clung to him and whimpered as they both trembled with the last shuddering remnants of their orgasms. Blaine's vision was blurred, his legs weak, his shirt sticking to him. He couldn't even think of the day ahead, or what he still had to get done. She filled his entire universe, she was all that mattered.

This no longer felt like business.

He drew back and kissed her. Her lips were wet like the rest of her, her skin sheened with sweat, her thighs slick, her pussy drenched. Her arms and legs were still wrapped around him, not as tightly, and she shivered.

"Oh my God." He smiled against her lips. He pulled back and looked into her eyes. They were bleary and heavy-lidded.

"Oh, wow." She grinned lazily. "I can't believe I waited so long to do this. Sex is great."

He laughed. "I wish we could keep going." He kissed her forehead.

She sighed blissfully. "Yeah, me too."

Unfortunately, they couldn't. Pulling out of her was as disappointing as sliding into her was glorious. She hopped down off the desk and grabbed her panties and sandal. He peeled off the condom and buried it in his wastebasket under the papers already in there.

"Is there a bathroom?" She wobbled as she lifted her foot and worked her shoe on. Her panties dangled from her other hand.

He tucked his cock in his pants. "Yeah, I'll show you." He needed it too. "Might want to hide those in your purse, though."

She looked at her panties and giggled. "Yeah, I better, huh?" She smiled. "I'll see you tonight?"

He zipped up his pants. He couldn't walk out to the bathroom with them undone, though he was making a mess of his underwear right now. "You bet. Make yourself at home."

"I'll try." She gave him a kiss and hurried to the door.

He watched her go, ruffling his hair, still breathing hard. He quickly grabbed the air freshener off the top of his bookcase and sprayed the room. Nothing like the scent of meadow flowers and sex.

Chapter Eleven

Blaine's apartment was bigger and nicer than anything Libby had ever seen, even the beautiful hotel suite they had for their wedding night. She felt weird stacking up her boxes and bags in the guest room, like she was some sort of homeless person couch-surfing—which, actually and factually, was the truth of the situation.

"Dang, Libs." Kellie stood in front of the huge windows in the living room that looked out over Central Park. "You hit the jackpot. I want a rich husband with a swanky place like this."

In addition to being big, practically the size of a house in floor space, it was also chic and modern, like something out of an interior decorating magazine. Every room was open and airy and the walls painted some neutral color with nice contrasting carpet. The kitchen was full of stainless steel and marble. But apart from a few personal effects scattered around the living room, it didn't look lived in.

She remembered him telling her the place needed some life. Had he paid someone to make it look nice, but couldn't make it homey?

"Well, just pay ten thousand dollars." Libby stepped up beside Kellie at the window. They were above the treetops, and buildings rose around them, a mountain range of glass and steel. "You can get a fake husband for six weeks too."

Kellie nudged her in the side with her elbow and turned to her with a grin. "So?"

Libby blinked. "So, what?"

Kellie rolled her eyes. "So, how was your wedding night?" She pinched Libby's hip, then wandered off across the living room toward a cabinet full of audio and stereo equipment. "Dang, he really does have some money."

Libby's cheeks warmed. She was still buzzing—practically vibrating—from what happened at lunch. That, and the events of her wedding night, were all she could think about. The pleasant ache between her legs and in her muscles was a constant reminder.

"I don't think it's polite to talk about things like that."

Kellie turned from the cabinet and popped her eyes wide. "It's only not polite to talk about it if something happened."

Libby turned back to the window, her cheeks heating up.

"Libby!" Kellie bustled back over. "What did you guys do? Come on, spill."

Libby couldn't keep a smile off her lips. "Well, we watched a movie…" She couldn't even remember the name of it now.

"Yeah, and?"

"We ordered room service." She *did* remember the waffles. She was ravenous and they were delicious, she didn't even care it was dinnertime and not breakfast. She wanted waffles, and Blaine got them for her.

"And?"

Libby fidgeted. "I said, it's not polite to talk about."

Kellie gaped at her. "Oh my God, you didn't … you did?"

Libby's smile and blush probably revealed everything.

"Oh my God." Kellie clutched her arms. "You totally *did*!"

"He's my husband." She pulled out of her grip. "What's wrong with that?" She headed off to check out the bathroom.

"I can't believe it." Kellie followed her. "How was it? How was he? Come on, I'm your BFF, aren't I? This is BFF privileged information."

Libby flipped on the light. The room was huge, of course. He had a shower and a big tub, and two sinks. Everything was black marble and brass, and it looked very classy. A rich person bathroom.

"I don't know." Libby shrugged.

"What do you mean, you don't know?"

Libby turned to her. "I mean, it was nice, really nice. But I don't know if he was good, I don't have anything to compare it to. It was my first time."

Kellie opened her mouth, then snapped it shut. She put her hands on her hips. "Was he good to you? He didn't hurt you, did he? He didn't force you?" Her tone turned serious.

"No! Gosh, no." Libby shook her head. "It was nice. He was really nice to me." She wanted to tell her everything, just gush about it, but she couldn't. She would die of embarrassment. Maybe she could text her the details later. It would be easier to talk about if she didn't have to look at her.

Kellie relaxed and smiled. "I'm proud of you, Libs."

Libby laughed. "For having sex?"

Kellie gripped Libby's shoulders. "You're a woman and you're making your own choices"

"I did wait until marriage, though." She pulled away and went to check out the kitchen again. She smiled deviously. "We did it again when I went to meet him for lunch today. In his office."

Kellie gasped and followed her. "Oh my God, I definitely need details. From virgin to hoe, that fast."

Libby cracked up. "Oh yeah. That's me, a big old

hoe."

They checked out the whole of the apartment, and Libby even peeked into Blaine's bedroom. It was the only room in the place that looked like someone spent time there. The bed was unmade and clothes lay around, in chairs and on the dresser. The scent of his cologne hung on the air. He had an en suite bathroom, but she didn't go in to check it out. She would be careful about respecting his privacy and wouldn't open any drawers or closets, though she was terribly curious.

"You're so lucky," Kellie informed her. "He's hot, he likes you, and he's rich. You chose well."

"The lucky part is that he's playing along, and he can deal with my father."

Speaking of her father, she would be getting a phone call soon.

"I'm going to feel really weird staying here," Libby admitted as Kellie got ready to leave. Libby didn't want her to stay there too long, as she already felt like she was invading Blaine's space and didn't want to be disrespectful by having friends over. "I mean, in six weeks we're getting divorced. I barely know him. And now I'm all up in his apartment."

Kellie tugged her jacket on. Libby could tell she didn't want to go, but she honored Libby's wishes. "I think at the very least you guys will stay good friends." She poked Libby's side. "Very good friends."

Libby shook her head, though she was wondering how much more sex they would have during this venture—part of her hoped lots. Part of her realized it wasn't very professional either, and would make it harder to leave him.

"You should hang out with his parents too," Kellie said. "They're really cool people. I was chilling with his mom during the reception and she was a total blast."

Libby frowned. "There's something weird about them, I just can't put my finger on it."

Kellie snorted. "You mean his dad isn't a total dictator and his mom isn't a doormat? I know that's what you're used to, Libs, but trust me, it's your parents who are the weird ones. You just haven't seen real human beings in the wild until now."

Kellie was nothing if not honest, and Libby liked her for that, mostly.

"It's not that." Libby folded her arms. "It's just the way Blaine acts around them. It's really, I don't know … formal?" She thought again of the way Blaine shook his father's hand as he was getting in the car outside the restaurant. Her dad was not huge on physical affection, but even he hugged her when they parted ways.

"You think so?" Kellie buttoned her jacket. "I don't know, his dad is a businessman too, maybe it has something to do with that. Your dad can be pretty frosty, that's for sure."

Libby played with the bracelet on her wrist, the one Blaine's mother had given her. "Yeah, I guess. I think it's strange he told them the truth about what we're doing, too, and that they're cool with it, with their son marrying a woman for money."

Kellie stepped forward and hugged her. "Stop freaking out, okay? Focus on what you need to do next. You're just paranoid." She drew back and smirked. "But have some fun doing it."

Libby took a deep breath. "Yeah, my father is supposed to call me today. That's not gonna be fun."

Kellie patted her arms. "You got this, girl." She kissed her cheek. "Call me tonight! Text me more details about your fun times." She grinned.

After she left, Libby wandered around the

apartment some more. She finally gave in to temptation and opened a few neutral things. The refrigerator, which didn't have much in it. The kitchen cupboards, which held pots and pans and dishware, but was lacking in the food department as well. Apparently, they'd be ordering out.

She peeked in the broom closet in the kitchen, and the drawers in counters, which were mostly filled with utensils and junk. Finally, she went and sat on the couch to watch TV and resist any further urges to snoop.

Blaine texted to make sure she'd gotten in. She told him she had, thanked him again, and smiled as she added a smiley face emoji. He told her he'd be home around seven and that if she needed anything there were several stores within walking distance.

She felt like a princess in a castle, looking out over the prince's kingdom. She slipped her sandals off and watched TV in a daze. Her mind kept straying back to Blaine's office, and the way the desk felt beneath her bare bottom, the way he felt inside her. The smell of his cologne clung to her dress. The salt of his sweat stayed on her lips.

How could she be so dang horny when she'd been screwing virtually nonstop for the past forty-eight hours?

As the afternoon waned, boredom and curiosity finally moved her from the couch. She went to Blaine's bedroom and opened the door. She would just take a quick look around, she told herself. She wouldn't touch anything, wouldn't mess anything up.

Being in his personal space gave her a giddy rush. She walked around, checking out the pictures on the walls. Pieces of tasteful art, like in his office. His sheets were navy blue. His alarm clock also had a radio. A half-empty water bottle sat on the stand next to the bed.

All the while admonishing herself, she opened the

closet and peeked in. It was a walk-in, full of suits and nice shirts, and rows of shiny, professional shoes. Ties hung on a rack. He had some more casual outfits too, and as she looked them over, she wondered what he looked like in jeans.

The attached bathroom was smaller than the main one, but still had both a tub and shower—only one sink, though. A few towels hung on a rack and an assortment of grooming products littered the sink counter. She picked up a square amber bottle and uncapped it. One deep whiff told her this was the cologne he wore. She closed her eyes and remembered the scent of it on his warm, slick skin, how it clung to his hair and all his clothes. Once again, she was in his arms, his hands on her waist, him buried inside her...

Her cell phone trilled in the living room and she nearly jumped out of her skin. Guilt washed through her and she quickly capped the bottle and put it back in its place. She ran to the living room.

Maybe he had a nanny cam and he'd seen her snooping? Her face burned.

The screen said it was her father. She was only slightly relieved.

"Hi, Daddy." She spoke brightly. Her heart raced and her hands trembled.

"Hello, Liberty." His stern voice filled her stomach up with dread, even more so now. "How are you doing today? How's married life treating you so far?"

She smiled genuinely. "It's good. I've just moved my stuff into Blaine's place."

"You've already moved out of the dorm?"

She struggled to remember the script they'd worked out. "Yes, Daddy. I've been planning on it for a while, so I was packed and everything." She sat down on the couch.

"Before you even knew if I would approve of you getting married?" He huffed. "You've gotten so impetuous. Hopefully your husband can work that out of you."

She clenched her fist on her knee. "Yes, I'm sorry."

He sighed heavily, as if her very existence taxed him. "That aside, we need to talk about your inheritance."

Libby took a breath. "Oh, yeah?" She tried to sound as causal as possible. "Gosh, with all the excitement, I haven't even been thinking about it."

He grunted. "I have. It's a huge matter, getting my accountant and lawyer prepared and an account all set up for you. But I did it for your sister, and I'm nothing if not fair to my children. I love you equally."

She blinked slowly. "An … account?"

"Yes, that's how I did it for Justice. I set up a joint account for us and put the money in. I'm still the main account holder, of course."

Her insides froze. She had never asked Justice how he gave her the money, she just assumed he gave it directly to her and that was how she and her husband got their nice big house and cars.

"A joint account?" She fought to keep the panic out of her voice.

"Yes. You think I'm just going to hand that much money over to either one of you, without making sure it's secure? When your sister needs money out of the account she lets me know. I always make sure her husband is aware of what she's withdrawing, though. I'll do the same with Blaine. He's the one between the two of you I trust to make sensible decisions. Maybe in a few years, you'll have your act together and you can discuss it with him."

Libby blinked rapidly. Her eyes burned with tears. Her throat was thick. "Oh ... I didn't know that was how you and Justice did it."

"Transferring that much money comes with a lot of fees and taxes." He sounded exasperated. "This way, the money is still technically in my name and I can avoid the IRS sticking their grubby hands in. Also, less legal paperwork needs to be drawn up. I know it sounds complicated, but ask your husband about it, he'll understand. He can explain it to you."

She barely heard his words. Her hand shook on her knee, her nails digging into her palm. Her vision blurred.

"We'll arrange a meeting later this week," he went on. "I'll get things set up to open an account at my bank and whatnot. You can let Blaine know about the money now, I'm sure he'll be pleased and surprised. It'll be a good partnership for him after all."

Libby couldn't speak. A tear escaped and slipped down her cheek. This was all for nothing, the marriage, the whole plot they'd concocted. If she couldn't withdraw the money without her father knowing when and why, she couldn't escape him, and she couldn't make this work. She couldn't even take out the five thousand dollars to sneak back into her mother's safe.

"Libby? You still there?"

She swallowed and wiped her face with a shaking hand. "Yes, Daddy. We'll get together later this week." Her voice almost betrayed her. She wanted to scream down the line at him, blow this all to pieces right now, tell him how horrible he was and how she had defied him.

"Hopefully, you'll make better use of it than your sister has. I was hoping she'd invest some of it into a trust fund for her kids, that way at least my granddaughter doesn't have to worry about going to school and working outside the home someday. That, or hire a maid." He snorted. "I've seen how she keeps house. She learned nothing from your mother. For all her faults, your mother kept our home clean."

Libby's tears unleashed and streaked down her cheeks. She had to get off the phone before she started sobbing.

"Make sure you do better." Her father spoke ominously. "You were lucky to catch a man like Blaine, as headstrong as you are. Try to make me look good, huh?"

"I'll try."

****

Blaine's apartment had a balcony, looking out over the park. Libby lay sprawled on a lounge chair out there, listless as a slug, staring at the sinking sun as it painted pink stripes across the deep blue sky. The air was chilly, but she hadn't moved to go inside or put a coat on. Her skin was as cold and hard as her insides now. In her right hand, she clutched the slide.

Blaine stepped through the sliding glass doors, still in his suit and tie, coat draped over his arm. He frowned.

"Libby?"

She rolled her head on the back of the chair and turned her face away from him. Her neck was stiff. Her eyes, in contrast to the rest of her, burned. She didn't want him to see the state she was in.

"I brought takeout, if you're hungry. I tried texting you." He lifted a plastic bag in his other hand. Worry filled his voice. "Are you okay? It's cold out here. Why don't you come inside?"

She swallowed. Even her saliva was cold.

"My father isn't going to give me the money." Her voice sounded alien to her ears, too flat and deep, and so distant.

He stared at her a moment, then lowered the bag.

"Come inside." He motioned through the doors. "Please, you've got to be freezing."

She hauled herself up, slowly and stiffly. Her muscles were still sore, but the reason for it seemed a vague, once-pleasant memory that might have happened in a dream. She held no joy in her hollow chest now.

She walked inside. Blaine had turned on the lights in the living room, and the TV was still on. He closed the balcony door. The warmth of the room felt good, despite not much else feeling that way. She shivered.

"What exactly do you mean, he's not going to give you the money?" Blaine dropped the bag and his coat on the couch, and walked over to her.

"Oh, he's going to give it to me. But in his way." She wrapped her arms around herself. "With his strings attached." She let out a dry, humorless laugh. "I should have known better. I *did* know better, but I went ahead with it anyway."

Blaine rubbed her shoulders and arms. His eyes shone with worry. "What do you mean? Tell me what's going on."

"It turns out when he gave my sister the money, he didn't give it to her without conditions. He put it in a joint account with himself as the main account holder. She can only take out money if she tells him first and explains to him what she's going to use it for. And of course, she has to have her husband's permission, as well."

Blaine slowed his rubbing.

"I can't take the money out without telling him first." Her throat tightened. "He says it's for tax reasons, but I know it's just so he can keep us on a leash. He would never want to see us make our own way in the world."

Blaine let go of her. He walked off to his bedroom and returned a minute later with a blanket. He draped it over her shoulders and led her to the couch. They sat down together, Blaine with his arms around her. She was still shivering, or maybe shaking. She felt sick. She was hungry too, but the sensation was lost under everything else.

"Well, then." He rubbed her fingers, working warmth into the icy digits. "We're going to have to figure out a way to get it out, little by little, and make up reasons for it."

He sounded, and appeared serious.

He paused as he noticed the slide in her hands. He took it gently, set it on the coffee table, and then went back to rubbing her hands.

"I can't drag you even deeper into this. I can't even drag myself deeper." She looked down. "I can't take out the money to go back to school, he would know. I don't know how to put on enough of an act to make him not realize what I'm doing. It's a lot of money, and he would want proof of where it's going. I know him."

Blaine tilted her chin up. He brushed his fingertips across her cheek, catching a stray tear. "We'll figure something out."

She sniffed. "It would take months—years, to take out all the money I need to make things work. I would have to pile lies on top of lies." She sniffed harder. "If he found out the truth, I don't know what he'd do to you, but it wouldn't be good. He'd make sure you lost your job, or have you arrested. And our agreement—it's only six weeks. We'd have to keep pretending to be married to make all the lies work. We can't do that. I can't ask you to implicate yourself in this for that long." She was on the verge of sobs again, and she'd thought she couldn't possibly cry any more. "I'd pay you for your time, but I just couldn't, I couldn't let you—"

"Libby, we'll figure this out." He pulled her against him. "I'll help you find a solution."

"I was an idiot." She burst into tears against his shoulder. "I should have known this wouldn't work. What was I thinking?"

He held her while she cried. She felt stupid, useless. She knew her father would win in the end. He always did.

"I owe my mother five thousand dollars," she choked out. "She doesn't know it, but I took it from her safe so I could pay for this marriage. I have to get it back in there before she finds out. How the hell am I going to do that?"

He rubbed her back. "I promise you, we'll think of something. I've come this far, I'm not leaving you on your own now."

She was so full of guilt she couldn't respond. Her father would make him pay, she knew that too. She didn't want him to suffer, this wasn't his fault.

The rest of the evening was miserable. She ate some of the takeout Blaine had brought, but she couldn't distract herself from her despair. Blaine made a few phone calls in his bedroom and told her he was going to contact some people to find out if there was a legal way for her to either remove all the money from the account or get her father kicked off it. Kellie texted her several times, but she didn't reply.

Blaine eventually rejoined her on the couch. He held her as they watched TV.

"What do you think of my place, at least?" He stroked her hair. "I hope you'll be comfortable here." She knew he was trying to distract her.

She looked around, her eyes sore and bleary. "It's nice. And clean."

He chuckled. "Yeah, I'm not here much. Always working. It kind of sucks that being able to afford a place like this means you're always working to pay for it." He sighed. "Plus, I have a maid come in once a week."

She thought of her father bashing Justice's cleaning skills and almost started crying again. Well, at least he could be proud of her on that front, if she stayed here. She didn't have to tell him it was a maid.

Blaine kissed her temple. "You can stay here as long as you need to."

She held his hand and played with his fingers. "I'll try not to be too intrusive while—until this is over, anyway." She'd probably end up back at Kellie's, or worse, at home with her mother.

"You're not intrusive." He sifted his fingers through her hair. "And you don't have to sleep in the guest room if you don't want to."

A smile tugged at the corner of his mouth.

She looked down. "I don't know."

"I'm sorry." He squeezed her shoulder. "I'm just trying to cheer you up a little. I know you're really upset. But believe me, Libby, I'm clever, and I'll figure something out."

She snuggled against his side. "I think I should get a shower. Do you mind?"

"No, you wanna use the shower in my room? The pressure is better in there."

She did. She wanted to get under the water and let it wash her cares away, make her forget, or at least try.

Blaine's shower was huge and had glass walls. He started to leave the room as she undressed, but she told him to stay. He undressed too, and showed her how to turn on the water. Then they were pressed together, wet skin to wet skin, her back against the slick glass. He kissed her neck and she closed her eyes, wishing everything away except the touch of his hands and the feel of his body against hers.

She never dreamed within two days of losing her virginity she'd have shower sex for the first time, but here she was, and it was just as sexy and hot as it looked on TV. Or maybe he was just good at making it that way. Blaine was strong and held her up, and when he filled her it was so exquisite, that thick hardness pushing up inside her, getting even deeper at that angle. She let out the shrieks and moans she'd wanted to release in his office, and dragged her nails up his back, helpless with pleasure as the warm water rushed over them.

He growled her name as he came, as he throbbed inside her. She felt so vital, so alive. He then dropped to his knees and used his tongue on her until she was thrashing against the glass and her knees would no longer hold her up. He clutched her hips, supporting her, and pleasured her until she was lost in bliss, until she was gushing into his mouth and not the least bit ashamed of it.

After, she was sated and wrapped in a warm, hazy fog that kept some of her sadness at bay. She stood under the spray and Blaine washed her hair. She had him, at least for right now, and he was so good to her. Better than she could have hoped for when she picked him out from a simple picture.

"We'll figure something out," he murmured and kissed her shoulder. "Don't despair."

Don't despair?

She would try, but it would be hard. Despair was something she was used to.

Chapter Twelve

"I don't know, Blaine. I'm not sure this is something I can help you with."

Blaine sat at his desk, work scattered across the top of it—work that he'd been neglecting, for lack of being able to focus. Having this meeting, even, was cutting into valuable work time.

"There must be a legal way to do it, Devon." Blaine stared at his computer screen, but Google didn't have any clear answers either. "Surely there's ways you can take someone off a bank account."

Devon Billings had been Blaine's lawyer for years and had helped him with all sorts of legal advice and tricky investing situations. More than a few times, he'd protected Blaine when an investor got bent out of shape and decided to turn on him for their losses. Devon had also helped him set up secure, high interest-bearing accounts for his imminent early retirement. He was just a damn good finance lawyer.

Devon shook his head. "From what you're telling me, the money is her father's, and he's simply putting it into an account they can both access. That gives him every legal right to be on it. You can't just kick someone off an account they set up with their own money. The only people who could take over something like that is the FBI, and only if there was some criminal investigation being conducted."

Of course, Coleman Dawson was too smart to get himself mixed up in a criminal mess, and Blaine wasn't smart enough to come up with a scheme to get him investigated. That wouldn't help Libby anyway.

Blaine rubbed his chin. He was still scruffy. He'd neglected to shave this morning again, not so much for Libby's enjoyment this time but because he was too distracted. He stared at the screen and clicked on another link.

"But…"—Blaine narrowed his eyes—"having the account in both their names means they both have access to the money. So, either one of them could withdraw all the money at any time, without first consulting the other? Or funnel it into another, single-person account?"

Devon shrugged. "Of course. That's what a joint bank account is. They both have free access to the money, anytime."

"And would her father have legal recourse against her, if she withdrew all the money?"

Devon was silent a moment, his brow furrowed. "You're talking about a lot of money here, and therefore, someone who has a lot of money to begin with. I wouldn't put it past someone in that position to use legal channels to try to get it back. And if the girl in question isn't ready to give a good defense as to why she took the money, she might not win a court case. He could definitely sue her to get it back."

Blaine sighed and slumped in his chair. He dropped his head back and stared at the ceiling. "Yeah, I figured as much."

"Blaine, I wouldn't advise this girl to take all the money and run. She of course would have every legal right to do so, and technically she wouldn't be breaking any laws, but that doesn't mean her father can't find a way to get it back. On top of that, she might not even be able to make such a large withdrawal without him signing off on it, depending on the bank. I would have to look at the details of the account to tell you for sure. But if he's as ruthless as you make him out to be, I'm sure he'll have fail-safes in place."

Blaine lifted his head and raked his fingers through his hair. He hadn't told Devon that Libby was his wife, just that she was a friend he was seeking advice for. Although, he was curious about the implications of her father finding out they'd concocted a sham marriage to get the money. Words like "fraud" and "extortion" danced in front of his eyes. He wanted to ask Devon about those things too, but maybe it wasn't such a good idea right now.

An idea struck him then, but it was crazy, crazier than anything he'd done so far. It would also mean getting much, much deeper into this and more committed than he already was. For what? The last ten thousand he needed to jump ship?

For a girl he'd only known a week?

He sat forward and looked at Devon. "But if she did take the money out with his signed consent, there's no way he could come back later and try to sue her, right?"

Devon splayed his hands. "I seriously doubt it. If he signed papers, without being coerced and not under duress, there's not much he could do about it. The law doesn't give you an escape hatch for choices you regret."

Blaine drummed his fingers on the desk. "I'll probably give you a call later this week. I want to set up a meeting with you and Brian, talk about some of my accounts and ways we can make them even more secure." Brian was his accountant, and along with Devon had been helping him manage and grow his nest egg.

"Sure, Blaine." Devon stood. "I'll send you a bill for today's consult."

Blaine smirked. "No freebies, huh?"

"You're in finance, Blaine, do you really need to ask that question? I'll give you a discount, though. I won't bill you for my commute."

"Your firm is on the second floor of this building."

"It's twelve floors to get here."

Blaine had to work through lunch to catch up, so he couldn't meet Libby. He wished he could, because she was in a fragile state and he was feeling rather protective. Every time he thought of her tear-stained face last night, and her cold skin from being outside, his gut knotted up and his back teeth clenched. He wanted to find her father and punch him.

Again, this was all over a girl he'd only known a week. A girl who had *bought and paid* for his services. Had sex really clouded his brain so much? When did he start ignoring practicality for self-indulgence? When did he start caring so much about these schemes he helped pull off?

He tried to focus and concentrate, and just ate a sandwich for lunch at his desk while having a conference call with several of his clients. Midway through the afternoon, he had made considerable progress and could no longer resist, so he called her.

"How are you holding up?"

"I'm okay." Her voice sounded flat and sad. "I hope you don't mind, I made some grilled cheese."

"You mean I have food in the house? I didn't even realize I had bread and cheese." He sorted through a pile of personal files to find his bank account folders.

"I went out to the store and got it. I needed to take a walk anyway, get some air."

"I have to do grocery shopping, I'm sorry." He rubbed the bridge of his nose. "I can call up a shopping service and have them bring a few things over, if you want."

"You can pay people to bring you groceries? That's a thing?"

"Yeah. It's pretty neat, and convenient." He pulled out one of the folders, but couldn't find the other one he needed, the one for his account that was just set up for savings. "You make up a list of things you need, give it to them along with the money for the stuff and their fee, then they go buy it all and deliver it to you."

"Wow. That sounds like a weird job."

Blaine was amused she had never heard of such a thing. Maybe they didn't do that in her old neighborhood in Yonkers.

"There's people who make a full-time job of it. It pays pretty well, from what I hear." He had traded stocks for a company that ran a grocery delivery service as their primary income stream.

"Maybe I can get a job doing that. Since everything else is going to fall apart. I'll need to live somehow."

"Don't talk like that."

He remembered then that the folder he needed was in his desk drawer at home. Not a big deal when it came to numbers, he could look those up online, but there was also information in there he wanted to brush up on. Details about account limitations, interest, and fees. He could always call the bank and find out the things he needed to know, but that would take a huge chunk of time out of his already tight schedule.

"It's hard to think positive right now." Libby still sounded glum. "I should have known there was no way to trick my father. He's way too crafty. I've been trying to come up with another plan all day, but I just don't see what we can do."

"Leave that thinking to me." He paused. "Sorry, I don't mean to sound bossy." He cringed at himself. "I just meant, I know more about financial and business things, and…" God, he was digging a hole. He didn't want to talk down to her or make it sound like she was stupid.

She chuckled softly. "No worries. You *do* know more about that stuff. You're just stating a fact, not lording yourself over me. Trust me, I know the difference."

He smiled. "I don't want to sound like your father."

"You don't. Believe me, my father would never apologize for being bossy."

He didn't want to tell her just yet what he was considering, in case it was impossible, or, he changed his mind. He realized, and quite profoundly, that this was moving quite fast and maybe he needed to think long and hard about investing massive, implicit resources and his motivations for doing so.

Still, there was no harm in merely tinkering with ideas right now.

"Libby, could you do something for me, when you have a second?" He shuffled through the folders again. "You know my desk, in the office next to the kitchen?"

"The room with the computer and bookcases in it?"

"Yeah. Could you look in the top left drawer and tell me if there's a dark blue folder in there with gold writing on it that says 'Morgan Stanley?' You don't have to do it right now, just check later and text me and let me know if you see it." He was sure it was there, but he was slightly paranoid. His organizational skills were not always at the level they should be. His assistant could attest to that, and often did, even without being prompted.

"Yeah, I'll check." She sounded like she might be eating.

"Not right now, finish your grilled cheese." He smiled. "I'll bring some real food home with me tonight."

"Okay. I might go see Kellie for a while, but I'll be back. I just … I need to clear my head, and try to think."

"I don't blame you." He plopped the other bank folder down in front of him. His thoughts quickly strayed from finances, though. He thought about waking up next to her this morning, how warm and soft she was in his arms, the scent of his shampoo in her hair from their shower last night.

That shower had been on his mind all morning, despite everything else that sat on his shoulders.

"You're being so good to me." Her voice was soft. "We don't really know each other, and you're putting a lot on the line for me. I don't know why you're doing it and I don't know how to thank you."

Giving voice to his own thoughts, but he was glad she felt the same way.

"I think you have a good heart, and your head is in the right place." He toyed with the edge of the folder, bending it back and forth. "I support your noble cause, and—" He wanted to choose his next words carefully, not just for her but for himself. "I can't stand seeing someone as good as you treated the way your father treats you. No one deserves that. I feel like it's my duty to step in because," he swallowed, "I don't feel like anyone has ever stepped in to help you your entire life, and that's just wrong."

Was *that* why he was doing this?

She was silent a moment, and her voice was shaky when she spoke again. "I think that's the kindest thing anyone has ever said to me."

He continued bending the folder, staring down at it. His eyes burned and he blinked a few times. "I know we don't know each other very well, but I feel like maybe you were sent to teach me something, and maybe I'm the hero you need right now." He gave a tremulous laugh. "Listen to me. Don't I have an ego?" He wiped his eyes.

"Nah." He could hear the smile in her voice. "You haven't said anything that isn't true. Just … thank you."

They fell silent. The overhead light buzzed, the soft sound of typing coming through the door from the outer room where his assistant was hammering out third-quarter reports. At least one of them was being productive.

"I hope you don't feel like I'm taking advantage of you." He lowered his voice. "I mean, in other ways."

"You mean sexually?"

"Yeah, I mean it's nice, but I don't want you to think—"

"It's better than nice." Finally, her tone brightened. "It's great. I mean, I hope you don't think I'm some kind of freak. I know we've been doing it a lot—like, a lot a lot, in the past day or so."

He grinned. "A freak? No. Trust me, it's normal to want to indulge when you get your first taste of something you really enjoy."

He wasn't sure if he was talking about her or himself. True enough, he couldn't stop dipping in either, because she was sweeter than anything he'd ever tasted or experienced.

He needed to stop thinking about it and get off the phone. He shifted in his chair.

"I've had my head in the clouds since we got married." Her tone was getting lighter and lighter, the first time she'd sounded this way since last night. "Even though my heart has been way, way underground. It makes it kind of hard to think."

"Tell me about it." He rubbed his forehead. "So—do you think we should stop? So we can figure this all out?"

"Um, well. Do you want to stop?" A touch of uncertainty.

"I…" He stared across the room. No, he sure as hell didn't. Should he? Yes. Would it be for the best? Probably. "Nothing in my body wants me to stop, trust me."

"Mine either."

The low pitch of her voice made his cock perk. Exactly what he'd been trying to avoid. He shifted again, but it didn't help. Thoughts came rushing in and he couldn't stop them—the sound of her whimpers, the way her naked body slipped against the glass wall of the shower as he pushed up into her, her soft folds around his tongue, so wet and swollen. The way she'd moaned his name when he fingered her from behind in bed this morning.

He closed his eyes and pressed his hand between his legs, over his fattening cock. Nothing could stop it though, it was relentless.

"We'll talk some more about it when I come home tonight." He tried to keep his voice even. "We'll decide if we're doing the right thing."

"Even in the middle of all this crazy, I can't stop thinking about it." Her voice was still low, soft and breathy. "I want it."

He almost groaned. He gave his cock a little squeeze, then popped his eyes open and looked at the door. No jerking off in the office.

"Do you want it right now?" he asked, unable to stop the words from coming out of his mouth.

What the hell was he doing?

"Yeah."

"Where are you?"

"Sitting on the couch."

"What do you have on?" Was he really about to have phone sex with her, at work? Did she even know what phone sex was?

"A dress." No hint of reluctance. "I like dresses."

"I like you in them." He rubbed his palm slowly against his crotch. "Do you have panties on underneath it?"

She giggled. "Of course I do."

"Take them off."

A subtle gasp, then shuffling on the other end. He closed his eyes and imagined slipping them down her legs for her, watching them puddle around her feet on the carpet of his living room floor.

"Okay," she whispered.

"Will you touch yourself for me?" He kept his voice down and continued to rub. He would not get his cock out in his office. Not ... like he did yesterday.

"Blaine." She whimpered.

"Are you thinking about me? Are you wet?"

He swore he could still taste her on his lips. Or the memory was so strong, it had flooded the parts of his brain that controlled his senses. He wanted to be down on his knees right now, sucking on her clit.

"Yes." She gasped. "Are you hard?"

He was so startled by her sudden boldness that his cock surged and pumped a heavy dollop of pre-cum into his underwear. Thank God he had black pants on.

"Very." His voice was thick on his tongue. "Rub yourself, make yourself come while I listen to you. Pretend I'm there, doing all the things you like. You don't have to say anything, just get yourself off."

She was quiet, but he could still make out the soft sounds of her pleasure in the silence. He strained to hear her fingers sloshing in her wet pussy, but the phone was too far away. Still, he imagined it. He kept squeezing his cock, resisting the urge to jerk it. He didn't want his underwear full of jizz and he still refused to pull his cock out and stroke it right there under his desk.

Her breath came harder, faster. He closed his eyes, the vision of her burning in front of him, his imagination painting a picture of her sprawled on the couch, one leg up over the arm, spread wide and rubbing herself frantically.

"Yeah," he whispered. "Do you feel me up inside you, all hard for you?"

A louder moan. "Blaine."

"I'm gonna fuck you so hard on that couch when I get home. Do you want me to fuck you?"

"Yes."

"Are you close?"

"Yes." A desperate whimper. "Please fuck me." It was a murmured, bashful plea.

Blaine almost came. He bit back a moan. "Libby."

She emitted a soft shriek on the other end, and there was a jumbled sound, like she'd dropped the phone. Her keening moans came through muffled, but they were the best music he'd ever heard in his life. He was sweating, breathing hard, helplessly rubbing the heel of his hand against the head of his cock. He was *definitely* going to come in his pants if he didn't stop.

She came back on, panting. "Oh, gosh. Blaine…"

"Did you come?"

"Uh huh."

"Good, thank you." He thought he might fall out of the chair. "I'll take care of you when I get home. Then we can clear our heads and try to … think." He couldn't think at all right now.

"Okay." Her voice was shaky. She laughed. "Oh, man."

"I really have to get off here. I'll see you soon, okay? Go clean up."

"Definitely need to." She chuckled, then made a kissy sound. "Bye-bye."

After she hung up, and he did too, Blaine tossed his phone on the desk and grabbed up the bank folder. He used it to shield his crotch as he made his way casually—or at least he hoped—to the bathroom.

Trying not to make a sound while having a mind-blowing orgasm at work, the kind that left his knees shaking afterward and made it impossible to stand up from the toilet, was the hardest thing he'd ever done. But it was also fucking awesome.

Chapter Thirteen

"God, I'm such a dolt." Libby rushed through the door of Blaine's apartment and dropped her purse on the floor. She checked her cell phone. The time was a little after five. Over two hours since Blaine had asked her to check and see if the folder was in his desk.

She'd been too busy fingering herself on his couch, and then after, going out with Kellie and trying to forget about everything. Part of that she could blame on him, the other part, not so much.

She hurried through the kitchen and into the room he used as his office. It was as big as any other room in the place and looked much like the office her father had at home growing up. This room didn't give her the heebie-jeebies, though. A wide desk sat near the windows on the opposite side of the room, a computer on top of it along with stacks of papers. Bookcases and filing cabinets lined the walls.

Libby stopped short in the middle of the room and texted Blaine. Her heart thudded in her ears.

I'm so sorry, I forgot to check for the folder before I left your apartment. I'm looking for it now.

"Dummy," she whispered to herself. *He asked for one simple thing.*

But she'd been so distracted, so full of misery and worry about how she could possibly still make this work, that his request had gone in one ear and out the other. Of course, it didn't help that he'd also distracted her with other things. She tried not to think too much about it, because it made her squirm like crazy. She couldn't wait for him to get home. She might just jump him when he came in the door.

She shifted her thoughts as she walked over to the desk, so she didn't get all horny again. At the coffee shop where she met Kellie, she'd tried to hold it together, but after telling her about her father's stipulations, she burst into sobs again and felt like an even bigger moron. People were looking at them and it just added to her embarrassment.

Kellie had taken her outside to get some air and dry her tears.

"We'll brainstorm," Kellie told her. "We'll figure this out. You've come this far, we're not giving up now. I've still got your back, sister. Screw him."

"Blaine said the same thing." Libby sniffed and mopped at her eyes with the tissue Kellie had given her. "He says we'll figure something out, but I can't drag him further into this. It's putting everything in his life in jeopardy. This is not what he signed up for."

Kellie smiled sadly and brushed Libby's hair out of her face. "Libby, he seems like a great guy, and a smart one. You got really lucky. Maybe the two of you will come up with something. Try to have some faith."

Libby had very little faith, let alone hope, and Kellie's reassurances didn't make her feel any better. She walked back to Blaine's building instead of taking a cab, in hopes the exercise would jog her brain. Halfway there, she stopped dead in her tracks and gasped. Her stomach sank.

"I forgot to look for the folder!" She moaned. "Dang it, Libby." She smited her forehead and ran the rest of the way.

Standing in front of the desk, she tried to remember which drawer he'd said to look in. Her brain had been offline since yesterday and apparently was no longer holding information.

A text came back from Blaine: **No problem at all, it's not really a big deal. I'll see you in a couple hours.** He added a smiley emoji, and a heart emoji.

She grinned.

She put her phone on the desk and chewed her lip, debating asking him which drawer he'd said. She didn't want him to think she was an even bigger idiot though, so she decided to just look through all of them. A blue folder, with gold writing. She remembered that much.

Most of the drawers were full of paper and folders, but she didn't see a blue one. She rifled through things, but he'd said on top, hadn't he? Going through his things wasn't polite, and he'd said it wasn't a big deal anyway. Was she just snooping at this point?

She opened a drawer on the right side of the desk, didn't see a blue folder inside, and was just about to close it again when something caught her eye. On top was a familiar, green folder with "Singles Arrangement Service Specialists" written across it. Libby paused and stared at it.

This, she supposed, was the agreement they'd made, the papers that Blaine had to sign on his end. She was still skeptical in believing any of it was legal, and the papers she'd signed herself weren't terribly complex. She'd given the ten thousand dollars directly to Monica in that meeting and the agency facilitated transferring it to Blaine. So, technically, Libby hadn't paid Blaine anything, she'd simply paid for the services of a dating agency and the rest was a gift to him. Their marriage was, for all intents and purposes, voluntary and outside the agency.

Libby started to close the drawer, but stopped.

It wouldn't hurt to take a peek and see what his paperwork looked like, right? This concerned her as much as it did him, so it wasn't something "personal."

"Stop being a big old snoop," she told herself. The admonishment didn't deter her, though. Curiosity won out.

She bit her lip and lifted the folder out. This one was thicker than the one she received, as Blaine had to sign a lot more papers, since he was technically employed by the agency.

She was startled to see another green folder beneath it, also emblazoned with SASS's logo. Wow, he *must* have had to sign a lot more paperwork than her. She didn't remember him getting two folders, but she had been so anxious that day she probably overlooked it.

She stood with the first folder in her hands and stared at it. She would just glance through it and put it back. Guilt roiled in her stomach, though.

She sat down in the big leather chair behind his desk, which was plush and comfortable. She opened the folder and leaned back, making herself cozy.

Inside the folder was a sheaf of papers, on top of which was their marriage license. For the first time in twenty-four hours, she genuinely smiled and picked it up. She read it over, thinking of their quick, simple little courthouse wedding. Maybe it wasn't so unromantic after all.

Her smile slipped away, to be replaced by a frown and a furrowed brow.

Blaine was listed on the certificate, but that wasn't her name. Beneath his name, instead, was the name *Amanda Gleeson.* At first, she thought she was just confused and that was the issuing clerk's name, but after she scanned the rest of the certificate, she realized it wasn't. The clerk's name was at the bottom. The date at the top was also from nearly a year ago.

She flipped through the rest of the papers. All of them were official forms from the agency that Blaine had filled out. Amanda's name appeared on several of them. Then, at the bottom, were court documents. She realized they were divorce papers. The date on them was a few months after the one on the marriage certificate. Not divorce papers, annulment papers.

Her mouth went dry.

She stared at the certificate again, then looked back down in the drawer.

Just close it, don't look at anything else. You've already seen too much.

Despite the dread building inside her, and despite the screaming voices in her brain telling her not to, she picked up the second folder. She dropped the first one on the desk and opened the second one.

The same sort of papers, and another marriage certificate. This time with a woman named Rebecca Host. The date on it, and on the annulment papers, was two years prior.

She stared across the room. Evening was coming on and the light was fading, turning the white walls deep blue. The apartment was silent. She couldn't even hear her own breath, and then realized that was because she was holding it. She let it out.

She wrestled with what she felt inside. Mostly, it was a weird, uneasy numbness. Her mind slowly connected the dots.

Of course, she wasn't Blaine's first wife. He'd been working for the agency for a while, and he'd married other women. She glanced cautiously down into the drawer, but thankfully, there wasn't another folder. Theirs must be somewhere else, not yet filed away into the past.

She struggled to quell the rush of disappointment and dismay. *Don't be stupid, why would you think you were his first wife? That's what the agency does, they hook people up with sham marriages. Why wouldn't he do it multiple times when he gets paid that much?*

She looked at the folder in her hands. A lump was forming in her throat. She felt like she might scream. She wanted to rip it up or throw it across the room. But that was dumb, so damn dumb, like the rest of this.

You aren't special to him. This is just a business. You knew that going in.

For goodness sakes, Libby, you bought *him. You have no right to get upset.*

She closed the folder, then mechanically made sure everything was secure in both, put them away, and shut the drawer. She rose from the chair. After standing numbly in front of the desk for a minute, she opened the top left drawer.

A blue folder sat on top, with gold writing across it.

She picked up her phone and texted him: **Found it.**

She stood in the ringing silence until he texted her back: **Great, thanks. See you soon.**

Despite all inner arguments to the contrary, the growing sick feeling in her stomach wouldn't go away. It made the despair over her father even worse. She was a moron, a fool, she'd taken a huge chance and it was going to ruin her life. When her father found out the truth, he would not only take away the money but disown her.

And she wouldn't even have Blaine when it was over. He would be on to the next woman who paid him to do her bidding.

She walked to the guest room in a daze. As she crammed the few things she'd taken out of her bags back in, her thoughts strayed to things she didn't want to think about.

Had he slept with Amanda and Rebecca too? Had

he as much fun on his wedding nights with them? Did he take them to some big fancy suite and seduce them with a cheesy movie and room service? She tried to picture what they must have looked like: tall, beautiful, rich women. Perfect women. The kind of women who could easily buy a husband and didn't have to rob their mothers to make it happen. She must be small beans in his world, the kind of girl who had to scrape money together to get some harebrained scheme off the ground, a scheme that wasn't even going to work.

The sick feeling intensified. She felt dizzy.

What about his office? Had he had sex with his other wives there? He had condoms in the drawer, ready to go. How dumb could she be?

And what about in the shower? In his bed?

She barely made it to the bathroom. After she got done throwing up, she rested her forehead on the cold porcelain of the toilet rim and cried. She'd cried so much in the past two days it exhausted her, but she couldn't stop. The tears just kept coming and coming.

"You're such an idiot," she snarled, curling her fists in her lap. "Just a stupid, stupid girl, just like he always said." Her father had been right, she didn't understand the real world at all, but now she was getting a big fat taste of it, as bitter and nasty as the bile on her tongue.

The future looked so bleak she couldn't even face it. Everything around her was just an ominous gray cloud of nothing and unhappiness, ready to swallow her up.

Chapter Fourteen

Blaine bought flowers on the way home, a bouquet of red roses from the bodega he always stopped at. They were cheap, but pretty, as all real florists were closed by the time he got out. He'd also bought some real groceries. Maybe he'd even cook tonight. He hadn't done any cooking in ages, and he loved to do it. Shoving things in the microwave for himself didn't count. Now at least he had someone to cook for, someone to impress.

When he entered the living room, he stopped short and frowned. He'd been expecting Libby to still be in a somber mood, but he wasn't expecting this.

She sat in the chair across from the couch, straight-backed and stiff. She was fully dressed, shoes and coat on. Her bags and boxes sat around her, as if she were ready to carry them out the door.

"Hi." Blaine put the grocery bags down next to the couch. "What's … going on?"

Her eyes were red-rimmed and puffy, her face solemn and blank.

"Kellie is coming over." She spoke flatly. "I'm going back to her place and staying there."

"Okay." Blaine walked toward her slowly, the flowers still in hand. "Why? I told you, you're not imposing on me. I don't mind if you stay here."

She looked up at him as he stopped in front of the chair. Her eyes glistened.

"How many times have you been married?"

Blaine froze, and then his shoulders sagged. His whole body felt like it deflated from the inside, like someone had stuck a needle in him and popped him. His stomach sank through the floor.

"I'm sorry." She looked down at her lap. "I wasn't trying to snoop, I swear. I couldn't remember which drawer you said the folder was in. And I saw ... I saw them."

Blaine's mind flew to his desk, to the folders and records he kept in there. He supposed, in that instant, he should have told her all this before now. He should have been honest from the second they met, and realized it mattered more than he considered it to.

"Libby—"

She held a hand up. "No, I shouldn't question you. That's wrong. It's not like I didn't buy you from an agency that specifically deals in pretend marriages. I mean, why on earth should I just assume I'm the first woman you've done this with?" Her tone wasn't accusing, more resigned. "I shouldn't have been so shortsighted."

Blaine turned and dropped the flowers on the coffee table, then grabbed the nearby ottoman. He pulled it up in front of her and sat down, elbows on his knees, hands clasped in front of him.

She still stared at her lap. Even so sad, she was achingly beautiful, and it twisted his heart to see her this way, to know he had made her like this.

"Libby, please look at me."

She glanced up. Her expression was guarded, her eyes wet.

"I should have told you." He spoke softly. "I'm sorry. You're the third woman I've been married to. All through the agency. I've never actually been married for real."

She swallowed, so hard he saw her throat convulse. If she cried, he'd feel even worse. He might cry too.

"And that's how it should be." Her voice was thick. "That's what the agency is, and this is about money. It never should have been about anything else."

"Yes, but..." He leaned forward. "It's always been for different reasons. I used to just do dates through the agency, then I realized I could make a lot more money with marriages."

She looked away.

"The first woman needed a new husband to piss off her ex-husband, something really public she could make a big show of. I was nervous about going through with it and I thought for sure I was going to end up getting arrested or something." He sighed. "But it was easy money and it only lasted a few weeks. Her ex-husband got jealous and they had a big blow-up that ended with them getting back together and getting remarried. It was a wild ride."

She looked back at him. Her eyes shone.

"The second woman did it to avoid marrying someone else, because she didn't want him to get her money. I never got too deep into the details because it was a huge tangled mess. Her family expected her to marry this guy and she had resources she didn't want him getting his hands on, because she thought he was colluding with her uncle. I stayed married to her for a few months, until she got all her assets in a safe spot, and she paid me double for it."

Libby sniffed.

He reached out and touched her knee. "And then Monica called and told me about you. She told me all about your situation."

She glanced at him through her bangs.

"It's been the most altruistic reason I've done this so far. The best reason, really."

She wiped her eyes. "You don't have to explain yourself. I know it's about money, first and foremost. You get paid a lot to do this. It's just work."

He withdrew his hand. His chest hurt. He should

have told her before now. He should have been honest and upfront. For some reason, "it's just work" sucked to hear, even if it was true.

"I *want* to explain myself, though." He folded his hands in front of him again. "You see, I've been doing it for the money because I don't want to trade stocks anymore. I'm working on an early retirement."

She tilted her head.

"The business world is a cutthroat one, full of people like your father." He shook his head and ran his hand back through his hair. "I've been in it since I was a teenager, and it's draining everything out of me that still feels human. I came up with this investment plan that would net me a huge return. I know investing inside and out, so why not put it to work for myself? The problem was, I needed enough capital to invest to get what I needed out of it."

Her hands were curled tight in her lap. She flexed her fingers.

"I found out about the agency three years ago, and I thought, why not? It sounded easy and fun, and like I said, at first I was just doing dates. But that was only bringing in a couple hundred bucks a pop. It wasn't the kind of money I needed fast enough. So, I looked into their higher-paid services."

Libby chewed her lip.

"You're the last one, Libby. Actually, it's some kind of twist of fate that we even met. I lost money this year and set myself back, so I needed to get married again."

She didn't say anything, nor did she appear to agree this was some romantic intervention from God.

"After you, I'll have all my ducks in a row, I'll have all the capital I need. In a year, maybe less, I'll be able to cash out and leave this world behind me for good." He rubbed the back of his neck. "I don't know exactly what I'm going to do. Maybe chill out on a beach somewhere for a while, maybe open another business of my own. I haven't decided yet, but I'll be out of the rat race."

"So, you're marrying women for money so you can retire." She spoke softly.

"It's just about money, Libby. It's not about love."

He thought she might be relieved to hear that—that it might allay her worries about the other women, but instead, she looked around at her boxes and bags, as her eyes filled up anew with tears.

"Kellie will be here soon." She stood, rubbing her face. "She'll help me get this stuff down to her car."

"Libby." He stood up as well. "I don't want you to go."

She looked at him, and a tear streaked down her cheek. His breath caught. He reached out to wipe it away, but she recoiled. He quickly drew his hand back.

"I need to go." Her voice was strained. "I have … a lot to think about. I'll get ahold of you so we can arrange the annulment."

"I still want to help you get the money you deserve." He stepped in her way as she tried to move. "I want to help you give your father what he's got coming to him. I never lied about that."

Her lower lip trembled. More tears fell. He wanted to yank her into his arms and hold her tight.

"My father will never be punished." She wiped at her eyes again. "He'll always have the upper hand. Trust me on this."

Blaine reached for her again. This time, she let him touch her. He held her shoulders, gently, but she wouldn't look at him. He had never had a feeling like this with any of the other women he'd married. They had never needed him like this. Hell, he wasn't even sure he'd ever felt this way with any woman he was dating for real. Seeing her so distraught made him want to do something crazy, anything, to make her smile again.

"I still want to help you." He schooled his voice to speak calmly. "I want to help you get that money."

Doubt flickered in her eyes.

"You said this has always been about money for you?" Her voice rose.

The pit in his stomach opened even deeper. Did she think he was trying to get a cut?

"That money is *your* money." He tightened his grip on her shoulders. "I don't want it, if that's what you're thinking. I want you to have it and I want you to go to school, to work on your project, to start your nonprofit and do what you've been called to do. I don't want a dime of it."

"I won't get that money, it doesn't matter."

"I might have an idea." He looked her in the eyes. "Maybe I can get your father to sign off on you taking out the money, so you can put it into one of my accounts."

She blinked.

"I don't mean so I can take it." He held up a hand. "So you can have it. Maybe I can make him believe I'm going to take care of it for you. I can say I'm afraid you'll take it out and do something stupid with it, so I want it in my account for safekeeping. It could work, if we really act the part."

She shook her head. "He won't buy that. He won't relinquish control of it."

"He might. I could tell him I think you're too impulsive right now. I'll really schmooze up to him if I have to."

"Why are you doing this?" Her eyes flashed. "Why are you helping me like this? You're an intelligent man, and I think you realize what my father could do to you if he finds out the truth. Why would you risk everything like that?"

Blaine wasn't sure how to answer. He wasn't sure if he *knew* the answer. Or maybe he did, but it was hard to put into words and would sound crazy even if he could. He had only known her a short time.

"This isn't like your other wives," she said. "This isn't making someone jealous or helping someone avoid getting robbed. My father will crush you. He'll crush both of us. I've seen what he does to people he doesn't like, to people who tried to get one over on him."

"Your father is a terrible man. He's a complete bastard." Blaine spoke this time without reluctance or tact. "I realized that from the moment I met him. I just want to see you happy. I want to see you get what's yours."

"I never meant for you to put yourself in harm's way like this."

"Maybe not, but I did it willingly." He drew her toward him. She took a step forward, but then stopped. "You didn't force me to do anything, Libby. You didn't ask me to, beyond the plan you laid out in the beginning. I could have said no. I want to do it, for you, and because guys like him are the reason I can't even do my job anymore. I can't even fucking stand going into the office, day after day, knowing I'm going to have to face pricks like him." His voice was climbing. "I can't do this anymore, and there would be no greater satisfaction than taking him down with me. If I crash and burn, so will he. Mark my words."

She shook her head. "It's all for nothing. He won't burn." She wiggled out of his grip. "In the end, he wins. And I've got to somehow keep him from finding out what we did."

"We don't have to give up yet, Libby." He dropped his arms. "We can figure out a way to make it work, still. I talked to my lawyer today. He said that—"

She cut him off. "Are your parents really okay with you doing this? They know all about these marriages, and why you've done them?"

He gazed at her a moment. He wouldn't keep anything else from her. He couldn't lie.

He looked down. "My parents are dead. My dad died from cancer when I was twenty-two, shortly after he helped me get my brokerage off the ground, and my mom died in a car accident when I was a kid." He lifted his head, cautiously, and met her eyes.

She stared at him.

"Those people are friends of mine, and I pay them to pretend to be my parents. They're great people though. Robert is in the trading business too. That's how we met." He realized how sordid it all sounded, once the words were out of his mouth.

"I thought there was something odd about them." Her eyes grew bright again. "This is all a big scam."

"Libby…"

"I guess I have no room to talk." She bent and snatched up a bag. "I mean, of course it's a scam. This whole thing is. I'm trying to scam my father, so I can't point a finger." She slung the bag over her shoulder. "I'm sorry, Blaine. I just—I realize I can't do this. I know I'm an idiot."

"You're not an idiot." He tried to help her pick up her other bags. Obviously, he wasn't going to be able to convince her to stay.

"I just wish…" She paused, biting her lip. More tears slipped from her eyes. "Yeah, I'm an idiot." She shooed him away and grabbed up the other bags.

"Libby."

Her phone beeped. She looked at it. "I have to go."

"Libby."

"I'll call you to make arrangements for the divorce."

He felt like the one who was an idiot. Everything she said was true—they were both involved in a scam, that was the bare bones of it. In the end, all the marriages he'd been involved in were just scams to make himself money. They were business transactions. Shady ones, but that was all.

So why did it hurt far more to watch her walk out the door than it had with any of the other women?

Chapter Fifteen

"I'm an idiot." Libby stared blankly at the TV. "I should have been smarter. I should have used my head."

Kellie stroked her hair. Libby was stretched out on her couch, her head on Kellie's lap, sprawled like a dead fish in the same spot she'd been sleeping before she moved in with Blaine. It was back to cramming her stuff in the corner of the living room, back to trying to figure out what to do next. Only this time, her options were limited and mostly terrifying. She could face her father or run away.

Neither one would get her what she really wanted.

"Why don't you trust Blaine to keep helping you?" Kellie tucked a strand of Libby's hair behind her ear. "I know this looks bleak, but he was willing to go the extra mile. Why don't you let him keep trying?"

Libby turned over, so she was looking up at Kellie. She sniffed. She wished she could stop crying. Her eyes burned. Her sinuses felt like they were swollen to the size of a hot air balloon. Her head throbbed.

"I'm his third wife." It even hurt to talk, her throat was so raw.

"Okay?" Kellie cocked an eyebrow. "You paid him ten thousand dollars to be your husband. Hypocrite much?"

She *knew* she was being a hypocrite. She had paid for him, as much as he had taken her money. They were both playing roles and she was just as implicit as him. It wasn't that, really. Of course, if he could make tons of money and put it toward some personal cause, why wouldn't he? No, it wasn't that he'd married two other women for money, the same as he'd married her.

She thought of their wedding night, and the

office, and the shower. Those thoughts made the pain in her chest even worse. The happiness she'd previously felt thinking about his kiss, his hands on her, the feel of his body, now filled her with sick regret. She tried not to picture him doing the same with those other women and failed, over and over.

"I wish he'd told me from the beginning." She had no way to explain to Kellie what was really bothering her, and was afraid how stupid it would sound anyway. "Shouldn't the agency have told me about it? Full disclosure and stuff?"

Kellie huffed. "So, you wanted to know how many times the guy you bought had been bought before? To what, make it more honest?"

Libby wanted to be cuddled and sympathized with, not fed the cold, hard, obvious truth.

"Listen, I love you, girl, you know I do." Kellie put a hand on Libby's forehead. "But I think you're upset and not thinking straight right now because of the bomb your father dropped on you yesterday. You've found your courage and you've come this far. Are you really going to give up now?"

Libby rolled her head to the side and stared at the TV again.

"Come on, Libs. You dropped out of school, you came up with this plan, you got the money together, and you married Blaine. You knew this wasn't going to be easy. You're just going to give up now that your dad has thrown another roadblock in your way? I thought you were braver than this, given your track record."

Libby sighed and looked back up at her. "There's no freakin' way I'm going to convince Daddy to put that money in an account without his name on it. What am I supposed to do?"

"Why don't you keep working with Blaine and

come up with something else?"

Libby didn't know if she could stand working with him still. She didn't know if she could be so close to him and deal with the feelings it brought up.

"I don't want to put him in any further danger." That was half true anyway. "My father will destroy him if he finds out the truth."

"Sounds like he knew that from the start." Kellie leaned over her and picked up her glass of wine from the coffee table. "You want some more?" She lifted the glass and took a sip.

Libby shook her head. "I think I've had enough. My head hurts, I don't want to make it worse." She rubbed her temples.

Kellie lowered the glass. "Blaine totally played along and sold the marriage to your dad. Hell, he met your dad and *still* decided to go forward with it. That tells me he's got your best interests at heart. He didn't run away screaming. So why don't you let him keep at it? I mean, at this point, if your dad finds out you're both dead anyway. You aren't saving him from anything. The damage is done."

Libby rubbed her eyes.

"Is this because he took your virginity?"

Libby removed her hands from her eyes and scowled.

"You're sweet on him now, huh?" Kellie smiled.

Libby looked away as hot tears pricked her eyes. She didn't want to cry again. "It doesn't matter, it's just a transaction."

"So? You can't like him? He can't like you?"

Her throat was thick and tight.

"I think he really likes you, Libs." She patted her stomach. "Is that what's bothering you? You didn't expect to get all emotional?"

"I'm his third wife." Libby could barely speak above a whisper. "It's all about money. Those people I met weren't even really his parents. He pays them to pretend."

"Wow, he's got it all worked out." She sounded impressed.

"I don't mean anything to him except a check."

"You bought him, Libs."

"I should have just stuck to our plan and not moved in with him or anything. I shouldn't have gotten involved with him like that."

"You *bought* him."

"I know!" She put her hands over her face. "I know, okay. I know I'm just as bad as him. I know I can't blame him. We're both lowlife scumbags, okay?"

Kellie peeled a hand off her face. "You like him. As a person."

She did, but she shouldn't have let that happen.

"He likes you too." Kellie peeled the other hand off. "Is that so crazy and far-fetched? You can't be lowlife scumbags and like each other too? I don't seem to remember that stipulation being in the contract when we went over it."

Libby sat up. She swung her legs off the couch. "He doesn't like me. He's just trying to retire." She stood up.

"Hm." Kellie took a sip of her wine, eyeing her.

"I'm just … I'm an idiot." She flopped her arms at her sides. She couldn't come up with a better word for what she was, because it fit so perfectly. "I'm a huge idiot, and this was all a big mistake. I'm meeting with my father and his accountant Friday to set up the account. And all this is gonna blow up in my face. It doesn't matter if I like Blaine. I screwed up my life even worse. His might get screwed up too."

No matter how much it hurt, no matter how betrayed and used she felt, the fact that he might get in trouble still wrenched at her guts. She didn't want her father to punish him, to destroy him, this close to his retirement goal. She didn't want Blaine to suffer because of her poor choices.

"You guys will work something out." Kellie said. "Clear your head of all these emotions and try to think, Libby. I know you can do it. You came up with this scheme, now see it through."

Libby wished she had as much faith in herself. She wished she could push her emotions aside and think rationally. But the future was black, and she didn't see any roads through that darkness except the one that sent her plunging headfirst into the abyss her father had created for her. She wouldn't drag Blaine in with her.

Instead of clearing her head, she just went to the bathroom and cried again, like the idiot she was.

****

"Hi, Mom." Libby tried to make her voice sound normal when she answered the phone. She didn't want her mother to think for one second there was trouble. If she found out, her father might find out, and this would all be so much worse.

"Hello, Liberty." As usual, there was no warmth in her voice, and Libby could use a little motherly affection right now. "I just wanted to call and check in on you. You sound groggy. Did you just wake up?"

Libby was curled up on the couch, the TV still on. Kellie wanted to cancel her date with Sean to stay with her, but Libby insisted she go. She wanted some time to herself. Time where she wasn't being reminded of her poor choices. Of course, her mother had to call and interrupt that.

"Yeah, I was taking a nap a little bit ago." She

rubbed her eyes and winced. They were so sore and swollen. Nothing compared to the ache in her chest, though.

"I wanted to give you a few days before I started being nosy. Let you settle in." Her mother paused. "How is married life?"

Libby lowered her hand and swallowed around the thick, permanently-wedged lump in her throat.

"It's fine, I'm just kind of trying to adjust." She didn't want to say too much. Doing so might lead to her breaking down again, and she had no lies ready to use in order to deflect. Her brain had turned to mush. "It's a different world."

Her mother hummed. "I'm sure it is. It all happened so fast."

Libby rolled her head on the pillow beneath her. She looked off the couch, down into her duffle bag sitting on the floor. She'd opened it earlier to get some Ibuprofen for her aching head. When she looked, she noticed the little white box inside, the one that held her slide.

Her eyes welled up again, though she was certain her tear ducts were shot by now. She swallowed hard a few times and quickly wiped at her eyes, trying to compose herself. She struggled to push the thoughts of her wedding day out of her head, of sitting in that serene little courtyard, with the rushing water and soft green plants. She tried not to remember what that slide meant to her, how it was supposed to give her the courage to conquer monsters. How it reminded her that Blaine really cared about her and what she wanted

But did he, really? Had he given his other wives gifts too?

She squeezed the bridge of her nose, eyes shut tight. "I've got a pounding headache right now, Mom."

Her voice was thick. "I can't stay on the phone too long."

"That's fine. I just wanted to see how things were going." She sighed. "I really hope you'll be happy, Liberty. I hope it all works out despite how fast you jumped into things. I guess—I suppose some people do make it. Though I'm inclined to believe that only really happens in books."

Libby thought she might scream, or barf, if she stayed too long on the phone listening to this.

"I know, Mom. We're going to try."

But they weren't. They couldn't. It was already over, and she'd have to face her mother's smugness and disapproval when she found out. She was right all along.

"Libby … before you go. I know your head is hurting. But I actually called to ask something of you."

Libby opened her eyes and rubbed her forehead. "What's that, Mom?"

A pause, so long Libby thought for a second they got disconnected. "I want you to stay in school."

Libby blinked a few times. She turned onto her back and gazed up at the shadowy ceiling. The only light came from the TV.

"What?"

"Don't drop out of school. I know you told your father you would, but I don't think it's a good idea."

This was strange, coming from her mother. She frowned.

"Mom?"

"Just listen to me. If things don't work out with you and Blaine, you need something to fall back on. You need a way to support yourself. Remember when your father and I got divorced, I was working two jobs just to keep us going? I ran myself ragged and I still couldn't make ends meet. I don't want that to happen to you."

Libby wasn't sure how to respond. That her

mother was concerned about such a thing was almost … comforting.

"I want you to have a good life, Libby. And that may not come through the help of a man."

Libby sat up and ran her hand through her hair. She was trying to think of something adequate to say.

"If your father won't keep paying your tuition, I'll find a way to help you."

"Mom." Libby sagged. "You couldn't—"

"I'll find a way." Her mother spoke firmly. "Just promise me you won't drop out of school."

Libby's vision blurred again, but this time the tears were for a different reason. Suddenly, she wanted to curl up in her mother's lap, like when she was a little girl.

"I'll try," Libby said softly.

"You asked me a question, on your wedding day."

Libby blinked a few times. She recalled them standing in the bathroom together.

"When I filed for divorce from your father…" Her voice was terse and tight. "It wasn't about me, not really. I'd endured so much from that man, we all had. But I could take it. I'd developed a thick skin, so as I said, it wasn't for me. I got to the point I couldn't justify raising the two of you like that anymore. I knew if I didn't act you would never have a chance. I had to save my daughters, and that's what gave me the courage."

Libby was stunned. The ache in her chest intensified.

"Not that it mattered." Her mother's tone turned bitter. "He never really left us, did he? He might not have lived in the house anymore, but his presence was always there. He never let go. Even now, I wake up sometimes in a cold sweat and think he's in bed with me."

"Mom." Libby dropped her head in her hand.

"You were too young, there were things I couldn't tell you. I had a card to play, but I swore to myself I wouldn't use it unless he pushed me to it. And of course, he pushed and pushed."

Libby lifted her head and stared across the room.

"Your father was having an affair, and I had proof of it. Damning proof."

Libby wasn't shocked, but her stomach immediately sank. Of course he had an affair. He had them under his thumb, but he couldn't be loyal. He couldn't be true.

"I'm sorry, Mom." She pushed her hair back from her face. "He's always been awful, hasn't he?"

She made a sound, somewhere between a gasp and a whimper. Was she crying? "Yes, well. The matter of the affair was one thing, but it was *who* he was having an affair with that made it truly deplorable. He was screwing around with the daughter of his secretary. The seventeen-year-old daughter of his secretary."

Libby's mouth fell open. She felt the blood drain from her face.

"What? Mom!"

"I told him if he didn't agree to the divorce and go, I would expose him. He might have gone to jail, and he certainly would have lost his reputation and his growing business would have floundered. That scared him. It scared him bad." She sniffed. "But it was the first and only time I've ever had power over him."

Libby wasn't sure if she wanted to scream, cry, or rage. She felt sick. She wanted to throw herself into her mother's arms and hold her forever.

"You were too young to know about any of that." Her mother seemed to be regaining control of herself, her voice leveling out. "Now you know."

Libby didn't know what to say. She hated her father more than ever. But he still had his hands around her throat, and she had no such power over him. That was years ago, and he had undoubtedly ended the affair, and if not, the girl was well overage now, and on top of that he had become infinitely more powerful and savvy since then. Her mother's old evidence wouldn't stand a chance.

"I want you to be happy, Liberty. And I want you to be something for yourself. To be your own woman. I don't want you to be a man's possession. Just because your father fills your head with these ideas of family and duty and loyalty, you know now he's a lying hypocrite."

She wished she could tell her mother the truth, just tell her everything. She was on the verge of doing it, but she remembered the money. The only way out of this was to take what she could get. The only hope she had left for the future was whatever scraps her father was willing to throw her.

"I know, Mom." Her words were strained, forced. "I won't let that happen."

"Don't tell your sister what I told you." Her voice had returned to its lofty, detached baseline. "It's humiliating enough for me as it is. But if it will save you from going down the same path, it's worth sharing with you."

"I won't, Mom."

"Get some rest. Take some aspirin."

After Libby hung up, she sat in stunned, frozen silence for a few minutes. Then she reached down and pulled the white box out of her bag. She held it in her hands and stared at it. For all the things he'd failed to tell her, Blaine wasn't anywhere near her father in terms of deceit. He wasn't anything like him, period. He just wanted money, and it wasn't like she didn't know that from the beginning.

She lowered her head and pressed the box to her forehead. Her whole existence felt shaken, like she would never get her footing again.

"Oh, God. Why?" She cried again, this time for her mother.

Chapter Sixteen

"Oh my God, Blaine! Aren't you a sight for sore eyes?"

Blaine grinned as Amanda threw her arms around him. She was just as boisterous and beautiful as he remembered her. She drew back and smiled wide. Her honey blond hair was pulled up, her light brown eyes sparkling. She looked him over.

"Seems you've been working out." She slapped his arm, hard enough to make him wobble. "You're looking really good."

"So are you, Amanda." Even in her business attire, she was a stunner. She had always been the kind of woman who commanded attention, for as long as he'd known her. Her demeanor and appearance was one of complete confidence and control. If she had been his first wife, he might have been too intimidated to ever go through the process again.

Amanda headed over to her desk, heels clicking on the bare wood floor. Her office was much more organized than his, and on a higher floor, providing a panoramic view of the Lower East Side.

"I hope I'm not interrupting your day." Blaine fidgeted with his blazer button. He should have worn a nicer suit. "I know you're a busy woman."

She waved a hand. "For my ex-husband, I've always got time." She sat down behind the desk. "How's the stock market treating you these days?"

He grunted. "Good, on the money side." He strolled over to the desk and she indicated for him to sit down in a chair on the other side of it. He did. "You know how it is, though. Sharks in the water, blood on the surface. Every day is a feeding frenzy."

She flipped through the contents of a folder and

arched an eyebrow at him. "Are you almost out?"

"Close." He smiled. "I got married again. Another short engagement, but this is the last bit of capital I need. I should be cashing out sometime next year."

"I'm glad." She folded her hands on the desk and smiled. "I know it's been sucking the life out of you. I don't want to see the light fade from those pretty blue eyes of yours."

Blaine chuckled and dragged a hand through his hair. "I thought it was what I was meant for. My dad was a broker for as long as I can remember, there was never any question if I'd follow in his footsteps. I was in it from the moment I could count, it feels like." He paused. "He never told me I'd get this cynical. The longer I'm in, the more all I can see is greed and underhandedness. I don't want to end up being one of them."

He considered all the things he'd already done to get out, and wondered if he wasn't on that road anyway.

"What *do* you want to end up like?" Amanda gazed intently at him. "What did I always say to you? Knowing where you want to go is just as important as the journey."

Blaine sat back. "I'm still working on that." He pictured himself lounging on that tropical island, but the image was so obscure, just something out of a TV fantasy. He needed something meaningful, something that would help him see the good side of humanity.

Something like Libby.

"I'll figure it out." He shrugged. "Meanwhile, I came here to ask for some advice."

She closed the folder. "Well, if I'm anything, it's a fount of wisdom." She smirked. "What's on your mind?"

"I was thinking about your situation. Our

situation." He pointed between them. "Back when we were doing our thing. About how you needed to hide your money. I remember some of the details, but not everything."

"Oh, yeah?"

"Yeah. Would you mind telling me more about it? Refresh my memory."

"It was pretty straightforward. My uncle had a scheme to get my father's money that I'd inherited. A harebrained scheme, but unfortunately he had most of the rest of my family backing it up."

He nodded. "I remember."

"And there was good old Jason, firmly lodged in my uncle's pocket."

Amanda had been engaged to a man named Jason Green, who, she had discovered after some snooping—suspicions had been piqued several months earlier when he'd let something slip—was colluding with her uncle. His plan was to marry her and snatch the money from under her nose. This, however, was foiled when she spontaneously married Blaine.

"You know I wouldn't marry a man unless it benefitted me." She flashed a wry smirk. "Jason was a business deal. We were going to merge our companies, and the marriage would be a legal anchor to build wealth on. Little did I know my uncle was his biggest shareholder, and *Jason's* wealth was going to come from taking *mine*."

"Yeah, I remember most of that." Blaine rubbed his hands together. "I'm talking about how you hid the money, after you and I got married. I don't think you shared a lot of that with me. Not that it was really any of my business."

"So why do you want to know now?" She sat back.

"Because I might need to do the same thing."

A curious glint filled her eyes. "I hid it by becoming a limited partner in a small privately owned company." She gave him her bright smile, but it was devious this time. "You can't touch capital secured in that sort of arrangement when you sue someone. And since I had no doubt eventually my frustrated uncle would go that route, I thought it the safest spot. The money still sits secure in a company it would be difficult to even discover my name attached to, thanks to limits on alter ego piercing laws. By the way, it's a clothing boutique in Brooklyn." She winked. "You know I like fashion. My partner is an ambitious divorced woman, like me, and she's grateful for my investment."

Blaine rubbed his chin. "You sank your money into a small business to hide it."

"In a manner of speaking. It's a bit more complicated than that." She sat forward. "Is that what you think you should do with the money you've made?"

He shook his head. "I'm asking about this for … my new wife. She's about to get a bunch of money and she needs to protect it."

Amanda perked up. "Do tell. This is my area of expertise."

Blaine told her Libby's story, leaving out no details. He tried to keep the bile out of his voice when he spoke about her father, but it was impossible. As he hashed it over, his anger intensified. He also felt that awful pit opening up in his stomach again. He didn't want Libby to fade from his life, he didn't want her to go forward without him. He wanted to be by her side, helping and supporting her. He kept seeing her tear-streaked face, her red eyes. He kept hearing the pain and anguish in her voice.

When he was finished, Amanda gazed

thoughtfully across the office, tapping a pen on the desk.

"If they're both on the account," she said, "of course she can legally withdraw the money at any time." She looked at Blaine. "It wouldn't be wise, but she could do it."

"Of course it wouldn't be wise. And her father would absolutely go after her. He would sue her for it, I have no doubt about that. I also have no doubt he has some powerful lawyers in his pocket. He would win."

"He certainly sounds ruthless. Even more than my dear uncle and fiancé."

"Do you think she could take the money out and hide it, like you did? In a limited partnership?" His spirits, and hopes, lifted a little.

She frowned. "Maybe, but it takes time to do that. Even if you have someone lined up to execute the partnership with, and you've talked things through and come to an agreement, it's not instant, it's a lot of paperwork and hurdles to jump. That's why I married you, Blaine, to give me time to execute the transfer without my uncle realizing what I was doing." She chuckled. "Remember, they thought I'd been having an affair with you and I broke Jason's fragile heart?"

Blaine's spirits sank again. "So maybe that's not the answer for her. If she withdraws the money, it's still going to take some time before she could sink it into an LLP. Time that he would have to take her to court."

"Yes, it could take weeks, or months. That's plenty of time for her father to discover what she's doing, plenty of time that she'll be open and vulnerable. She could always go on the run, I suppose."

Blaine sighed. "No, that won't work. Something tells me he could do a lot of damage even if she was hiding from him."

"Your best bet, of course, would be to play the

long con."

He wasn't sure what she meant.

"Take the money out slowly and pretend it's for some business the two of you are starting up." She shrugged. "It could take years, though. But in the meantime, you could be sinking it into a limited partnership or even starting your own LLC to protect it."

Blaine scowled and rubbed the back of his neck. That wouldn't work.

"If you wanted to stay married to her that long, it could be profitable for you. You could spend your early retirement as a pampered house husband." She smirked. "While you figure out what you want to do with yourself. It could be a good arrangement, being a professional husband."

Blaine patted his hands on the arms of the chair, trying to think. "I don't think she's going to let me do that. I don't even know if she'll let me help her at all now." He looked away.

When he glanced back, Amanda had narrowed her eyes.

"You ... you're sweet on this girl, aren't you, Blaine?"

He scoffed. "It's a business arrangement."

"You have feelings for her." Amanda gaped. "That's why you're so worried about this. If you were just in it for the money, you'd take your fee and run. But you're trying to figure out how to help her!"

"Her father is an awful man." He spoke defensively. "I deal with guys like him all the time. I'd love to see them all taken down a peg."

"You like her."

"She doesn't deserve the way he treats her. She's brilliant and kind and ambitious, despite him."

Amanda sat back and slapped her hands on her

thighs. "I know the face of love when I see it. I see that look in your eyes." She laughed.

"I've known her a week!" He huffed. "That's not enough time to fall in love with someone."

Amanda smiled coyly and turned to a shelf next to her desk. "Isn't it?"

"I admire her and what she's trying to do. I'm concerned about her."

She pulled down a book and turned back to him. "Yes, I can see that." She held the book out to him. "Limited partnerships, by the way, are a great way to grow your wealth over time while taking a low risk, especially if you're really good at investing. If you know what's profitable, what works, and what doesn't, you can pick the right company that will have you reeling in the profit hand over fist."

He frowned and took the book, and looked at the cover. It was titled *Limited Partnerships: All You Need to Know About Investing Your Wealth for the Future in a Protected Environment.* Why did business books have to have such ridiculously long, descriptive titles?

"And I think you can spot a profitable company when you see one, can't you, Blaine?"

He glanced up from the book, brow furrowed.

"I mean, if someone had a large accumulation of capital to sink into just the right partnership, one that's growing and sure to be profitable, they could reap those profits over time and grow their investment, without worrying too much about losing it." She titled her head. "And still retire."

Blaine looked back down at the book.

"And of course, you'll also be helping the business owner, someone who wants to grow their product." She tapped the pen on her desk again. "Someone who needs the money to help get their idea off the ground. Wouldn't that make you feel warm and fuzzy inside? Wouldn't that be *human*?"

Blaine looked up at her. He opened his mouth, but didn't say anything.

"But I guess that's up to the investor." She smiled and sat back. "How far they really want to go to help someone they're concerned about. When you don't have concrete plans for your future, I think something always comes along to guide you in the right direction. That's been my experience in life anyway. I've always been guided by the sweet hand of fate."

He chuckled. "You believe in fate?"

"I believe in destiny. And there's a million ways to get to your destiny. Sometimes, it means taking the dirty money of a dirty man, and sometimes it means building something together, without any dirty hands involved."

Blaine considered the book. He didn't know a whole lot about limited partnerships, but if there was anything he caught on quick with, it was business and investment projects. Maybe the future wasn't about changing things radically, but just enough to make him like the world of money again, to see the human side of it that wasn't burgeoning with fangs and claws.

"I have a lot to think about. Thank you, Amanda."

She walked him out to the reception area. Her main job was an investing firm, which was why she had picked him as a husband to begin with. They had a lot to talk about, and honestly, she'd given him some of his best tips over the past couple of years.

She hugged him.

"You let me know what happens." She gripped his shoulders and gazed into his eyes. "She's a lucky girl to have you helping her."

He took a deep breath. "I hope so. Maybe you're right about destiny, Amanda." He smiled. "Maybe meeting you was destiny too. How come we didn't work out, huh?"

She rolled her eyes. "You know exactly why, Blaine. You had to be saved for a princess you could rescue from her wicked father." She kissed his cheek. "Read that book, cover to cover, brave knight, and do your research. And then, decide how you want to spend the rest of your life."

He tucked the book under his arm. "I will, Amanda. Thank you again."

He left her office. Standing outside on the street, under the bright sun, he felt doubt, but also a twinge of hope. He had a lot to do. He just hoped Libby would listen to him and let him help her. Wiping those tears away forever was his true destiny.

On the way back to his office, he made a phone call.

"Blaine Parker." The man on the other end sounded surprised and delighted. "I haven't talked to you in far too long. How's it going?"

"Great, Sheldon. I hear you're starting a new business venture."

"Did you now? You know me, always have to keep moving onward and upward."

"Pharmaceuticals. It sounds like it's going to be profitable. The world needs medicine."

"I seem to have a knack for profit." He chuckled.

"Yes, you do. I was just wondering—do you have all the capital you need to get it off the ground yet?"

Chapter Seventeen

"I can't believe you're going to do this." Kellie pulled the car into the lot. "Libs, you know this isn't the answer."

Libby sat in the passenger seat, squinting in the morning sunlight. Her skin was warm, but she was cold and empty inside. She clutched her hands in her lap. Just the thought of facing her father in a few minutes made her heart pound against her ribs and her breath short.

"Then what exactly is the answer?" Libby asked. "Do you know where else I can get half a million dollars?"

Kellie whipped the car into a parking spot. She had on sunglasses and gold dangly earrings that flashed in the light. Libby had dressed conservatively, in a knee-length skirt and sweater. She didn't have any makeup on and had just pulled her hair back. Even as a married woman, she couldn't appear as anything other than mousy and plain in front of her father. The last thing she needed today was a lecture about a married woman looking like a slut.

"Have you talked to Blaine?" Kellie shut the car off and turned to her. "I bet he's working on something. Or maybe he can talk to your dad and convince him to do this another way. He's been a good actor so far."

Libby pulled down the visor in front of her, to check her face in the mirror on the back of it. Her eyes were still a little puffy, but she could pass it off as allergies. "I don't want Blaine involved in this. It's best he just take his money and go."

Kellie flung her hands up. "Jesus, Libs."

"Kellie, what the heck am I supposed to do?" She snapped the visor back up. "You and I both know there's no way anyone, not even Blaine, is going to talk my father out of doing it this way. He wants to keep control of that money and he's not going to let it go." Her voice was strained. "He wants to keep control of me, and he won't give that up either."

Kellie pressed her lips together. "Right, he wants to keep control, so do you think you're really going to get to use any of it?"

Libby looked down at her hands.

"You think he's going to let you take out any of that money once you and Blaine get divorced?" She leaned closer to Libby. "You think he's going to let you take out a big chunk of it all at once so you can go back to school and take the classes you need to? No way. No way in hell."

"I don't have a choice." Libby spoke through gritted teeth. "He won't do this any other way."

"You'll never see that money, Libs."

Libby put a hand over her eyes. "Maybe I can talk to Justice, see how she took it. I'll figure something out."

"Don't you owe your mom five thousand dollars? How are you gonna get that out?"

Libby wiped her eyes and glanced at the clock on the dashboard. "I have to get in there. I have to sign the paperwork and get the account set up with him."

She opened her door and got out. The morning was cool and breezy. A beautiful day, but she could see and feel only darkness. She slung her purse over her shoulder and took a deep breath. Her chest hurt, tight with tension.

Kellie got out too, and slammed her door. "I'm coming in for moral support, no matter what he says. You'll need it."

"You have to stay out in the lobby. Daddy won't want you in there."

Kellie tossed her hair over her shoulder. "Yeah,

he doesn't want anyone with common sense around." She scowled at Libby. "Sorry."

Libby walked around the car. They headed toward the building. Every step felt like marching toward doom. This was the only way to get the money in her name. She would figure out how to use it later. Hopefully.

As they reached the front steps, a voice called out behind them.

"Libby, wait!"

Libby stopped, hand on the railing, and turned. "Blaine?"

Blaine rushed toward them. He wore just a dress shirt and pants, no tie, no jacket. The sunlight made his hair look lighter and it bounced as he hurried toward them. Libby's stomach clenched at the sight of him, as well as her heart. He carried a folder, which he was waving.

She glared at Kellie. "Did you call him here?"

"No!" Kellie held up her hands. "Geez, Libs."

Blaine rushed over to them and stopped, breathing hard. He gazed at Libby, his blue eyes bright.

"Don't go in there," he said. "I have an idea."

Libby swallowed. "Blaine, there's nothing that can be done. Why are you even—"

"Hear me out." He held up the folder. "I've been working this out for the past few days. I think I've come up with a solution so you can have the money you need and not have to get it from your father. And it's not the transferring the money to my account thing. I agree, that was dumb."

Kellie gaped and looked at Libby.

"What do you mean?" Libby glanced up the stairs, twisting her hand on the railing. "I have to get in there, we have an appointment."

"Just wait a minute." Blaine gripped her arm. She looked down at his hand. His touch was firm but gentle, and it made her ache worse. "Wait," he said softly, and withdrew his hand. He opened the folder. "Do you know what a limited partnership is, in business terms?"

Kellie inched over and tried to peek in the folder.

Libby shook her head. The anxiety inside of her was almost too much to bear. If she was late meeting her father, he might not give her the money at all.

"Okay, say someone starts a business." Blaine raked his hand through his hair, something he was always doing when he was keyed up. "Any kind of business—a boutique, a bar, a trading firm, a pharmaceutical distributor, anything. They start the business, but they need money to run it. Not just the loan to get it started, but the actual means to keep things running until they have enough business to turn a profit."

Kellie moved to his side. "You mean like, to pay for overhead and stuff?"

"Yes, exactly. They need money for everyday expenses, like upkeep, paying employees, stuff like that. So they seek out investors, people who believe in the business and think it'll grow and become profitable. These investors sink their money into the new business, with the expectation they'll eventually share in the profits."

Libby had no idea what this had to do with her or her father's money, but Blaine seemed eager to share the information, and she found herself glad to be in his presence again, even just a tiny bit.

"The problem is," Blaine looked between them, "investors are taking a huge risk when they do that. If the company goes under, or gets sued, or goes into debt, they stand to lose more than their initial investment. They're on the hook when stuff goes wrong. They might have to pay out as well."

"When my father first started his business, he had a lot of investors." Libby folded her arms. "I guess everything turned out all right for them."

"Well, there's another way to be an investor that comes with less risks." Blaine pulled some papers from the folder and handed them to her. "You can read up about it, but I'll give you the short version. Limited partners are investors who put money in, but the only risk they take is their initial investment."

Libby furrowed her brow and looked at the papers.

"A limited partner has no liability if someone brings a lawsuit against the company, or creditors start coming after the owners. They'll lose their investment if it shuts down, but that's it. And a lot of times, limited partners are also able to conceal their identity if things like that happen. It's not always easy to find out the name of a limited partner, but,"—he waved a hand— "that's not important here. What's important is, it's a lower risk, and if the business turns a profit, it's all returns for the investor."

Libby was thoroughly confused. She flipped through the papers. "What does this have to do with my father's money?"

Blaine closed the folder, and gazed at her. His face was full of anxiety, but there was determination in his expression too. "I have a huge chunk of retirement money, and I know this guy, he's a hell of a good businessman. I've been involved in his trading for years. He's starting another business and I trust him, I know it'll turn a profit in no time. He's savvy. He's smart. He's got a great idea."

Libby stared at him, still unsure where he was going with this. Did he want her to become a limited partner?

Blaine drew his shoulders up. "I'm going to put my retirement money into his business, as a limited partner. And I'm going to give you the profit that comes from it."

Kellie's mouth dropped open. Libby stood frozen.

"I *have* half a million dollars right now," Blaine said. "I'll have even more in two years, maybe three, with this partnership. And the extra is yours to have, if you don't take the money from your father."

Libby was trying to unscramble her brain.

"Libs!" Kellie gripped her arm. "Are you hearing this? Do you understand what he's saying?"

Blaine shook his head. "You don't have to be under his thumb anymore, Libby. You can walk away from him and never have to worry about having him in your life ever again." He stepped toward her. "The money is yours. You don't even have to stay married to me. We'll come up with an agreement, a legal one, and make sure everything is above board so you know no matter what happens, you'll still get your payout."

Her mouth had gone dry. Her heart was pounding again, but for different reasons.

"What … if the business fails?" She hesitated. "You'll lose all your retirement money, won't you? If I understand your explanation correctly?"

Blaine nodded. "I trust this guy, like I said. He's good. I've done my homework. He's ready for me to come on board too. It might take a couple weeks to get set up, but it will happen."

Libby was trembling.

Blaine took her hand. He squeezed. "Don't take your father's money. Tell him to stick it."

Tears pricked her eyes. Hope glimmered on the horizon, but something obscured it: the pain in her heart, the memory of Blaine on top of her in their wedding night bed. The way she felt used, just another investment in his business world.

"Do it, Libs." Kellie was still clutching her arm. "This is the perfect solution. I told you he'd come up with something."

Libby pulled her hand out of Blaine's. "You're very good with money and investing. You're a good businessman."

Blaine frowned. He was so beautiful, and it just twisted the knife in her heart. She should have known better than to get emotionally involved.

"I'm the third woman you've done this with." She stepped away. "I know this is about money, you said that." The bitterness finally burst out of her. "How much sex did it take to convince them to go along with your plan? Probably more than it took for me, since I'm just a silly little girl."

Blaine gaped at her.

"Libby," Kellie gasped. "What the hell?"

"You didn't have to get me into bed to convince me of anything." Her voice shook, the words hard to get out, but she needed to say them. "You could have done all this without playing with my heart. I know the other women probably liked it, but I actually thought for a second that we … that you…" She wiped hard at her eyes with the heel of her hand. Now her eyes were going to be even puffier.

"Libby, I didn't—"

"Thank you for the offer." She dropped her hand. "You've done a great job." Her lower lip quivered. "I have to go get this account set up."

She turned and hurried up the steps, before she had to stare into those blue eyes another second, or be fooled by that stunned, hurt look on his face. Yeah, he was a good actor. A damn good actor.

"Libby!" Kellie charged up after her. "Oh my God, are you out of your mind? He's offering you a way out so you can tell your father to get lost!"

Libby stopped and whirled around. She shoved the papers Blaine had given her into Kellie's hands. "I have to go take care of this. Stay out here, I'll be back."

As she turned, she caught another glimpse of Blaine's face, from where he stood at the bottom of the steps looking up at her. The concern, the anguish, she couldn't be fooled by it, couldn't believe it. She wouldn't be swayed by how beautiful he looked or the memories of their time together, still burning bright in the back of her mind, and beneath her skin. She made her way to the front door.

"Libby!" Kellie screeched after her.

She opened the door and went inside. Maybe this wasn't her best option, but she needed the option that didn't also leave her with a broken heart on top of everything else.

****

"Where is your husband?"

Libby stood next to her father in the small waiting room, clutching her purse in front of her. He was straightening his tie and seemed to have one eye on the clock. He had to take an hour out of his busy day for this. He'd reminded her of that three times already.

"Working." She stared straight ahead, and struggled to keep her face blank and passive. "He couldn't get away."

"And yet, I'm far more busy and essential than he is, and I managed to make it."

Libby didn't have any story made up beyond that. Or beyond today, even.

"No matter." Her father turned to her. "Tell him

to call me tonight. I want to discuss this account with him. It's important that he oversees any of your withdrawals. It's vital that you discuss the use of this money with him. He is your husband, after all."

Libby just nodded.

Her father gripped her shoulder and turned her toward him. She stared at him, breath held.

"This is a huge gift." He stared back, into her eyes, his gaze hard and shrewd. "A huge and *generous* gift. It's to help you set up your future, the way I did for your sister."

"Yes, Daddy."

"It'll get you a nice house, a car, the start of a college fund for your future children. You won't have to scrape and struggle the way your mother and I did when you and Justice were little. God forbid."

Libby didn't remember "struggling." Her father had always been an astute businessman, even before he started his own company. They'd lived in a somewhat smaller house back then, true enough, but she knew kids at school who had it far worse. They always had food, and a car, and new clothes. They always felt like they were in a safe neighborhood.

"Your husband will help you manage this money properly." He patted her cheek. "You made a good choice, Liberty, not letting your youth and eligibility slip away. I'm sorry I doubted you. Waiting around is never a good idea for a woman. Even if your choice was a bit rash, you didn't have many other prospects, and you jumped on the first chance you got. That's my enterprising spirit I've instilled in you."

She forced a smile. "Thank you, Daddy."

A door to their left opened. A short man with glasses stepped out. "Mr. Dawson?"

"Ah, Martin." Her father released her and walked

over to him. "Thank you for making time for me today. Sorry to give such short notice."

"Anything for you, Mr. Dawson." He shook hands with her father. "I put some of my lesser clients on the back burner for you. Wouldn't want to keep the CEO of Dawson True Life Products waiting. That would just be bad for business." He chortled.

Libby wondered briefly how much her father paid this man to kiss up to him. It didn't matter, though. Her father did that with everyone. His ego was far too fragile to allow anyone to disagree with or inconvenience him.

So much so, he'd grant her mother a divorce to avoid scrutiny.

"This is my youngest daughter, Liberty." Her father beckoned her over. "We've come to set up her trust fund account."

"Ah, yes, Ms. Dawson." Martin shook her hand. His was warm and squishy. "Your father talks so much about you."

"It's Mrs. Parker now," her father corrected. "She's a married woman. I was worried I wouldn't live to see the day."

A flush filled her cheeks. Mrs. Parker. Yes, that was her name now. But not for long. Would she take her old name back when they divorced? Her father's name? She blinked a few times, in a desperate attempt to fight back the sting of tears.

"Congratulations." Martin beamed at her. "Please, come inside my office." He ushered them through the door.

The interior of the office was cozy but modern, and smelled like coffee. She barely noticed the décor, though. She sat down next to her father, in a high-backed chair on one side of the desk, and stared across the room in a daze, toward windows looking out on the bright sunny morning.

She remained like a corpse sitting there, stiff and blanked out and numb, as they started discussing the account and transfer of money, as they rifled through papers and Martin showed her father things on his computer screen. Numbers, interest, withdrawals, security. Her father wouldn't ask her opinion anyway. She would just sign where she needed and he would take care of the rest.

Her dreams were vanishing into the mist that seemed to fill the room around her. She wouldn't be able to go back to school. She wouldn't learn the things she needed to learn. Her nonprofit would never be realized, her invention would never come to fruition. All the people she could have helped would die. The places she could have gone, the work she could have done, was no more.

When she and Blaine divorced, she would probably move back in with her mother. Her father would take her off the account and hate her forever. She'd get a crappy job so she could pay her mother back the five thousand dollars she'd stolen out of the safe. Hell, her parents might just disown her and she'd be out on the streets, or Kellie's couch, for all eternity.

She looked down at her hands in her lap. Her chest was so tight she could barely breathe, the pain inside her so sharp she couldn't function.

A voice came then, muffled, from somewhere in the building. Shouting. It sounded like a man. Her father and Martin were talking so she barely noticed it at first, then it got louder, closer.

She lifted her head.

"Libby!"

She gasped and jerked around to look at the door. She recognized that voice, of course. He wouldn't do this. He *couldn't* do this to her, wouldn't humiliate her like this in front of her father and destroy his own life in the process.

"Libby!" Even closer now and clearer. Another voice joined in, what sounded like someone arguing with him.

"What the hell?" Her father turned in his chair. "Who's hollering?" He eyed her, as though suspecting it was her fault. "Is someone yelling for you?"

"I'll go see." She quickly got up. "I'm sorry, Daddy."

"You can't be in here!" a woman cried. "Sir, I have to ask you to—"

"Libby!"

She yanked the door open. Her heart was in her throat.

To no surprise, Blaine stood in the waiting room. Kellie had followed him in. A woman in a pencil skirt and sweater was scowling at Blaine, hands on her hips.

"Sir, if you don't have an appointment, you need to wait downstairs," the woman informed him. "Mr. Gunther is in an important meeting right now. Don't make me call security."

Blaine ignored her. He stared at Libby, breathing hard. One hand was clenched at his side, the other still holding the folder. Kellie stood behind him, looking smug.

"Libby," Blaine said. "I need to talk to you. Don't sign those papers. Don't open that account."

"What are you doing?" Libby could barely get her voice to work. "Go away, Blaine. Please."

Her father stepped out around her. "What on earth is—Blaine?" He sounded mildly surprised. "Oh, you made it after all, good."

"Blaine." Libby shook her head. Dread cemented

her in place. "Please don't. Don't do this."

Blaine stepped forward, his expression stony, eyes filled with fury as he focused on her father. "No, Libby. I think it's long past time to do this."

Chapter Eighteen

Blaine stared down Coleman Dawson, the worst of the worst. That tall, cunning, heartless, evil bastard, the very embodiment of all Blaine had come to hate, the figurehead of all the cruel, self-serving, twisted, soulless rhetoric that had made what he was good at unbearable. Coleman was every cutthroat investor, every businessman who squashed smaller people under his heel, every fat cat who drank his expensive wine and smoked his cigars, and disrespected the humanity of everyone around him. The ones who cheated on their wives and neglected their children. The ones who simply saw other people, even their own families, as stepping stones to be stomped on in their rise to power.

"She's not opening that account with you." Blaine marched over and grabbed Libby's wrist. "She doesn't want your goddamn money."

Libby gasped and stumbled forward as he pulled her from her father's side. She gaped at him, her face pale, her eyes luminous and terrified. It was time to help her face her fear, time to make it so she never had to be scared again.

Blaine kept hold of her wrist and thrust the folder at her. "I'm a good investor, I know a healthy business model when I see one. I promise you, within two years you'll have the money you need. And then we'll pull out of it. I just need your patience and your trust."

"What the hell is going on here?" Coleman stepped toward them, eyes flashing. The rage building behind his expression was dangerous, but Blaine knew this wasn't going to be easy, or pretty. "What are you talking about? I don't have much time to screw around here, I already rearranged my schedule so we could do this."

"Please." Blaine moved closer to Libby, gazing into her eyes. "I promise you I can make this work. You don't have to live with me. You don't have to be around me. We'll make it a purely business relationship."

"Blaine, stop." She tried to pull out of his grip. "You can't do this."

"You can't do *this!*" He pointed at the confused man in the doorway, who Blaine assumed was Coleman's accountant. "He has you by the throat if you do this. You'll never escape him."

Libby looked wild-eyed at her father, then pulled at Blaine's grip again. "Please don't..."

"What the hell is going on?" Coleman stormed over. "What are you saying to my daughter?" He pushed at Blaine's shoulder. "Unhand her."

Blaine let go of her, but only so he could turn on Coleman.

"Back the hell off." Blaine advanced on him. "You're a goddamn monster, but this is where your path of destruction ends."

Coleman looked shocked and then deeply affronted, and then rage blossomed in his eyes. Blaine steeled himself.

"I don't know who the hell you think you are—"

"I'm her husband!" Blaine yelled in his face. "And I'm not going to let you run her life anymore."

"Blaine." Libby gripped his arm. "Stop. Please stop!" Her voice cracked.

Blaine turned and grabbed her shoulders, making her look at him. Her eyes were bright with tears. Her lower lip trembled.

"Libby, I didn't have sex with Rebecca and Amanda. I didn't touch either one of them."

Libby blinked, her lashes glistening.

"Rebecca was so hung up on her ex-husband it

never even crossed her mind. He was all she talked about. I told you, she went back to him right after. And Amanda." He let out a laugh. "Amanda is a lesbian. She was only going to marry the man I usurped because they had a business arrangement."

Libby continued blinking. Her face softened, though. "What?"

"I never touched either one of them." He pressed a hand to her cheek. "Hell, I haven't even had sex with a woman in over a year, not until you. The last time was because I got drunk at a company Christmas party."

Libby stared at him. A tear slipped from her left eye and wetted his hand. He brushed it away, gently.

"But…" She opened and closed her mouth. "Then why … with me?"

Blaine clutched her face with both hands. "Because. I know it's not been very long and this has all been crazy, but I think … I'm in love with you."

She drew a sharp breath.

"I never meant to hurt you, Libby. You're one of the best people I've ever met. You give me hope again. You remind me there's still gentle, good, beautiful people in this world that can be ambitious without destroying others."

She pressed her hand over his, the one not holding the folder. "Blaine."

"Please, Libby. Let's do this together. I don't want to see you trapped."

"Excuse me!" Coleman bellowed.

Blaine looked over his shoulder at him. The rage on his face had turned murderous. He stalked toward Blaine.

Blaine pushed Libby behind him. She gripped his arm. Kellie rushed over too.

"She's not taking your money," Blaine said. "I

have a business proposition for her. She doesn't need you anymore."

"What the hell is going on here?" Coleman loomed over them. "This is absolutely out of line. I knew I shouldn't have trusted you. What the hell do you think you're doing?"

"I'm doing the right thing." Blaine tilted his chin up. "I want you out of her life."

"You have no say in this." Coleman's shoulders trembled. "How dare you. How dare you insinuate yourself in our private family business. Just because you married her doesn't mean you can stick your nose in. I want to know right now what the hell is going on."

"What's going on is that she's not going to sign papers for that account. She's not taking your money."

"She's my daughter, she'll do as I say." He flashed his burning gaze to Libby, over Blaine's shoulder. "You get over here, right now. You're going to explain yourself, young lady. You're going to apologize and stop this nonsense. Don't you think you're so much better now that you tied a man down. You're going to get rid of that uppity attitude right now."

Libby dug her fingers into Blaine's arm. "Daddy, don't."

"Get over here." He pointed forcefully to the spot beside him. "Right now, Liberty Ann Dawson."

"No!" Libby shrieked. She stayed behind Blaine, but her voice was suddenly stronger than he'd ever heard it. "I married him to trick you. I'm not in school anymore, and I'm not going back, except to take the classes I want to. Science, engineering, biology. I'm going to invent a way to purify water in disease-stricken areas. I'm starting a nonprofit to help people all over the world."

Coleman boggled at her.

"I'm not your little girl anymore." Her voice shook, but remained strong. "I was going to take your money and do what I wanted with my life. What you would never let me do. I'm not going to be a mother and a housewife. I'm not going to turn into what you turned my mother into."

Blaine slipped his arm around her waist and pulled her close. She was shaking.

"I'm going to get her the money she needs to do all that," Blaine said. "And there's nothing you can do or say about it."

Coleman glared at his daughter like he might snap her in half. Blaine had never seen a father look at his daughter that way, and it made him sick.

"You were going to take my money and go wild with it?"

Kellie snorted. "Helping people is going wild?"

"You tricked me?" He still glared at Libby.

"I don't want your money." Libby clung to Blaine. "And I don't want you in my life anymore."

Coleman turned his gaze on Blaine, and Blaine's stomach dropped. "You encouraged her to do this?"

"I didn't know her until a little over a week ago, but yes, I fully support her decisions." Blaine braced himself for whatever was about to happen. "You're an evil, rotten bastard. You don't deserve the things you have in life and you sure as hell don't deserve a daughter as good as her."

Coleman lunged at him. Blaine quickly let go of Libby and pushed her out of the way. He'd seen a security guard downstairs, but the guard couldn't get up here fast enough to stop what was about to go down. It had been years since he'd boxed at the gym, but he'd do what he could.

Coleman swung to punch him. Libby jumped

between them, screaming.

He just barely missed her. Kellie shrieked. Blaine lurched forward and tried to grab her, but she flew at her father.

"Don't you dare!" She pelted his chest with her fists. "Get away from him, you bastard. Get away!"

Blaine gaped at her. Coleman stumbled back, looking genuinely startled. Libby withdrew, sobbing, but she wasn't done with him.

"You're a terrible father!" she yelled through her tears. "You treated us like animals that needed to be trained. You taught us we couldn't be anything more than a man's property. You ruined my mother's life, even now she's afraid to be herself."

Blaine eased toward her, but Libby wasn't done.

"I won't be your docile little pet anymore." She was sobbing, but her words were powerful and loud. "I don't want your money. I want to be free of you, and I want to do what matters to me. Blaine supports me. Blaine believes in me. He doesn't try to own and control me."

"Liberty." Coleman spoke gruffly and tugged at his tie.

"It's Libby!" she screamed. "I hate that stupid name. Go to hell!" She started pummeling him again.

Blaine grabbed her and pulled her back. He had no doubt her own father would have her arrested for assault. She spat on him as Blaine dragged her away.

Libby bared her teeth, seething. "I know about the affair. Mom told me."

Blaine had no idea what she was talking about, but for the first time since he met him, Blaine saw fear in Coleman's eyes. His face went white as he stared at his daughter.

Libby pointed at him. "If you ever, *ever* interfere

in my life again, we'll tell everyone."

Whatever she was talking about, Coleman stood stock still, but looked like he might topple over. Blaine was stunned and impressed.

"Come on." Kellie grabbed Blaine's arm. "We should get out of here before you get in trouble."

Blaine held Libby in his arms. She clung to him, crying. He had to hold her up practically, but it didn't matter. She'd said what she needed to say her entire life, and he didn't blame her for feeling completely deflated. She'd had a lot of air to let out.

"Come on," Blaine said to her. "Let's go." He steered her toward the door and glared back at Coleman. "We're going, so you can get back to work. We know your time is very valuable."

Coleman glared after them in return. His tie was skewed.

"Go then!" he yelled. "Fine, if this is what you want. Good-bye, daughter. Have a good life. Have a good life being a dirty, disgusting, willful little whore. That's all you'll ever be, a bullheaded slut that will never be good for anything but having a man stick his cock in her."

Blaine saw red. He pushed Libby off on Kellie.

"Blaine," Kellie gasped. "No."

Blaine rushed toward Coleman, fists clenched. His boxing training came back in a flash.

"Blaine!" Libby yelped.

An assault charge was well worth the satisfying crunch when Blaine's fist connected with Coleman's jaw.

****

The tall blond woman introduced herself as Amanda and shook Libby's hand with a firm grip. She was gorgeous. She also had a powerful aura about her that was all business. Not like Libby's father, not as intimidating as that, but Libby would trust her to take charge of a situation.

And, she was.

"I guess I can't call him a goody two-shoes anymore." Amanda smirked as she filled out the check for the bond. "Assault. Who would have thought Blaine Parker had it in him?"

Blaine had called Amanda and asked her for the favor of bailing him out. Amanda had then contacted Libby, who had been in the process of freaking out over how she would do it herself.

"It's kind of my fault." Libby stood in front of the window with her, on the other side of which a police officer sat. "I should have made him leave before things got out of control with my father."

She *had* been leaving with him, though—it was her father's instigation that caused this. She needed to stop making excuses for him, starting right now.

"But," Libby added, "my father drove him to it. We could have left peacefully, but he had to have the last word."

Those last words hurt, for certain, but Libby could shake them off easier than she ever had in her life. He was a liar. A cruel, twisted liar who deserved everything he got.

Amanda glanced at her. "From what I've heard, it sounds like your father has been asking for someone to haul off and punch him for a long time."

Libby couldn't suppress a smile. "Yeah, I can't say it wasn't fun to watch."

Amanda finished filling out the check and slipped it through the slot beneath the window. The officer passed her back some papers to sign.

Libby fidgeted. "We'll pay you back as soon as

the business starts turning a profit. I wish I had enough money right now to do this myself."

Amanda waved her pen. "Consider it a gift. If it wasn't for Blaine, my uncle would have found a way to take all my money by now." She smiled. "And I'd be married to a gross, slimy guy who doesn't deserve me." She stuck out her tongue. "Men."

Libby giggled.

After Amanda paid Blaine's bail, they went back to the lobby to wait for his release. Of course her father had pressed charges, and dramatically went to the hospital, though he was diagnosed with nothing more than a bruise. Blaine had been in jail for two days, awaiting his bond hearing this morning. Libby missed him horribly. She sat down next to Kellie, who took her hand and squeezed it.

"You okay, Libs?" She rubbed her thumb over Libby's knuckles.

Libby took a breath. "Yeah, I am."

She felt empty inside, but not the way she had almost forty-eight hours ago, sitting in that office next to her father. Instead, she felt as if all the tension, fear, despair, and self-pity she'd carried around since childhood had drained out of her. She felt as if all the things that had kept her nervous and edgy since the day she was old enough to be aware of her father's behavior had washed away. The space left behind was jagged and raw and gaping, but it would heal in time. She would fill it with other things eventually, if she was lucky. Purpose. Strength. Education. Ambition.

Love.

Blaine looked tired and ragged when he emerged, his shirt untucked, blazer draped over his arm. His hair was tousled and he had dark circles under his eyes. But he was smiling at her. He looked kind of sexy like that, truth be told. Her hero.

She needed to clean him up and tuck him in bed.

Libby ran to him and threw her arms around him. She wrinkled her nose. He smelled kind of funky too.

"You okay?" he murmured. He kissed her ear.

She drew back and grinned wide. "Me? You're the one who spent a couple nights in the clink. How was it?"

He rolled his eyes. "Boring, mostly." He smiled again, and his eyes glittered. "I met a guy in there who wants to create an investment portfolio. Drug dealer, needs to diversify his funds. I don't think he'll be out for a couple years, though. I might be retired by then."

She grabbed his hand and peered at it. "How's your knuckles?" They looked red and slightly swollen.

He flexed his fingers. "Ah, not too bad. Throbbed like hell the first night, but they gave me some ice. Your father has a hard jaw to go with the rest of his hard head."

She wrapped her arms back around him. "Thank you," she whispered. "I didn't want you to go to jail for me, but thank you."

He rubbed her back. "Doubt I'll get much but a fine out of it. My record is squeaky clean. And hell, the judge might even take pity when I tell him why I did it."

He kissed her. Her breath caught, her cheeks warming at the fact they were being watched, but she kissed him back. She glowed bright and hot inside. Maybe that hole would fill up faster than she imagined.

Kellie and Amanda walked over. She broke the kiss and turned to them. Blaine slipped his arm around her shoulders.

"Thanks for bailing me out, Amanda," he said. "Twice, really." He looked at Libby. "She suggested the limited partnership."

Amanda put her hands on her hips. "I had to meet the woman who finally captured your heart. The ambitious, altruistic woman you wanted to sacrifice it all for."

Libby's cheeks got even hotter. Had he really said those things? She wrapped her arm around his waist.

"They're such a cute couple, aren't they?" Kellie beamed. "Just gorgeous."

"Yes, I look like a male model right now." Blaine ruffled his hair. "I need a shower and some clothes without sweat and jailhouse grime on them. Thank you again, Amanda. I'll wire you the money as soon as I get home."

Amanda held up a hand. "No. I don't want it back. This is for everything you did for me in my time of need."

"Amanda, I can't—"

"Put it into your new business." Her tone was no-nonsense. "The faster it grows, the faster you'll be helping this one out."

Blaine smiled gently. "Thank you."

"Yes, thank you," Libby piped up. She bit her lip. "He told me about that limited partnership thing, but I'm not sure I completely understand it. I'll figure it out though, because it's a lot better than taking my father's money."

Amanda reached over and patted Libby's arm. "Don't worry, I'll give you an education." She smirked at Blaine. "Make sure you bring her around my office. I like her. A young mind I can mold."

Libby wasn't sure what that meant, but if Amanda wanted to teach her things, she was willing to learn. She was exactly the kind of strong, brilliant woman Libby wanted to be someday.

"Have you heard from your father?" Blaine's tone

turned grim.

Libby shook her head. "He called, but I didn't answer. My mother has been calling too, but I've ignored her as well." Her stomach knotted up when she thought about how she would inevitably have to confront them, but it wasn't the same as before—in fact, it was more like expectation than terror.

"Block them," Kellie said. "You know your father is gonna stomp his feet, but there's nothing he can do. You didn't take any money from him. He has nothing to hold over you anymore."

"I'll have to talk to my mother eventually, though. It's not her fault. I don't want to cut her out of my life because of him. There's still hope for her."

Blaine squeezed her shoulder. "You and I have to work out our agreement too. Are we going to stay married, at least for the duration of the deal? It might be better for tax purposes."

Libby looked into his eyes. "I guess we need to talk about it."

From the corner of her eye, Libby saw Amanda wink at Kellie.

Blaine kissed her cheek. "I want to clean up and then get some real food, instead of the awful stuff they serve here. You hungry? I can make us some lunch. I think I have a few things at the apartment I can throw together now."

"Why don't you let me cook?" Libby grinned. "You've had a rough couple of days."

They headed toward the doors and Kellie practically skipped in front of them. She seemed happier with this relationship than Libby, even.

Was it a relationship? A real one?

"Or, I know this coffee shop." Libby leaned against his side. She could still detect a faint trace of his cologne, and he was so beautiful, it didn't matter if he was grubby and smelly. For the first time, she allowed her heart to soar, free from restraints, and allowed herself to feel the heady thrill she'd been trying to suppress because of all her worries. "You know, the place where we first met?"

He smiled wide. His smile was dazzling, and it was all for her.

"I have to stop somewhere and get some flowers."

Epilogue

"Libby?" Kellie peeked around the doorway. She gasped. "Oh my God, look at you. You're beautiful!"

Libby turned from the mirror, smiling. "It's crazy, isn't it?"

"It's not crazy at all." Kellie walked into the room, balancing perfectly on her high heels. Libby still couldn't manage heels, but it didn't matter. She was much more relaxed in her skin these days, and she celebrated, rather than brooded over, the differences between her and her graceful best friend. Kellie looked great in her green dress too, it fit all her curves just right.

"It's amazing, Libs." Kellie gripped her arms and looked her over. "It's the best thing ever." Her eyes welled with tears.

"Oh, stop it." Libby swatted her. "This isn't even the real deal, it's just a do-over. Don't start crying. At least not yet. Save it for the ceremony."

"I can't help it." Kellie dabbed at her eyes. "It's not so much that, it's that I'm going to be losing my best friend. You're going away and I'm all emotional about it."

"I'm not going away forever. I'll be back at the end of the year." Libby turned to the mirror again and fussed with her hair. She'd had some platinum highlights put in a few months ago and she absolutely loved them. The look felt much more like "her," or at least, the her she was these days. The real her.

"I'm so proud of you." Kellie wrapped her arms around Libby's shoulders from behind and beamed at her in the mirror. "You've worked so hard for this."

Libby was about to turn bashful, but that was the old her. She *had* worked hard. Four years of courses, lectures, practical field work, and long nights had finally paid off. All that education came to fruition when the prototype for her water filtration system received both an award and a grant. Tomorrow, she'd be getting on a plane to fly across the ocean and help implement it. Her ingenuity was already being touted in technical journals, her face was all over the internet, and all the attention was overwhelming and amazing at the same time.

"All this focus on me is really helping the organization boom." Libby grabbed a tube of lipstick from the table next to her. "Thanks to that, we can start funding the real work. That prototype has so many limitations. I have to figure out a way to implement it on a much larger scale." Her nonprofit organization—Water of Life—was a small-time charity that she'd been financing her research and work through. Suddenly, it wasn't so small.

Kellie chuckled. "No talking shop today. You have months of that ahead of you. Just try to enjoy the moment."

Libby let out a laugh. "Enjoy it? Did you see how stressed my mom was about the table settings? She's micromanaging this to death and it's driving me crazy. I don't even care how many flowers are in each centerpiece." She started applying the lipstick, a vibrant red.

"Speaking of your mom, her and Rob are here already. I just saw them."

Libby smoothed the lipstick on, then smacked her lips together. "Of course they are. God forbid a balloon be out of place."

Honestly, her mother wasn't nearly as much of an uptight freak as she used to be. Rob had a lot to do with that. Libby liked her mother's boyfriend. They'd been together almost two years now, and he brought out the best in her. And he was absolutely nothing like her father.

Days like today brought out the old Mom in her though, and Libby had to make sure everyone enjoyed the event to the fullest, including herself.

She checked herself over one more time, then went with Kellie to intercept her mother in the reception hall, before she decided the tablecloths were the wrong color because they clashed with the ribbon on the party favors, or something equally asinine. She found her mother browbeating the caterers who were trying to set up the buffet line.

"Mom, give it a rest. They've got this under control, don't worry."

Her mother turned to her. She put a hand over her mouth and teared up. Libby would have to deal with a lot of that today, apparently.

"Just look at you." Her mother gasped. She strode forward and fussed over Libby's dress. "This is gorgeous. You look amazing."

The long white gown was fit for a princess on her wedding day, and Blaine had insisted she spare no expense. So much white satin and silk. She'd had it made strapless, because she had great shoulders—and now arms, from working out—and she wanted to show them off. This was the only deviation from her childhood fantasies of her wedding dress. She wasn't so conservative these days.

"Thank you, Mom. Please try to relax, okay? Go find your seat and settle down."

Rob strolled over, smiling. He was a handsome, dark-haired man in his late forties. He had sparkling eyes, a kind smile, and a deep, soothing voice. In addition to being great for her mother, he was great for her too. A good listener, supportive of her goals, and always sending her little gifts and emailing her words of encouragement, or taking her calls when her mother was busy at her new job and Libby was melting down over something not going well at school. All things a man should do for his daughter.

"You look gorgeous, Libby." He kissed her cheek. "I'll try to collar your mother."

Her mother scowled at him. "This is my daughter's big day. I just want it to be perfect. I'm not being unreasonable!"

"It's my second big day, Mom." Libby gathered up the skirt of her dress so she wouldn't step on it. "We're just doing this so we can have a real wedding, instead of something in front of a judge."

"I wish you'd consider waiting a few days before you leave." Her mother followed her as she walked down the buffet line, doing a visual check. She trusted the caterers, but it would make her mother feel better. "You could take a little downtime, have a honeymoon."

"I have to leave tomorrow. The project starts next week, and I'm the only one who knows how to get everything set up just the way it needs to be." As she suspected, the food looked fine. "It *will* be a honeymoon, of sorts. Just a working one." Blaine was coming with her. He was the manager of her nonprofit, after all.

"Your father called me. He wanted to come, but I told him I didn't think that was a good idea." Her mother wrung her hands.

Libby was unruffled. "If I wanted him to come, I would have sent him an invitation."

"I know." Her mother gripped her arm, stopping her. "He wanted to give you a wedding gift, some money. I told him maybe that wasn't such a good idea either."

She touched her mother's hand. "Don't worry about him. He's out of our lives. He made his own bed, now he has to lie in it. Neither of us needs to answer to him anymore. Let him sit in his lonely ivory tower and watch us live our lives." It had taken over a year of therapy for her to be able to say that and mean it, but today she did, more than ever.

His tower wasn't so tall these days either. Last she'd heard, the discrimination and unfair labor practices lawsuits he'd been slapped with over the past few years had tanked his business and sent his stocks plunging. She could only imagine the monetary gift he wanted to give her was something like twenty bucks. She and her mother never had to reveal the disgusting, vile truth about him—he'd managed to show his true colors quite well on his own.

"Margie," Rob called. "Let's go sit. Everything is fine here."

Her mother sighed. Then she smiled, her eyes shining. "I'm so proud of you, Libby. You're everything I hoped my kids would be. You and Justice both."

"Is she here?"

"Yes, she and the kids are already sitting down."

Justice was doing much better these days too. She'd taken the money their father had given her and started her own business—yet another upstart, bucking the notion of what women should be. She ran the day-to-day operations of her little interior decorating consulting firm and her husband helped with the books. Libby also had a new niece, and she was cute as a button.

Maybe, when she came back, she'd start working on giving her sister some nieces and nephews as well.

Her mother headed off with Rob, to the room where the ceremony would take place. Libby's heart sped up. Half an hour. She didn't know why it was so nerve-wracking, she'd been with that wonderful man for years, it was hardly new. They'd recently cashed out on the limited partnership. Blaine made his investment back and more, which enabled them to go on this trip and fully launch the project to get the filtration systems in place. Even with the grant and award, they had to fund additional expenses themselves.

They also paid for this wedding with the cash out.

You give me direction and purpose, he often told her. *You show me the heart of humanity.*

She always blushed when he said things like that. He'd done just as much for her, and things that were just as important. He'd given her the strength to be herself, to follow her dreams, to grow and change. He'd given her courage and support. But most of all, he'd given her the kind of love that saw her through all the ups and downs of life.

And today, they were going to reaffirm that love.

Everything at the buffet table was in order. As she walked back toward her dressing room, she passed by a blond woman bent over a tray of cupcakes. A jolt of recognition hit her. She stopped short.

"Monica?" Libby blinked in surprise. She was sure she'd seen the face of the woman who had brought her and Blaine together. Was she moonlighting as a caterer?

The woman looked up, and Libby realized at once it wasn't her. She was a little younger, her face narrower. They could be sisters, though. Libby felt dumb.

"Pardon?" The woman smiled. "You look beautiful, by the way. Congratulations."

Libby shook her head. "I'm sorry, I thought you were someone I knew. Thank you." She paused. "You don't happen to have a sister named Monica, do you?"

The woman chuckled. "Sorry, no. Only child."

"Oh, sorry."

Kellie hurried in, heels clicking on the floor.

"Come on, we don't have much time. You have to finish getting ready. You don't want to miss your second walk down the aisle, do you?"

"It's technically my first. I didn't walk down an aisle before." Kellie was still the only person who knew exactly how she and Blaine met, apart from the truth she'd screamed at her father, of course. They stuck with the story of him visiting her school. It seemed a lot less tacky than having bought him.

Though honestly, it was the best purchase she'd ever made.

"Don't forget this." Kellie held out a sparkling crystal tiara.

Libby giggled and took it. "I want the full princess look." She delicately placed it atop her head. "Do I look like royalty?"

"You look like an angel." Kellie teared up again.

Half an hour flew by. Kellie helped her finish getting ready. Rob came to get her and offered her his arm with a smile.

"Thank you for letting me give you away. Not having any kids, I never thought I'd get to do this. I'm excited."

Libby grinned and took his arm. She gave it a squeeze. "You're the father I never had. You're so good to my mom, and to us. I'm proud to have you walk me down the aisle."

"Your husband is sweating bullets."

Libby chuckled. "Is he? That's cute."

The room where they were getting married—remarried—was perfect, decorated right out of her dreams as well. Chairs were arranged to form an aisle, a white carpet leading up to the altar. The walls and ceiling were mostly glass, and the sunlight streamed in, making the air glow gold. White and green flowers adorned everything. At the front of the room, a wooden arch had been erected, woven with flowers and white ribbon. They would say their vows beneath it.

Everyone stood as she walked down the aisle: family, friends, colleagues. As she approached the arch on Rob's arm, she caught first sight of her sweating husband.

Blaine was handsome and splendid in his gray suit, tailored like a second skin for his tall, broad-shouldered frame. A prince for a princess. He had his hair tied back—it was much longer now than when they'd first met, and Kellie often teased him that he was turning into a stereotypical environmentalist hippie. His clear blue eyes shone as she stepped up to him.

He took her hand. He hadn't shaved off his scruff, because she liked it, but he looked very dignified.

"You're beautiful," he whispered. "I'm the luckiest man in the world right now." He clutched her hands beneath the bouquet.

Libby giggled. "Times two?"

"Times a thousand."

The ceremony was everything she'd hoped for in a wedding—the exchange of passionate vows, a ring slipped onto her finger—they were just using the rings they already wore, upgrades from their original cheap rings they'd gotten a few years ago—and gazing into the loving, adoring eyes of a man who still took her breath away, even four years later.

Kellie sat in the front row, clutching Libby's mother's hand, both dabbing their eyes. Kellie started openly weeping when Libby and Blaine lit a candle together.

"To the next step in our future together," Libby murmured. "And making all our dreams come true."

The officiant pronounced them man and wife—

again—and then came the good part. Blaine swept her up in his arms and gave her a hard, passionate kiss. For one breathless moment, she really was a princess, caught in the arms of her Prince Charming.

The crowd stood again, clapping and cheering as they walked up the aisle together, arm in arm. Such a contrast to their first wedding.

The reception was also far better than the first one too.

"It'll be hard to top our first wedding night, though," Libby cheekily remarked as she sipped champagne with Kellie. She watched Blaine greet people and shake hands. Amanda was there, with her new girlfriend, and they were laughing it up.

Kellie nudged her in the ribs. "I better get details. More details than the first time, preferably."

"What about you and Sean? You think you guys will have your big day eventually?"

Kellie's boyfriend was at the catering table, loading up a plate. He was a fun guy, and Libby thought he matched Kellie perfectly in wit, charm, and brashness.

Kellie shrugged. "I'm not the marrying type, Libs."

"I used to think I wasn't either. I had to pay a guy, remember?"

"And your life is magical now." She took Libby's hand and twirled her around, and they both dissolved into laughter.

Next to the wedding cake—the big, beautiful wedding cake—Libby displayed her slide in a picture frame. Lots of people asked her about it, and she got a continuous kick at how their expressions turned from curious to horrified as she told them the story. Her mother fretted a bit that the bacteria might get out and give all the guests cholera, but Libby patiently explained it was a dead sample, and it was securely sealed in the slide.

"So morbid, Libs," Kellie informed her. "And yet, so you. Proudly displaying your bacteria. Your bacteria of *love*."

"I want everyone to know what I'm going to be up against in my work too. It's really a tiny monster. Most monsters are, and they're easy to fight when you're brave and smart enough."

"Maybe we should have just set the reception up in a lab. You'd feel more at home."

"That would have been cool, but I think Blaine would be against it."

Libby's mother seemed much calmer during the reception, as she'd stopped her fussing and fretting. Probably because she had a glass of champagne in her hand as well, and Rob was careful to steer her away from any distractions.

After mingling enough to be polite and answer all sorts of questions about their trip, she and Blaine met out on the patio. It overlooked a garden of sculpted shrubbery and rosebushes, the sinking sun coating everything with a pink and gold frosting.

"Hey there, sweetheart." He slipped an arm around her waist. "Fancy meeting you here."

She finished her champagne and plunked the glass on the railing. "I'm not one to miss a wedding. I'm a huge romantic, you see."

Blaine stroked her cheek and gazed into her eyes.

"You ready for this?" he murmured. "We've got a lot of hard work ahead of us. You, more than me, but I promise I'll be by your side every step of the way."

She nodded. "This is what I've wanted. I'm ready for it."

He pressed his forehead to hers. "I still can't

believe we're here. I can't believe after the way we met, we actually made it. We got this far, and we're going even further. I only had to marry two other women first to find you, huh?"

"Don't they say the third time is a charm?" She played with a lock of his hair. "And I didn't even have to pay you ten grand to be here today."

"Speaking of ten grand." He drew back and locked his arms around her waist. "We've got some money left over. I was thinking maybe we could start a college fund."

She tilted her head. "For you? Are you thinking about going back to school?"

"No." He smiled. "I was thinking more for our future children."

She smiled in return.

"After we come back," he said. "After your project gets going. And of course, after you completely finish school. I know right now isn't a good time, but I'm in this for the long haul, obviously, and I thought hey, maybe someday."

She wrapped her arms around his neck. "I would love to have your babies. But you're going to have to get a job, so we don't go broke." She grinned. "Play the stock market or something."

Blaine cracked up. He had more than enough in his retirement fund for them to live comfortably for decades, even when they factored in traveling the world and trying to a run a nonprofit. He was, after all, an amazing investor and he still understood money far better than she did.

He lifted her off her feet and spun her around. She shrieked in delight and clung to him. He put her back down and they shared a slow, deep, knee-weakening kiss.

She entwined her fingers with his. "I'm so glad I

found you in that book," she murmured.

"I'm so glad I wore my best suit for that picture and caught your eye." He took a breath. "So, what do you want to do next, Mrs. Parker?"

She gazed up at him and grinned. "How about we head up to our room and watch a movie?"

The End

www.meganmorganauthor.com

THE MARRYING TYPE

EVERNIGHT PUBLISHING ®

www.evernightpublishing.com